A pair of breasts first made an appearance as they were unburdened from the harness of a brassiere. Thomas found himself amazed at their infinite variety, for no two sets were ever quite the same. However, he much preferred the kind with extremely large areolae and nipples. It mattered not whether the cushiony foundations were grand or diminutive just so long as their crowns were at least the size of plums. If a chill breeze blew in through the open windows, the rubbery tips would stand out all the more, prompting Thomas's lips to burn with the desire to wrap themselves around them.

Also by M. S. VALENTINE:
*The Captivity of Celia*

# Elysian Days and Nights

BY M. S. VALENTINE

MASQUERADE BOOKS, INC.
801 SECOND AVENUE
NEW YORK, N.Y. 10017

*Elysian Days and Nights*
Copyright © 1997 by M.S. Valentine
All Rights Reserved

No part of this book may be reproduced, stored in a retrieval system, or transmitted in any form, by any means, including mechanical, electronic, photocopying, recording or otherwise, without prior written permission of the publishers.

First Masquerade Edition 1997

First Printing July 1997

ISBN 1-56333-536-0

First Top Shelf Edition 1997
1-56333-905-6

Manufactured in the United States of America
Published by Masquerade Books, Inc.
801 Second Avenue
New York, N.Y. 10017

*The Elysium Spa...a woman's paradise!* proclaims the full-page color advertisement in the back pages of *Ladies' Society*, a glossy high-priced magazine that one finds only in the best newsstands in the greatest cities in the world. Those in the know consider it their personal bible, for how else can a woman of beauty and means keep up on the latest trends in popular culture, fashion, diet, and exclusive vacation spots?

Within weeks, other periodicals catering to a similar audience began to carry these slick pronouncements, touting the spa's merits as the much-needed tonic for the fast-paced and exhausting lives of women of means. However, if one could decipher the subtext, it immediately became clear that the Elysium Spa specifically targeted a certain kind of woman: a woman of youth and beauty, neglected frequently by a wealthy older husband. Although the advertising copy did not specifically state such preferential criteria, an exhaustive application process due to "the abnormally high demand for our services" filtered out any undesirables, thus leaving only the crème de la crème of young womanhood qualified enough to mail in a hefty deposit—payable in U.S. dollars only, please.

Like clockwork, every month the small staff waited eagerly for the arrival of the spa's private plane as it brought with it a new group of specially selected guests. Since the facility was located on a tiny patch of scrubby land in the Mediterranean, there was no other means of access to the spa, unless one wished to land a small plane or moor a boat illegally on the isle—something that occurred rarely. Indeed, few boats ever ventured out this far from the civilization of the small Greek village of Aristos on the main island in the archipelago, their skippers preferring instead to sail around the safe cluster of islands closest to its modest port. Hence, anyone on the secluded island had a good reason to be there.

The location's remoteness was what had originally made it attractive to the unusual gentleman who had signed the deed to the land, consequently saving an elderly Greek archaeologist from spending the rest of his years in poverty. The tales of ancient treasure had never been realized, but this foreigner imagined riches beyond those of the material. He'd had a vision one day—a vision that led to the development of the Elysium Spa, and a vision that led invariably to the never-ending fulfillment of his greatest fantasies.

On the younger side of middle age, Dr. Emile Bronski was a man of indeterminate origin who, like the people he hired, possessed a cultivated European accent along with striking good looks. In addition to his other duties, the doctor took complete charge of determining which women would be receiving formal acceptances to their requests for a visit, choosing from the thick stack of applications only the most beautiful and wealthiest of women. Since he would be the one to administer the rigorous daily physical examinations of his patients, Dr. Bronski wished to see only those of the highest in physical standards. Of course, money was also an important factor. However, the doctor did have his standards...

...standards which proved extremely difficult to live up to. Like many of the staff, Dr. Bronski had a special predilection—a predilection he had pursued relentlessly throughout his life. He suspected that he was probably rather unusual in his tastes when compared with other men of his caliber; thus he considered himself somewhat of a pioneer, finding pity in his heart for the sorry sods who had neither the imagination nor the discernment to appreciate the finer things in life.

To be specific, the doctor possessed an unquenchable passion for the clitoris—or, to be more precise, a lady's "passion petal." However, not just any passion petal would do, but only the most colossal ones—the sort that protruded out from between a woman's thighs even if they were crossed—imposing plump pink beauties that waved proudly like a giant banner of victory—clitorises like the one that adorned the labia of his former wife, Dorothea. Sometimes he thought he would spend the rest of his days searching for a substitute, although, granted, his quest brought him tremendous pleasure.

Unfortunately, Dr. Bronski was unable to determine the quality of a woman's clitoris merely from the photograph and financial statement included with her application materials; hence he would often forgo the daily exams for those of the ladies he considered not quite up to his exacting standards. He couldn't very well send her packing, for what reason could he give to someone who was willing to spend thousands of dollars just for a few weeks on what amounted to a desert island? Such lapses in judgment happened, and one had to make the best of it. Yet, when the doctor encountered the right sort of woman, he would throw himself completely into his work by scheduling several physicals a day, exhausting both himself and his overstimulated patient.

Due to his single-minded pursuits, many times Dorothea had accused her husband of being mentally unbalanced, a fact that inevitably led her to flee the Bronski home outside of Zurich. However, the doctor paid no mind to such denunciations. He was a professional man practicing the art of medicine, and the amateur diagnosis of a woman with no interests save for fur coats and young boys could not possibly be given much heed. Indeed, Dr. Bronski was simply a devoted connoisseur of this distinctive female feature and there was nothing the least bit sinister about it!

Now that he had the freedom of bachelorhood once again, the doctor could do as he pleased without the critical eye of his wife upon him. And one of the first things he did was put his plan for his dream spa into

# ELYSIAN DAYS AND NIGHTS

operation. As the compound itself underwent construction, so did his private house on the island—an airy whitewashed villa much like any of the upper-class residences dotting the arid hills on the Greek islands. Dr. Bronski had kept the design plain and functional, for he was more concerned with the interior of the structure than the exterior. After all, this would be his first *real* home—a home that would be decorated entirely to his preference and he went all out, commissioning the most alternative of alternative photographers for the special brand of artwork he required to make his new domicile truly complete. The doctor knew these shady characters were bilking him heavily, but it did not matter so long as he got what he wanted from their cameras.

The day the large wooden crates began arriving on the island signaled the beginning of Dr. Bronski's new life. These celluloid artists had definitely done themselves proud. The doctor reckoned that at even fifty times the price it would have been worth it. Just the sight of the delivery boat mooring at the tiny dock gave the doctor an erection. And when he got home and removed the contents from these crates, semen spurted out of him like water from a fire hose, completely soaking the front of his white linen trousers.

Giant prints of giant clitorises had been mounted onto board and set into simple steel frames ready for hanging. The fleshy subjects had all the sharp clarity of the real thing, the colors as vibrant and intense as the juiciest of clitoral youth in various stages of arousal. Why, one could practically taste and smell them, so faithful to life were these portraits. Dr. Bronski did not dare ask to whom they belonged or how the men he had paid ever managed to photograph such a wide variety. It was enough just to know that he had not been cheated, for each clitoris possessed its own special uniqueness, whether in shape, shading, or fringe.

Hence the walls of the doctor's home were soon festooned with images of this lustrous female appendage. Yet he still remained faithful to his former wife, keeping a framed 8"x10" color photograph he had taken of her clitoris at his bedside along with a wallet-sized one in his billfold beside his medical license. Dorothea had truly been a lady to be reckoned with, for never in his life had Dr. Bronski encountered a woman with so massive an organ. To this very day, he continued to marvel at it. How it irked him that others were now enjoying what by rights should still have been his to enjoy. If it hadn't been for the Elysium Spa, the doctor believed that he would have spent the rest of his years as a resident in a psychiatric institution, so haunted was he by images of handsome young males fingering and sucking the juices from Dorothea's grand extremity.

Indeed, Dr. Bronski's unusual fancy had provided the original inspiration for him to choose gynecology as a profession, for he could think of nothing better than to sit and admire clitorises all day—*and* be paid handsomely for it to boot. However, much of his enjoyment would be curtailed by the annoying presence of his starchy, prune-faced nurse who, no doubt, probably wished to look at what he himself gazed upon so adoringly. This, along with the rise in malpractice suits among his American colleagues, put somewhat of a damper on Dr. Bronski's joy. Hence the opportunity to acquire the tiny island came along at an opportune moment.

It would be only a matter of time before he completely relinquished his two practices to his partners, the luxurious office in Manhattan giving him the most pain to abandon. Yet the doctor had a higher calling—a calling that required a man's total dedication to his chosen art. One particular occasion during the normal course of a business day had changed Dr. Bronski's life. He considered it a sort of epiphany for him—a turning point that made him realize he needed to help the women of the world achieve the ultimate in pleasure, even if it meant lining his pockets a bit in order to do so.

On a Monday morning an anxious young woman arrived at his office for an examination—a woman he had never seen before and, indeed, would never see again. From his preliminary questions, Dr. Bronski discovered that she was from a small African village and had arrived in America only recently. Looking forward to the examination with his usual anticipation, the doctor seated himself before the woman's splayed thighs. However, when he lifted the sheet covering her genitalia, he nearly fell off his low stool. To his horror, this new patient did not possess a clitoris. All that remained in the region where it should have been was a slight thickening and puckering of the delicate plum-colored skin. Dr. Bronski knew this was no mere birth defect. Indeed, this had been a cold, calculating excision of flesh done by some jungle witch doctor. Why would anyone wish to cut off a woman's access to pleasure, not to mention an object of such lustrous beauty? He raged inwardly, fighting to stop his anguished tears. He only hoped that this transgression had been committed at an early enough age so the poor woman would never have known about—let alone missed—the ecstasies which should, by rights, have been hers to experience. The doctor had heard of such primitive practices and was grateful that at least the butcher who had committed this crime had not sewn the tender amethyst slit of her vagina shut as well. Thus Dr. Bronski vowed to dedicate the rest of his life to this spectacular female appendage by spending his days paying daily homage to it and seeing that it received its much-deserved happiness—especially if the clitoris happened to be one of monumental proportions.

From the very beginning, the doctor made it a rule to hire an international staff for his beloved spa—especially Europeans. He knew that a cultivated accent would work wonders on the young ladies, many of whom had made the long journey all the way from the United States. The guests' nationality proved to be no accident, for Dr. Bronski had a special liking for American women. His former wife was an American, and he found that as a general rule they possessed far more sizable clitorises than either European or Asian women. And, for the doctor, *nothing* could be more important than that.

The specially selected females who visited the Elysium Spa suffered from various maladies—some physical, the majority imagined, the most obvious of which was the lack of attention paid to them in their matrimonial arrangements. Being young and inexperienced at the time of wedlock, they suffered from neglect by their wealthy and powerful husbands—men who were continuously in pursuit of still more wealth and power and, being somewhat older than their wives, had chosen these women more as trophies than as partners. Hence these young ladies were ready to believe virtually anything in their hopes of ending their chronic headaches and fatigue; and Dr. Bronski, in his wisdom, designed a therapeutic program specifically with these factors in mind. According to his philosophy, a physician needed to treat the entire body and not merely the obvious afflictions. Therefore, his patients seldom questioned his rather unorthodox methods. Nor did they dare to question the doctor's daily gynecological checks, all of which were done without the customary examination gloves. Dr. Bronski could always anticipate his anxious patient's silent questions and answered them immediately in a soothing masculine voice, explaining that the stricken one needed the touch of healing hands in their purest form in order to get well—and this meant the absence of any artificial accouterments like latex gloves or paper gowns. So desperate were these women to believe in a cure to their psychosomatic ailments that the doctor rarely received any protest. Instead, the patient would lie back totally naked on the examining table, placing her feet cooperatively in the widely spaced stirrups, the gnawing sensation of wrongdoing in her belly quickly being overridden by an uncontrollable fluttering between her parted genital lips.

To aid the doctor in his single-minded pursuits, he had designed and constructed a special device exclusively for his patients at the spa. It consisted of two separate belts that looped around a woman's upper thighs, with a padded clamping mechanism attached to each end. Dr. Bronski fitted these straps around each outspread thigh, pulling them taut to take up any slack. The small clamps would then be gently but firmly clipped onto each of the labia majora and with one more minor adjustment of the thigh straps, the belts would become as tight as a hangman's noose, hence completely unrolling the female lips and revealing what would usually be, by the time the doctor had finished with his meticulous tinkering, an upstanding and very flushed clitoris.

This contrivance would be accepted quite easily, for Dr. Bronski explained that a woman's true physical health could be determined accurately only by the healthful condition of her clitoris. He spoke of this in very clinical terms, tossing in a number of multisyllabic medical terms in order to reassure even the most skeptical of patients that all was completely aboveboard. Indeed, the doctor proved quite an orator and had been the envy of his fellow university students throughout his academic career. And at last it was paying off in the most charming of dividends.

Not every guest would be receiving the healthful benefits derived from Dr. Bronski's many years of experience, for not every woman could measure up where it most mattered. Yet once the doctor had determined via his stringent set of criteria who among his patients were the most clitorally endowed, he would initiate a course of therapy. The chosen one would be instructed to lie back on the examination table and relax as the doctor made himself comfortable on his stool. The clamping apparatus would have already been secured and after a dramatic show of knuckle cracking and exercising of the finger joints, he got straight down to business, unzipping his trousers and releasing his stiffened penis which, because of his low proximity to the patient, could not be seen by her. Now facing the fully splayed vagina before him, Dr. Bronski began to slowly manipulate the newly unmasked clitoris with his index and middle fingers, incorporating a finger from his other hand to tickle the tiny slit below. By this time the crimson opening would have grown extremely liquescent and as this wetness trickled onto the other opening of lesser repute, a finger would slide in and tickle the hot walls of the woman's rectum.

This specially prescribed treatment caused a great deal of writhing and moaning on the part of the patient, not to mention a painfully delicious throbbing on Dr. Bronski's part, for he had acquired the unusual habit of wearing a leather ring around his penis. As the purple shaft strained and swelled and became further constricted within its leather noose, he almost lost consciousness several times, so intense was the feeling. While the doctor worked on his patient, he would move in as close as he dared in order to fully appreciate the hot, musky scent between her thighs—a scent that grew so much more aromatic as the woman neared orgasm. When the moment finally arrived and she cried out with her own private pleasure, Dr. Bronski would stifle his own cries as his bulging penis emptied its turbulent fluids out onto the pristine white tiles beneath his feet.

Every woman who received this treatment assumed it to be one designated solely for her and for her alone, and the doctor, in his wisdom, encouraged such beliefs among his patients. Indeed, the doctor was not a particularly capricious man. His finicky tastes led him to select only a handful of ladies from each new group that checked into the Elysium Spa. For obvious reasons, guests never discussed their therapy with each other. Hence, the doctor remained completely free to continue with his harmless deception, for it was all in the name of medical science.

On occasion, Dr. Bronski would modify his methods by sitting on his low stool, not even touching his patient, but merely staring spellbound at the inspiring vista before him. No doubt the woman harnessed by the clamps was not totally immune to the doctor's heated gaze, for her fully exposed clitoris soon began to wriggle and flourish on its own, swelling larger and larger before his eyes until he could no longer remain immobile. During such moments as these, he preferred to keep one of his hands free for self-manipulation. However, he had plans for the other and he would riffle through the cabinet drawers to select from a series of vibrators whichever model he deemed most appropriate for the situation. Although sold to the medical profession solely for health-related reasons, Dr. Bronski found these extremely handy for his purposes. After all, the instruments *were* utilized for health reasons, for what could be more healthful than a woman's pleasure?

These phallic devices came in several lengths and widths. The doctor employed them at his discretion, usually placing the largest of them against the hood of the woman's clitoris and holding it there firmly. When he twisted the base to activate it, what squeals of delight it incited from the recipient of its therapeutic effects! Indeed, the doctor even fell a little bit in love during these moments, for the immediate flush suffusing his patient's labia minora proved most compelling to a man of his generous heart. Yet there was still more to come, for he would amplify his treatment by inserting slimmer varieties into the woman's vagina and anus. A lubricating jelly aided the vibrating tool's admission into the less-practiced rear orifice. It would be only a matter of time before he introduced the largest in his collection to this newly awakened entrance. Switching on the tools to full speed, he thrust them in and out of the openings in unison, his focus never once vacillating from the twitching florid pennant his clamping apparatus had unmasked.

When a clitoris proved particularly impressive, the doctor drew it into his mouth, sucking hard upon it as if it were a piece of candy. Indeed, this was precisely the sort of treat for which the doctor had a sweet tooth. He relished all the slight variations in flavor his palate encountered. He thanked the gods every time his examining table was blessed with a visit from a big-clitted female, and thus he would do his utmost to pleasure her, offering a stimulating finger to her two orifices as he nursed upon the fleshly delight so fully erect and at attention that it reminded him of his own penis.

The lovely Carla easily became one of the doctor's favorite ladies. Yet the first time he had placed her in the stirrups, he was disappointed. Although an orange-brown nub projected out well enough from its nest of coppery hair, it looked merely above average—nothing warranting any special treatment on the doctor's part. However, when he fitted his contraption onto the puffy lips and they opened up like two segments of a juicy orange, Dr. Bronski altered his opinion immediately. As if sensing that it was being measured against the strictest set of standards, Carla's clitoris rose to the occasion, showing the doctor that it could compete with the best of them. Now *this* was a passion petal! Indeed, he didn't even get a chance to release his penis from his trousers before it exploded, leaving a warm, glutinous mess in his expensive undershorts. However, the price of one pair of English silk boxers seemed a small price to pay in exchange for the breathtaking display before him. Even Dorothea would have found Carla's clit a most worthy adversary.

Dr. Bronski had many more opportunities to indulge his infatuation for Carla's sumptuous endowment and he would make the most of them, incorporating every technique and device available to him in order to help her clitoris attain its most extravagant dimensions. Only then would he finally take the feminine tentacle into his mouth to feel its fleshy plumpness flutter excitedly as it divided into two distinct morsels. With the tip of his tongue, he forced up the retractable hood, only to blaze a trail from the now-unprotected vermilion glans down between the unfurled segments, slipping and sliding joyfully through the dewy silken trough until reaching the core of moisture, and then traced the path all the way back up again. The doctor would repeat the process over and over until Carla's slit quivered uncontrollably from his adoring tongue, the sappy wetness virtually pouring from it and forming a viscous puddle on the vinyl surface of the examination table beneath her. Dr. Bronski would lap up these offerings with each repeated visit, returning once more to nurse upon the object of his enchantment. Carla came again and again in his mouth, for he would not stop after her first orgasm, but instead continued on with his licking and sucking even well after a second round of his semen splattered the already-sticky tiles below.

Like the rest of the spa compound, Dr. Bronski's private examining room had hidden cameras. One had been stationed in the cupboard directly above his head, the innocuous-looking faux-brass fitting its judgmental eye. Because of the angle of the examination table and the doctor's low seating arrangement, there would never be anything to obstruct the camera's view. Hence the film collected from these physical examinations would always be of the highest caliber, leaving little doubt in the mind of the viewer that the woman was a most willing participant.

Dr. Bronski had employed his younger brother Thomas to man the surveillance equipment. A social misfit in every respect, it was either a job at the good graces of his brother or the inevitable fate of jail. Hence the doctor had given him the only position he thought he could manage, hoping this dark-eyed malefactor linked to him by blood would not botch up this generous and very unique opportunity. The court had been most lenient in releasing Thomas into his respectable brother's custody and the doctor had rushed him out of Switzerland before he could get himself into still more trouble. Dr. Bronski believed that had Thomas continued on as he had been, sooner or later he would have ended up having his head shot off by some woman's enraged husband. And in this day and age, there weren't many judges or juries who would have condemned such extreme measures.

Generally a passive fellow not particularly inclined toward confrontations with the opposite sex, the doctor's sibling had a special penchant—a penchant modern society found totally unacceptable. Thomas liked to watch ladies. However, he preferred to watch when they did not know they were being watched. To him an open window offered a direct invitation: a handwritten gold-border sheet of creamy parchment paper presented to him personally by a delicate feminine hand. Thomas knew all the best neighborhoods in suburban Zurich—neighborhoods with many first-floor bedrooms and nice big windows, windows that served as his private movie screen. Experience told him that the very best time for viewing was in the evenings when the women were busy readying themselves for bed. Thomas stationed himself outside a window where the drapes or shutters either had not been closed or else were only partially so, thus enabling him to observe the ritual nightly disrobing of his chosen victim.

A pair of breasts first made an appearance as they were unburdened from the harness of a brassiere. Thomas found himself amazed at their infinite variety, for no two sets were ever quite the same. However, he much preferred the kind with extremely large areolae and nipples. It mattered not whether the cushiony foundations were grand or diminutive just so long as their crowns were at least the size of plums. If a chill breeze blew in through the open windows, the rubbery tips would stand out all the more, prompting Thomas's lips to burn with the desire to wrap themselves around them.

Stockings were next unhooked from lacy garters and down they would roll, one at a time, pale thighs parting slightly as the woman perched on the edge of the bed attending to this divestment. Discarded to the dusty world of the floor, the nylons retained the ghost of a shapely leg even long after the delicious warmth of her body had gone from the fibers. Thomas couldn't help feeling sorry for the stockings as they suffered silently in their careless abandonment.

Once this simple task had been accomplished, the unknown woman would then stand so that the silken wisp of panties could slide down over the dizzying swell of her bottom, each charmingly dimpled knee lifting up high as she stepped out of the leg holes, the once-pristine gusset now darkened from the wetness of a long day. Thomas strained to catch a glimpse of the hidden treasure that had caused this liquid phenomenon, frustrated when his view was obscured. From his vantage point beyond the cruel barrier of the window, all he could ever hope to see would be a triangle of curly dark hair which, unfortunately for him, did an excellent job at hiding the lush womanly details beneath it. And when the observed one turned her back to him, even though Thomas enjoyed the presentation of the perfectly halved roundness of her buttocks, he wanted to see more. He wanted to see the secrets that lay between them.

So Thomas Bronski, along with his coworkers at the Elysium Spa, had finally found the job of his dreams—a job he would have happily done for free. And it turned out he was quite the whiz when it came to technicalities. Aside from monitoring the closed-circuit cameras stationed about the facilities, Thomas was in charge of editing the film, a task he considered of the greatest importance to his brother's financial empire. Although he would have preferred a job somewhat more in contact with the guests, his peculiar disposition had pretty much ruled out such a possibility. However, despite Thomas's inability to possess these beautiful young women physically, thanks to the cameras he could possess them in another way. He took some solace in this knowledge, his hand frequently stroking the stumpy length of his yearning penis in the privacy of his cramped little control room.

Thus Thomas lounged in his oversized black leather swivel chair at the base of operations, feeling like a god. And perhaps he was a god, for he was certainly all-seeing and all-knowing. The lovely guests could have no secrets from him; indeed, he saw them wherever they went, capturing their most intimate moments on film, the reels of which were carefully cataloged and filed away on the row of shelves behind him, the name of the female subjects written on their respective labels in Thomas's meticulous hand. The nuns at his grammar school had always given him a gold star for penmanship and he often wondered what they would think if they knew what his fine calligraphic talents were now being used for.

Yet too many years of always being on the outside looking inside soon took its toll upon Thomas Bronski. He needed more—far more than sitting in his cramped little office and monitoring television screens could ever give him.

As the surveillance man simmered silently like a pot with its lid ready to blow, the daily business of the spa went on as usual. Guests came and went. The demand was so heavy that very soon a waiting list had to be drawn up. Applications arrived from every corner of the Western world. Each woman vying for an invitation was more beautiful and wealthy than the next. Word had gotten around in the most elite social circles that the Elysium Spa was the place to go to cure one's ailments. Yet no one actually knew what really went on within the compound itself—and those who had discovered the truth firsthand did not dare to speak of it. With so much success, Dr. Bronski began to consider the possibility of expanding. Indeed, any man in his position would have been planning an early retirement. However, the doctor had found his private Elysium and had absolutely no intention of abandoning it—*ever.*

The spa prided itself on its wide range of healthful

activities, making certain that no guest ever became bored during her stay—nor lacked the pleasures so rightfully due her. The extensive psychological profile Dr. Bronski had compiled on each woman helped him to define her unusual needs. Hence, an individualized treatment plan was created and administered in accordance with his findings. Oddly enough, one patient's therapy did not much differ from another's, for most suffered pretty much from the same afflictions. The only differences would be in the quantity of a specified treatment and here the doctor allowed his attractive staff members to exercise their own expert judgment. They knew just how far they could go with a guest—which apparently was as far as the physical limits of her body would allow.

Dr. Bronski considered it extremely important for each patient to establish a routine and stick to it religiously. Being away from home and family often produced a great strain on the nerves. In order for a guest to get the most from her stay, there needed to be some semblance of normalcy—a prearranged schedule that differed very little from one day to the next. Therefore in addition to Dr. Bronski's therapy, part of the daily ritual would be massages. The doctor hired only the best—and that best was André. His appointment book would always be filled to bursting with names and times, for once the ladies discovered his multiple talents, they made certain to schedule themselves for one of his special massages as often as possible during their stay—and as many times as possible within a single day. André's leonine eyes, powerful hands, and the rich scent of his dark skin—skin that glowed like molasses and smelled just as sweet, left these women with little desire to refuse his attentions, no matter how intimate these attentions became. Had he not been under exclusive contract to the spa, André and his portable massage table would have been busy with many happy clients for many years to come....

Happy clients like Carla, a slender redhead whose tranquil temperament did not seem to match the coppery fire atop her lovely head—nor the coppery fire between her thighs. At first André took her for the usual type of client who frequented the spa—rich, spoiled, beautiful, and bored. Yet she would soon become his favored lady. He would even go so far as to break house rules, bribing Thomas to make some stills from the reels of film she had been featured in unknowingly—a bribe that did not involve money, but rather an opportunity for the doctor's brother to indulge in some firsthand observation of André's technique. Although the masseur would not allow the surveillance man to watch him with Carla, he did not particularly mind the young man's peculiar presence in the courtyard when another of the ladies lay facedown and rump up on the padded massage table. Indeed, she would be so involved in her own pleasure that she failed to notice the diminutive figure hovering nearby—nor did she notice the warm, foamy puddle that had been deposited on the sparkling blue tiles beneath her widely spaced feet. The bargain struck between these two extremely different men had benefited them both. Thomas had achieved the immediate gratification he craved. For André, such gratification would be less immediate; for, in his old age, he would treasure the precious photographs Thomas had made, studying them in the privacy of his retirement villa and remembering the sweet taste of Carla's hot anus upon his tongue.

It immediately became apparent to André that he was being used by his employer for sinister purposes. Yet he did nothing. His powerful desire for the dainty hollow and the opportunity to have free rein of so many made him indifferent to his exploitation or exhibitionism. Besides, the pay was excellent—as indeed were the generous tips bestowed upon him by his shocked—then later, grateful—clients. André felt truly blessed to be at the spa performing work that he loved. He also felt truly blessed with the shape of his penis. Having to initiate young ladies whose rear apertures were pure and unsullied and consequently closed to intruders, its tapered shape made the work to be done far easier for both himself and the unsuspecting woman lying before him. André considered himself an expert on the subject. He could always tell when an opening was untried by noting the anxious contraction that occurred whenever he pulled a shy pair of buttocks apart. So chaste a physical reaction served as a personal challenge, for the masseur took great satisfaction in converting a woman's stubborn back entrance into a welcoming chamber of pleasure for a man's penis.

Hence, in the beginning, André went slowly, starting off with a regular massage in order to get the ladies used to the feel of his strong dark hands on their pale bodies. He would set up his padded table outside in the courtyard beneath the clear azure sky, the hot fingers of the sun joining his as he rubbed the rich scented coconut oil on the neglected flesh before him. After a couple of these relaxing sessions, the ladies became enough at ease with his touch to unwrap them from the fluffy white towels that hid their nudity. Then André commenced with demonstrating his *real* talents.

Expert hands squeezed and stroked the women until they felt as if they were melting into the table. Once they had reached this languid state, André began work on their buttocks, kneading and kneading the ripe young cheeks until they glowed, his hands driving them up and apart so that the sun could kiss the heretofore-unexposed mouth of their delicate anuses. The openings yawned luxuriously from such a spreading, showing André a tantalizing hint of the radiant pink just beyond the overstretched rim. Per Dr. Bronski's highly detailed instructions, he kept the cheeks apart an instant more than prudent for the camera lens to view all the subtle nuances therein. He took this opportunity to leisurely admire the secrets he had just unveiled, comparing each crinkled nugget to the many hundreds he had already seen and experienced in his short lifetime. No two were ever quite the same, for each possessed a uniqueness in character that only a man of André's sophistication could discern.

The masseur's first discovery of this all-too-often-unexplored treasure was as a youth barely out of his starched school uniform. She had been his first love and, like so many other girls of his day, interested in having sex but deathly afraid of getting pregnant—especially in the highly pious West Indian village where they had both been born and raised. Utilizing the lesser-esteemed opening of her anus for their mutual pleasure seemed like an obvious alternative. Already a budding masseur among the elderly and ailing in the community, André had at the ready a bottle of oil—oil he had painstakingly pressed from the fruits of papaya, mango, avocado, and coconut and he squirted a generous portion into the girl's tight dimple. Before realizing it, he had emptied half of the container. Then, wanting to make certain the act would be completed with the least amount of discomfort, he added a bit more for luck.

Young André's entry proved far more effortless than he had originally imagined and he began to regret squandering so much of his precious massage oil when only a little might have done just as well. Within seconds he was pumping away happily inside the newly deflowered rectum of his maiden love who, judging from her deep sighs and moans, appeared to be enjoying the act as much as he. Unfortunately, the excitement of the moment drew a quick response from André's penis. His fluids gushed out before he had taken his fill of the narrow passage. He slid out sadly, surprised at how small his shrinking organ looked. Suddenly the girl clutched her abdomen and groaned, bending forward at the waist. The combination of too much rich fruity oil and thick boiling semen had gotten the better of her and she squatted in shamefaced agony, the contents of her rectum purging noisily from her along with the contents of her bowels. Her face twisted itself up with the onslaught of tears as she comprehended what had happened—and what she had just done in front of her lover. Before hysteria took her over completely, he pulled her to him and hugged her trembling body, kissing away her tears.

However, all was not lost. The quick-thinking André took charge of the situation quickly by cleaning the soiled girl thoroughly with a wet cloth. And his penis went sliding right back into the hot slick opening it had departed from prematurely only moments earlier, finding himself even more welcomed the second time around. Indeed, the young couple would indulge themselves in their new practice as often as possible, the frequency of these meetings priming the girl's rear opening to accept him unconditionally.

So André knew how much oil was too much oil and he vowed never to make the same mistake again—especially here at the spa with ladies of this caliber who, no doubt, would rather die than allow a man to witness such a purging. Of course he always knew why they often took flight after he had finished with them, but at least with his less-liberal application of the oil, they had enough time to make it to the privacy of their bungalows.

Despite these occasional yet decidedly unpleasant aftereffects of such a union, André could tell that not a single woman had ever regretted being taken in this manner. Hence he always looked with great eagerness toward introducing yet one more beautiful female into these uncustomary pleasures, certain that she, too, would become as addicted as he himself was. Who better than he to initiate all the exquisite young guests at the spa? Surely no one would dare to question his status as a master in the anal arts.

Indeed, André always knew best how to proceed in these matters—*and* with the least amount of opposition from the unsuspecting lady. To help prepare an uninitiated client for the next step in his special massage therapy, he would insinuate a well-oiled finger into her anus, stealing himself for the surprised gasp he knew would be forthcoming along with the involuntary muscular clutching at his embedded finger—which he found almost as exquisite as the moment of penile penetration itself. He refrained from doing more, however, leaving the affronted woman wondering whether the entire incident had been completely unintentional or a figment of her overwrought imagination. André could picture every single one of these ladies lying in their elegant beds in their elegant bungalows and puzzling over this extraordinary event, their silken vaginas steaming with musky molten heat as they relived over and over again the all-too-fleeting moment when André's coffee-colored finger had pressed into the never-before-invaded rings of their fiery little anuses. No doubt the forbidden shade of his skin added a great deal to their excitement, for he knew that women such as these had never experienced a man of another race— nor, indeed, had they probably ever experienced *any* man other than their husbands.

When the ladies returned the following day for their scheduled massages, André felt reasonably certain that they would not object to another trespass. And when he had once again gotten them into their languid state, he concentrated all his efforts on their buttocks, kneading and squeezing and spreading them until they appeared to want to remain parted of their own accord. His oily fingertips gently grazed the dainty ruffled rim of the hot sun-licked opening between them, teasing until it contracted on an almost-continual basis, transmitting a secret message that only he could decipher. Once the women had reached this condition, André took matters a step further by sliding two fingers inside the snug chasm and waiting for the customary gasp and muscular tensing. If no opposition seemed imminent, he assumed the way was clear and with his foot he tapped a black button protruding from one of the floor tiles, consequently alerting the control room that something of major importance was about to transpire. This in turn alerted Thomas to confirm that the camera hidden in the tree branch above the massage table was fully operational. André sometimes thought he could hear the camera whirring from its precarious perch, but concluded that it was merely his imagination—an imagination perhaps tainted with an element of guilt as well.

As a matter of economics, the masseur had been instructed to depress this alert button only when something of a highly incriminating nature was about to transpire, for it was impractical to spend so much employee time sifting through hours of useless film when only a few choice moments were all that was really required. Of course, Thomas Bronski had his own method of doing things. The task of previewing reel after reel of sexually explicit film well into the early morning did not annoy him in the least bit. He would filter out those segments showing the beautiful young guests at their most salacious extremes, and retain the rest for his own personal film library. Indeed, sleep had become a virtual stranger to the surveillance man, for who could afford to shut his eyes when such lustful activities went on?

With the camera activated, André's oiled fingers took on a life of their own, boldly plunging in and out of the submissive anal opening before him. He held his breath in anxious anticipation, waiting to see if the woman would scream for help. This happened rarely, which was why the masseur had been instructed to alert the control room whenever he planned any kind of intimate maneuver—even if a penile penetration was not yet on the schedule. There was always a possibility that one of the ladies might become difficult about such matters, and the spa simply could not risk the early departure of an unhappy guest, not to mention a financial opportunity gone to waste. In these particular cases, *any* film was better than no film at all.

Shortly after André had begun working at the Elysium Spa, such an eventuality did actually occur. Had he been more experienced, perhaps he might have anticipated that a certain Mrs. Cyril Oliphant III could be a problem. However, André was eager to please his new employer— and Dr. Bronski was eager to be on the road toward financial success. Such is the formula for a mistake and, with the arrival of Mrs. Oliphant, the spa sustained a big one. The doctor's usual meticulous screening process had failed, nearly bringing so much hard work and dedication to a dismal halt. Dr. Bronski had suspected that his new patient might not be up to the rigorous routines at the spa, for upon his physical examination of her—of which she would allow only the one, he found her clitoris to be extremely stunted and bland both in color and aroma. Normally he would have anticipated such findings merely from a woman's mouth, for his many years of medical experience had led him to the unshakable conclusion that lips were the same whether located on a face or between the thighs. And Mrs. Oliphant had extremely thin lips—miserly, in fact, which should have been sufficient warning that her other pair of lips would possess the very same stern attributes—certainly not an appropriate atmosphere for a clitoris to thrive. It also became immediately apparent that the woman had lied about her age. The photograph she had submitted had been taken years ago—no doubt during happier days before she had married Mr. Oliphant III.

Such observations should have alerted the doctor immediately, and he took the blame for his miscalculation. He apologized profusely to the anguished masseur, who nearly quit after his harrowing encounter with the shrewish woman. In retrospect, Dr. Bronski realized that what he should have done was send the woman packing, but he had let greed get the better of him, hence ignoring the obvious signs of a female who was totally incapable of either lust or passion. He concluded that the sexually repressed Mrs. Oliphant III did not even know the true purpose of the pea-sized bit of flesh above her vaginal opening. As a result of such ignorance and neglect, André's gentle probings in the dour-faced pucker of her backside had been met with a shriek of the most strident nature and the spa with the threat of lawsuit which, luckily for all, had never materialized.

Despite the apparent lack of appreciation on Mrs. Oliphant's part, André's massage treatments usually went according to plan. After the repeated introduction of his skilled fingers into a client's unexploited anus, the situation could only escalate. Then his skilled penis would have its opportunity. The masseur knew precisely how to position a client on his table so the camera could record every salacious detail of their union. Often the lady's excitement would be so great that she reached back to spread her buttocks for him, leaning her torso forward like a jockey on a racehorse, her splayed thighs straddling the sides of the massage table as she rubbed herself to orgasm against the nubby texture of the towel beneath her. Yet no matter who she was or where she came from, each woman wondered what her husband would have done if he could at this very moment have seen her with her uplifted backside being sodomized aggressively by a throbbing ebony penis. Of course, in her romantic innocence, she had no idea that he might very well have seen exactly this indelicate scenario had she refused to pay what the management called "supplemental fees" upon her departure. Indeed, the thought of the cuckolded spouse—a spouse who consistently neglected the physical needs of his lovely young wife yet expected her to remain his and his alone—made this unwholesome transgression all the sweeter. In turn, the recipient would slam her buttocks back onto the invading penis so that her usually dormant receptacle could be packed more fully. André knew that the contrast of

## Elysian Days and Nights

his oil-glossed blackness—for his organ was truly the darkest part of his body—slipping in and out of these fair furrows made a dramatic statement on film—a statement none of these privileged young ladies could afford to make known to her spouse, let alone anyone in her social circle.

The handsome masseur had awakened new passions in these proper society ladies, so returning to home and hearth offered little satisfaction. Performing their wifely duties on the usual Saturday evening or—if a spouse were particularly amorous, a weeknight—provided little solace for the loss of the molasses-skinned islander and his tapered organ. The risk was far too great for a normally submissive wife to request such an unheard-of penetration from her husband. Therefore, several of the more daring ladies used their initiative to trick their mates into performing the act they missed most. As men of limited imagination, they would usually do the marital deed in the dark and beneath the safety of the bedclothes. Hence it proved relatively easy to relocate the marital penis under such circumstances. With an exaggerated sneeze worthy of ejecting even the grandest of male members, the woman would raise her knees, placing the yearning mouth of her anus in the location where her vagina had just been. In his eagerness to resume seeking his pleasure, her spouse would immediately hoist himself back inside the opening that ostensibly had rejected him, plugging himself unknowingly into his wife's bottomhole. Thanks to his selfish pursuit of orgasm, he would neglect to notice the hotter and dryer nature of this slimmer channel and, as his climax approached, ram into her rear thoroughfare with tremendous force. The darkness would prove a blessing in more ways than one, for the woman knew that her husband would be utterly horrified to discover what entrance his penis had invaded. Thus, in the shadows of the night, she would close her eyes, imagining the tiny black braids atop André's head dancing and swaying as when he and she were last united in this fashion.

The masseur often reflected upon all the beautiful young women he had serviced throughout the day, conjuring up scenes of them sitting together eating dinner at the communal dining table, his still-hot semen leaking out of their glowing anuses and forming an oily spot on the pristine white of their panties. Had he entered the dining room on any given evening, no doubt he could have claimed carnal knowledge of every single one of them—a carnal knowledge of the most forbidden kind!

André so enjoyed possessing white women. Although he knew all about the psychological concept of forbidden fruit, he dismissed so simplistic a rationale. There was far more to his unusual desires than any psychologist could possibly explain. These fair-skinned ladies appealed to André in a very special way; their bewitching little crinkles always looked so pale and unripe—so deliciously innocent compared to the girls he had known in his youth. Indeed, there was a certain rawness in appearance about them that he found exciting—a rawness that made what he was doing to them so much more intimate and erotic.

Monika had by far been the fairest woman André had ever encountered in his tenure at the spa—and perhaps in his entire lifetime. Barely out of her teens, the slender Dane possessed a perfect curtain of shimmering white-blonde silk that reached her waist. She had the unconscious habit of tossing it back over one delicate shoulder whenever it threatened to get in her way, never once realizing the devastating effect so routine an action had upon all the males who witnessed it. Had she known, she might have refrained from doing so, for the glossy tresses brought about many wicked fantasies in the minds of men, of which the most common involved a nude Monika coiling the perfect tendrils of hair around a bursting penis.

Only a smattering of down marked her long arms and legs. When André, in his very first session with his new client, placed her facedown on his massage table and removed the protective cloak of her towel, he discovered Monika to be virtually devoid of hair within the slender crack of her buttocks. Shivering with desire, he began to caress them, running his oiled fingertips lightly over the projecting slopes. The masseur could not believe his good fortune, for not only was she absolutely exquisite in his area of interest, but compliant as well. Not a hint of protest could be heard from her lips. Indeed, the Dane remained lying obediently on her belly, apparently unconcerned about her nakedness. Nor did she appear concerned that the man who had been enlisted by the spa to provide her with a therapeutic massage seemed to be acting in an entirely unprofessional manner—or at least unprofessional if one expected a garden-variety massage.

Several minutes passed. Even after it had become apparent to the reposing Monika that André had no intention of giving her a massage on this warm, sunny Mediterranean morning, still she made no effort to remove herself from his presence. Instead she continued to lie quietly on the table set out in the center of the blue-tiled courtyard, her face half-turned toward the masseur as she rested her head within the crook of her arm, one slate-gray eye open and watching his dark figure expectantly.

The gods had presented André with a gift, and he knew he would have been a fool to refuse it. Indeed, Monika's supple backside was a masterpiece created expressly for him and his trembling hands moved over it with even greater boldness, his slippery fingertips finding their way stealthily into the heated cleft. Upon parting the gracefully molded cheeks, a modest opening the hue of a pale tea rose came into view. Unable to remain immune to such perfect beauty, André bent down, placed his lips against it, and kissed it in reverence. Such a delicate pinkness caused his heartbeat to accelerate. When he finally fitted the ebony head of his penis into the rosy aperture, he wished he could have frozen the moment forever, so lovely was the striking contrast between light and dark.

Monika accepted him inside her easily, her sultry passage seeming to defy the apparent minuteness of its entrance. She lay there passively, allowing André to go as deeply as he pleased—*and* for as long as he pleased, the only sound she made being the fluid suctioning emanating from her repeatedly penetrated anus. With his every stroke, her bottom rose up to oblige him. The masseur stuffed her rear passage all the way to the thick root of his penis and would have gone still farther had there been more of him remaining. The unique tapered nature of his organ allowed him to observe Monika's chaste little rim as it expanded more and more to absorb his increasing width until the tender pink flesh looked ready to tear, so widely had the anal mouth been stretched.

That morning André came inside her three times without even once having to withdraw, providing some excellent footage for the spa, not to mention a fine orgasm for the man in charge of capturing it all on film. Thomas Bronski was kept so busy with his own continually sputtering penis that he'd nearly neglected to activate the camera in the dry sauna, where one of the maids had just gotten a guest into a position of the most illicit nature. Indeed, very little would be dry by the time the engaging young domestic had finished her duties.

Without fail, Monika continued to turn up for her morning appointments with the masseur, her warm, naked body obediently taking its place on the padded table that was still warm from the naked bodies which had preceded hers. However, despite her seeming passivity, her hunger for André's particular brand of courtship became more and more urgent and he soon found himself inside her hot, needy rectum as many as four times within a single day. And it did not stop with the sunset, for every evening the Dane would be waiting for him in her bungalow. Lying nude on her stomach, a red and a blue kerchief served as her only garb—she had tied one around her head to cover her eyes and the other to cover her mouth. A coil of rope rested beside her on the bed and her fingers stroked the scratchy fibers blindly as she awaited the masseur's arrival. If perchance he was late, she would place the length between her thighs, fitting it into the continuous seam from tailbone to pubic mound and drawing it back and forth to excoriate the delicate tissue. No wonder André frequently found the rope damp, not to mention Monika's pale tea rose glowing like a hot ember. Indeed, had he taken the trouble to check, he would have found that the silken tongue of her clitoris had ignited into a blazing flame as well.

André caught on instantly to her powerful desire for submission. Without uttering a word of greeting, he bound her pale wrists together above her white-blonde head. A jar of expensive French emollient would always be at the ready, its lid screwed off beforehand by Monika so there would be no unnecessary delays. André scooped up a generous portion with his fingertips, greasing her expectant opening and his own expectant organ with the rich cream, cooling the fire of the rope's enthusiastic abrading. Monika relished this intense contrast of scourge to balm, knowing that she was in store for yet another delicious dose of the former. Feeling his slick fingers probing her, Monika raised her buttocks into the air and they separated of their own accord, issuing the invitation André had been waiting for.

Since his penis had already taken its fill of sweet young anuses that day, the masseur now had the leisure to maintain an erection for a considerably long while, and Monika mumbled from beneath her gag, urging him not to spare her. She wanted to be punished, so she confessed that she had been a very naughty girl with one of the maids earlier that evening while in the sauna. And indeed, the Dane still had the piquant taste of Françoise—the prettiest of all the domestics at the spa, on her tongue. Hence André obliged, ramming himself roughly into the dainty inlet, Monika's hoarse cries urging him to do his worst with his cruel ebony weapon.

All who would view the film of these encounters—and there would be many—marveled at the dramatic sight of André's glossy blackness sluicing in and out of Monika's tender pink bud. Even the women watching the footage of these impassioned moments could not help wishing that they had witnessed the alliance in person. Indeed, Dr. Bronski's brother went insane with desire each time he played and replayed the explicit images.

Suddenly an idea came to him. Fed up with his lot in life, Thomas decided to expand his duties beyond that of lowly film technician. Since no one actually kept tabs on him, he made plans to take an extended coffee break from the stuffy semen-smelling room where he spent all of his waking hours. Hence a hastily scrawled note signed with André's name was dispatched to Monika's bungalow. It seemed unlikely to Thomas that she had ever happened upon a sample of the masseur's handwriting. Thus she would have no way of knowing that *he* had actually been the note's author. A staff meeting had been scheduled for the usual time André would have paid her a call. Not wanting the lovely Dane to be disappointed, Thomas generously decided to take his place.

Wanting everything to be perfect, Thomas took the liberty of bringing along an extra coil of rope, for surely one would not be sufficient for what he had planned this evening. When he arrived, the door to Monika's bungalow was unlocked, as he'd expected it to be and, upon entering the sexual theater of the bedroom, he found her waiting exactly as he had observed her so many times on camera: lying on the grand stage of the bed with her slender, almost-frail body deliciously naked, her smooth, pale buttocks quivering as they awaited their fate. The small oval of her face was turned away from him, the kerchief covering the cool slate-gray eyes behind it. Having anticipated that he would not have lasted a minute with her, Thomas had earlier taken a hand to himself, squeezing out an initial outlay of semen before coming to her bed. As he stared down at Monika's submissive form, he felt confident that he would be able to make a good show of it. So with great eagerness, he pulled the rope out from under her fingers and tied her wrists together as he had seen André do. However, he also bound them tightly to the bed railing in the event that she might suddenly realize the stumpy plug in her rectum was not the elegant tapered instrument she was usually accustomed to and then might attempt to wrest off her blindfold to discover the impostor.

Thomas took his time, knowing that this might be his first—and would probably be his last—opportunity to indulge himself with Monika. He spent several minutes just letting his fingers explore her pale body, relishing her provocative scent as it grew stronger and stronger with his intimate investigations. He had never in his entire life possessed a female as beautiful as this and would have preferred to experience all three of the young woman's orifices. But the passing of time and Monika's impatient pleas for punishment forced Thomas to expedite matters. Indeed, her appeals soon became so urgent that despite the muffling cloth of her gag, he had to take his belt to her in order to quiet her down, fearful that the guest in the next bungalow over would hear and come running, concerned that some harm was coming to her usually silent neighbor. To his surprise, Monika seemed to enjoy the feel of the dull leather against the nearly translucent skin of her rearcheeks and she raised them so high the twitching pink of her anus became fully visible along with the swollen pennant below as it jerked wildly within its puffy labial housing.

In a rush of inspiration, Thomas reached for the length of rope he had cut expressly for this meeting. He could still smell the salt of the sea in the twisted cords, for he had procured it from the tiny dock at the end of the island. It was far more crude and rough-hewn than the one that now bound Monika's wrists. It usually moored small boats. Although the surveillance man had originally intended to use the piece to tie her ankles together, it would serve its new function quite well. He lifted Monika onto her knees, pushing her head forward so that it rested on the pillow. Her backside projected high into the air from this new posture, the belt-reddened cheeks dividing in an impassioned plea for Thomas to do his worst. The rosy dimple between them twinkled merrily, seeming to advertise and, indeed, *promote* its services.

With his heart beating so rapidly that he could barely remain on his feet, Thomas grasped the rope about halfway down, leaving a few inches of slack at one end. Drawing back his arm as far as it would go, he struck Monika within the satiny fissure of her buttocks, crying raucously when contact had been made. She shuddered with the shock of the first blow; in her blindness, she had no way of anticipating what was coming. However, as the rope continued to gain familiarity with the terrain, her body lost much of its resistance and she held her pose firmly as the stinging blows turned into a full-fledged whipping.

Thomas aimed directly for Monika's anus, reveling in the sight of it flinching with the impact of the lash, only to burst back open like the seeking mouth of a hungry child. He lashed out again and again, the prickly tip of the rope licking the wildly contracting hollow. No doubt this lusty hatchway had never met up with the likes of Thomas Bronski. He grinned widely, watching in victorious satisfaction as liquid honey poured from the unattended sliver of Monika's vagina, drowning the convulsing tongue of flesh below and spattering onto the braided fibers of his makeshift crop. This provided him with additional inspiration. When the muscles in his arm finally became too exhausted for him to continue, he gathered up the rope's slackness and began to insert one end of it into Monika's abused opening. The muffled moans coming from beneath the inadequate gag of her kerchief encouraged him. He fed as much of the abrasive material into her as he could manage. The well-utilized status of this particular entrance made his task considerably easier. When it appeared that the Dane had had enough, he wrenched the rope out in a single draw, leaving her to squeeze her thighs together in orgasm.

Unable to restrain his ravenous organ any longer, Thomas's trousers fell to the floor. He hoisted himself into position behind her, straddling her trembling thighs and stuffing his weeping organ into the hot hole between her buttocks, nearly weeping himself, for he had dreamed so long of this moment.

Monika pushed her bottom toward him, waiting for the exquisite burning sting this penetration always brought. Indeed, it was the pain and discomfort that made it so pleasurable and, in fact, preferable to the other method of coitus. By offering her compliant backside to an interested penis, she thus placed herself completely at a man's mercy, rendering herself utterly helpless by this thorough and inescapable impalement. Yet instead of the sweet torment she expected, the male extremity inside her felt very comfortable—odd, considering that she had been used several times by André already this day—and had been for several days in a row now.

Suddenly Monika worried that she had become permanently altered by so much activity in this region and felt a brief twinge of fear that her husband might discover her disgraceful secret. However, in all the time she had been married, he had never once bothered to look, let alone to touch her there. When she had finally gotten up the courage to suggest that he might like to investigate such a possibility, she became humiliated when he declared that he considered these parts highly unclean and suitable for one purpose only. Indeed, Monika's husband was truly a man of little imagination.

Happily ensconced inside of Monika, Thomas tried to emulate what he had seen the masseur do. To his delight, he felt his inadequate penis lengthen and thicken inside the hot elastic cavity. Perhaps he was *not* so poorly endowed after all, for not only did he feel every subtle bump and ridge on the rectal walls, but he swore that he felt every microscopic particle of scratchy fiber that his rope had left upon its hasty exit. Perhaps what Thomas had needed all along was simply a bit of conditioning to bring out his full potential—conditioning that his stroking and squeezing hand could not provide. And Monika appeared to enjoy his newfound skills, for she cried out with each deep thrust, begging for the man she believed to be André to hurt her. Of course Thomas was more than happy to oblige the lovely Dane. The tortured sounds of her pain excited him as he had never been thrilled before and filling him with something he never had—namely *confidence*. Hence he decided to expand upon what he had learned from his lonely post in the surveillance room. He withdrew from Monika briefly, only to slap her airborne buttocks with the flat of his palm, then stuff several of his thick fingers into the breached opening before thrusting himself right back in again.

Monika came with a tortured howl, as did Thomas, who felt as if every drop of fluid in his entire body was squirting into her smoldering rectum. How he would have liked to take her in this fashion yet one more time, for his still-drizzling penis was very much intact and deeply entrenched inside her pulsating chamber, which gave little indication that it wished to release it. However, the risk of discovery seemed far too great, for surely the masseur was on his way over to the bungalow this very instant.

Indeed, Thomas nearly collided with the handsome islander. He had to dive behind a bush to avoid being seen, experiencing his own form of torture as the verdant brambles pricked his flesh right through his thin cotton clothing. Tiny specks of crimson formed on his white shirt, making him wonder about Monika's unusual desire to receive pain. Yet who was *he* to question such a need, for hadn't he taken pleasure from inflicting it?

When André entered Monika's bedroom a few minutes later, she raised the florid cheeks of her buttocks even higher than usual, ecstatic that he had returned to punish her burning hollow one more time. However, in the waning light, he failed to notice the unusual signature left by his predecessor—the glowing stripes of red crisscrossing the normally flawless mounds of her backside. Nor in his haste to possess her did André detect the surveillance man's more personal endorsement—the angry inflamed pinstripes marking the delicate pink within.

Several days later, Monika disappeared from the Elysium Spa. In fact, she disappeared from the entire island. André had arranged a private appointment with her far from the prying lens of a hidden camera and they had agreed to meet on a secluded beach a good mile and a half away. Despite Dr. Bronski's prohibition against personal involvement with guests beyond that of the professional duties set forth by the spa, the masseur had begun to have romantic intentions toward the exquisite young Danish woman and her pale anal rosebud. Hence he vowed to have her all to himself—even if only this one time—and that meant breaking the strict rules the doctor had set forth.

Monika lay naked on the beach, awaiting her dark lover with her blindfold and gag in place and a rope looped around one slender wrist. She had discarded the plusher comforts of her beach towel, preferring instead to be at one with the raw elements. She shimmied about on the hot sand like a creature born to it. Aroused by the chafing grit against her thighs, breasts, and belly, she shifted her body to continue feeling the scalding grains against her bare flesh, reaching down and parting the pink bloom of her labia so the tender pendulum between them would benefit as well.

When André found her, she was close to orgasm. He bound her wrists together quickly above her head, the way she preferred it. He also made certain that the two kerchiefs were in place over her eyes and lips, tightening the knots securely at the back of her head. Unlike before, Monika's gag would do a far more thorough job of covering her mouth, imprisoning her tongue. Thus, whenever she tried to speak, her words were muffled. No longer could she communicate her desires to André intelligibly. Monika's servitude was now complete. She shivered beneath the bright yellow ball of the sun.

Kneeling within the wide V of her thighs, André placed his palms on her buttocks, forcing them apart until the unlighted crevice had flattened out completely. The glaring light from above cast away all shadows from the satiny strip, illuminating a floret of rubescent pink beyond any hue that nature could have endowed it with. Indeed, the opening the masseur had come to service was already moist and gaping. He slid through it with ease, finding it as burning hot and gritty as the sunbaked sand against his bare knees. The coarse granules scouring her broadened anal ring and being deposited continually within her rectum only heightened the experience for Monika. A couple of strong pumps sent her reeling into her first orgasm, for André's weight had also caused her unveiled clitoris to grind itself hard against the sand.

The sun at the beach felt so much more intense than it did back in the sheltered cove of the courtyard, and its sensual benefits were not lost on André. Each deep thrust into Monika's rear cavity forced his own buttocks to divide. Fire crawled furtively between them, kissing the inky wreath of his anus. Suddenly he understood why all his ladies seemed to take so much delight from these alfresco meetings.

Unbeknownst to the couple, three youths from a neighboring island had moored their tiny fishing boat a few yards away and were now in the process of observing these unusual activities from a nearby grove. They had spotted Monika's naked form approaching on the beach shortly after their boat had drifted ashore and had hidden both it and themselves from view, believing that she was just another tourist out to get a bit of color on her sun-starved limbs. They had heard about the groups of foreigners visiting the island, but had never been particularly interested in what went on. However, had they known that these foreigners were all sexually charged women who went around unclothed for most of the day, no doubt they would have come snooping around a lot sooner.

Having lived their entire lives within the confines of their own tiny island, they had never come across a female of such exquisitely fair beauty as Monika. They studied her in enraptured silence from their hiding place. The slender grace of her young body was quite unlike the stocky girls of their own parched little landscape—indeed, quite unlike even the girls in the well-thumbed magazines they bought from the sailors passing through their village. Long white-blonde hair shimmered around Monika in a silken mantle. When she tossed her head back, sunlight bounced off it in platinum glints, sending a searing jolt through the young men's unseasoned loins. They would continue to feel these powerful jolts of desire as their eyes coveted what their bodies as yet could not have.

As Monika moved nearer to their hiding place, the enchanting details of her femininity became much more distinct to her three male admirers. The symmetrical pink-tipped spheres of her breasts were as perfect as

## ELYSIAN DAYS AND NIGHTS

those of any Greek goddess, possessing all the sophistication of a woman, yet still maintaining a girlish charm as they rested proud and high on her rib cage. Occasionally a coil of hair would catch on one sharp nipple, encircling it in a lingering caress. However, where this lustrous fringe ended, another one soon began, for fine flaxen curls crowned the gentle rise of Monika's pubic mound, reminding the boys of spun sugar and looking equally delicious. A pulpy pink nub protruded from this savory nest, seeming to point directly at them. Their first sighting of it prompted the three to lick over their lips in imitation of an act they had as yet no knowledge of and it took a self-control beyond their years to stop them from ambushing her right then and there.

A yearning such as they had never known plagued them, yet each boy feared this tantalizing young female—or maybe what they feared most of all was their own unexplored desires. Hence they remained hidden from view, trembling as they watched the nude woman rub herself against the sunbaked sand in a strange dance of erotic torment. However, their cowardice served them well in the end. Apparently, the pale foreigner had been expecting someone—someone who would add a flush to her Northern European flesh. For perhaps Monika's skin had looked almost transparent when she had first emerged on the beach, but it now radiated a glowing heat as the man stooping over her fed his ebony penis to her prone body.

Although not much older than Theo, the oldest of the three young men, Monika had seemed so removed from them, so *untouchable*—indeed, almost as untouchable as the flat images of the naked females displaying themselves so explicitly on the tattered pages of their magazines. Yet why would these women show their bodies if they didn't want to be touched? Perhaps this woman on the beach wanted to be touched as well. And later, when the other figure arrived on the scene—a figure far darker and more masculine than the one that had up till now been occupying their attention—the boys knew they were right.

The three young men had been exposed to sex via the village tart, a chubby young woman who would do their bidding for a pack of cigarettes. Nevertheless, no amount of amateur coupling could have prepared any of them for the bizarre activities taking place on the beach. This business with the rope and kerchiefs was totally alien to them, yet—despite their ignorance of the pleasurable use of restraints in such matters—highly arousing. However, when André rolled Monika onto her back and hoisted her thighs high into the air, the boys began to bicker quietly among themselves, the oldest insisting that it was the woman's rear hole the man's penis was inside of, his two companions insisting that this was impossible. However, when the couple again shifted position, with Monika crouching on her knees, it became instantly clear that Theo's assertion had been accurate, for the breached cheeks of her bottom became visible beneath the rocking hips of her lover. His black polelike extremity vanished repeatedly within the mysterious furrow between them. They observed this unusual junction like a team of scholars doing research, nearly chuckling aloud at the sight of André's dusky testicles slamming repeatedly against the woman's outthrust buttocks. The masseur held tightly to her waist, lifting himself up and offering the boys a glimpse of the unoccupied vermilion sliver of Monika's vagina as it rained its sweet, creamy droplets onto the thirsty sand below.

Despite their one-sided opinions of their own carnal worldliness, such a penetration had never occurred to them. But apparently it had to their penises; three fleshy staffs of young manhood rose in unison, making their wishes known. Unable to ignore such needy throbbing, each removed his penis from the safety of his shorts and, oblivious to the presence of his friends, gave it a few firm jerks, watering the shrubbery proudly with a foamy shower as Monika came violently from the rhythmic digging in her rectum. Her full young breasts swayed like an ocean wave as André bucked wildly against her well-cleaved buttocks, his own buttocks clenching and unclenching with the force of his orgasm.

Then André ran back to the compound. He was already late for a massage, and his clients did not like to be kept waiting. With the fetters of her kerchiefs still in place over her eyes and mouth, the Dane dozed peacefully on her stomach, oblivious to the turmoil she had created a few feet away. Little did she know that in agreeing to meet the masseur on the beach, she inadvertently had changed the course of her life—and the lives of three other people as well. There could be no turning back for these young peasants, whose simple lives had consisted of fishing and an occasional hurried fuck in exchange for a package of smokes. Something inside them had come undone—like a bolt being lifted from a door that had never been opened.

They sprang from their hiding place, coming upon Monika so unexpectedly that she thought that her dark lover had returned to her. In anticipation of further pleasures, she raised the blooming half-moons of her buttocks high, disclosing the well-used dimple of her anus. It twinkled invitingly, offering itself to all comers. However, when Theo tied the discarded length of rope around her wrists and knotted the ends snugly—far more snugly than André would ever have done—she became suspicious immediately. The nearby shuffling of two pairs of bare feet further alerted Monika that all was not as it should be and when she began to struggle, the boy who had bound her hands sat down heavily on the backs of her thighs, his weight preventing her from escaping.

Being the eldest and wanting to substantiate what both he and his somewhat more skeptical friends had witnessed, Theo—who was not known for his shyness—wrenched Monika's sand-chafed buttocks apart unceremoniously, exposing the orifice in question to the candid glare of the sun—and to their candid appraisal. Its reddened rim yawned widely, framing a glistening black pearl. However, its recent provocative usage had stretched the fragile perimeter enough to defy the circumference of *any* pearl the boys had ever seen.

Theo smiled triumphantly as the others gathered around, the fronts of their stained twill shorts taking on a life of their own. Now that he had an audience, he decided to show off. He slid his middle finger into the unfathomable groove, pushing as far as it would go. The forbidden nature of what he was doing to the helpless young woman elicited several startled gasps from his friends, not to mention a constricting of the rectum by his violated victim. His smile grew even broader, a newly discovered power urging him to continue and, indeed, even to accelerate his outrageous behavior. Although Theo hadn't quite known what to expect from such curious terrain, Monika's interior felt so steamy against his finger that he decided to insert one more. Gauging there was still plenty of room for another, he added yet a third. Thus, with the wide eyes of his two friends upon him, he began to thrust this makeshift cock in and out, trying to emulate the fluid movements of the dark man's penis.

Having spent the majority of his young life working the brilliant cerulean waters of the Mediterranean, the unrefined digits of Theo's thickset fingers received little care. Hence, his nails were always torn and ragged, the sun and sea-dried skin as rough as the coarsest sandpaper. Yet, rather than detracting from Monika's pleasure, these crude conditions served to enhance it. She moaned voluptuously through her gag stifling, her buttocks rising up to meet these unkempt intruders and take them in deeper.

Suddenly Theo knew what he wanted to do most of all….

Unfortunately, his plans would be temporarily delayed as Monika found herself being examined by two other inquisitive sets of equally crude fingers, only to be rolled over onto her back for a more thorough going-over. Without having been instructed to do so, she held her thighs open, giving each young man a chance to pull apart the lightly haired puffs of tender flesh and inspect the feminine mysteries between them. They swarmed around the object of their curiosity, their noses informing them of an unusual fragrance—a fragrance like a flower, yet not like a flower—a fragrance unlike anything within the limited world of their experience.

A trembling pink tongue greeted them, seeming to grow larger and larger beneath their scrutiny. Because of Monika's earlier exertions, a few grains of sand had adhered to the surface of her bud and the surrounding rosy sheaths. The youngest man tried to pluck them off. However, the silken flesh proved so moist and sticky that he had to wet his finger with saliva in order to wipe away the errant particles. He needed to repeat the process several times to cleanse the unfolded blossom thoroughly, his actions prompting the florid projectile to branch out into two candy-pink flaps. Directly below this highly elastic structure was what first appeared to be a tiny slash made by a sharp knife. However, closer scrutiny showed the wound had simply been an illusion; instead of blood, the incision was speckled generously with whitish beads. Theo well knew the pleasure-giving function of this crimson sliver, and it, too, was explored by many curious fingers, all of which would be licked discreetly afterward.

When everyone's fingers had become fully familiar and scented with the outer and inner contours of Monika's body, Theo took charge once again. Like an uncompromising choreographer assisting an undisciplined ballerina into a difficult plié, he positioned the nude woman on widely spaced feet and lowered her into a broad squat, making certain that she kept her knees pointing in opposite directions. Her legs quaked from the abnormal strain being placed upon them and, in her blindness, she nearly toppled face-forward onto the hot sand. However, Theo crouched down behind the elegant curves of her buttocks, using his body to support her back. His fingers gripped the tensed cheeks, splitting them wider, and she leaned into him, her shackled hands dangling uselessly between her outspread thighs. He motioned with his chin at one of his companions, who moved quickly into place, kneeling before Monika and consequently shoring her up from that end as well. The youngest of the group remained standing, his excitement rendering him immobile as he hungrily contemplated the beautiful and unresisting figure sandwiched between his two best friends.

As Monika was forced to maintain her immodest pose, it instantly became clear to each of them the wide-ranging potential of the female body—especially a body that had already been well primed for every conceivable entry. There would be no need for consultation as three pairs of shorts were sloughed off, presenting an unseeing and unspeaking Monika with three upstanding and very purple stalks, their foreskins peeled so far back they were barely discernible from the shaft. Theo nodded to his partner, stationed at her front, signaling that he begin.

Accordingly, he himself up into the dripping slit of Monika's vagina, stretching it into a large vermilion gash as the humid channel beyond filled with his eager youth. Then Theo fitted the bulbous head of his penis into her anus, straining to push himself in the rest of the way. Monika's captive buttocks projected out toward him and although the fiery hollow between them was still extremely slick from its earlier amusements, it failed to yield to his rigid bulk. The masseur had been far less amply endowed than his younger competitor, thus enabling him to coerce even the most stubborn of rear entryways into compliance. Nevertheless, the heretofore unacquainted Theo could not have known this important piece of information. Indeed, he had never expected to be greeted with such extreme reluctance and he blamed his friend's penis for using up all the available space, thus significantly crowding the slimmer and drier passage he himself was in the midst of penetrating. So impossible a challenge only increased his youthful determination. He attempted to enlarge the overburdened opening, using the tips of his thumbs to retract the snug-fitting elastic seal from around the muscular knob of his thwarted organ. He rapidly discovered that this method, although entertaining and—to the lovely recipient, a sophisticated form of punishment in itself—was not the most efficient way to solve his dilemma. The thin lip of tissue proved nearly impossible to hold, especially when it had already been stretched beyond the breaking point.

Suddenly Theo recalled what his more expert predecessor had done. His frustration led to success as he spread Monika's buttocks as wide as they would go and, pushing with all his might, slid slowly all the way inside of the cramped cavity, with André's leftover semen aiding his way. He pressed his face into the sweet-smelling silken mane of her white-blonde hair and, imagining it to be the flaxen thatch of curls he had admired earlier, began to pump the enlarged socket of her anus.

Having thoroughly trapped their fair-skinned booty between their lithe bodies, the young fishermen could now devote all of their efforts to the fulfillment of their own pleasures and they filled Monika's two passages to capacity. Working as a team in their small fishing boat had prepared them well for this moment. Thus, while Theo continued to keep her bottomcheeks open, his partner made certain that her knees remained outspread, each particular service benefiting not only the one performing it, but the group as a whole. As the interlocked trio performed their complex ballet, fumbling fingers dislodged the gag from Monika's mouth. The saliva-dampened cloth was replaced by a dribbling penis, which she began to suck immediately, her mouth greedy for its raw masculine flavors.

With every major orifice occupied and her arms, legs, and eyes in bondage, Monika had attained true happiness. Without freedom of movement and the distraction of vision, her body had become highly sensitized to even the most subtle sensations. She could give herself over completely to the piercing barbs of pleasurable pain as the two boys forced her to accept them into the constricted tunnels of her vagina and rectum. Even the taste of the youth in her mouth seemed somehow sharper—more tart and earthy. It mattered not that her breasts were being squeezed cruelly and her delicate pink nipples bitten savagely by one of her seducers, whose teeth were evidently intent on drawing blood. Such a thorough invasion into her body combined with the briny tang of the youth's penis in her mouth made her want to stay like this forever.

Indeed, had Monika only guessed that her wish would come true.

Just as she became acclimated to the unique rhythms of these ambitious appendages, Monika had to reorient herself to a whole new set of rhythms. The young men switched places. The wet, fragrant penis from her vagina was then placed in her mouth, the one she had been so hungrily sucking now jabbing its way insistently into her backside. Theo plunged the stout head of his organ into her slit, battering it hard as his friend worked his slightly smaller version in and out of her sore and overextended rectal canal. However, almost as soon as Monika had readjusted to the change, the trio alternated yet again, Theo driving his hot shaft into her mouth, where the combined flavors of her two passages and the three penises exploded on her tongue, sending an urgent message to her clitoris. This went on for several rounds until finally the young men could no longer contain the storm threatening to break and all three of her orifices were generously flooded with male fluids.

Monika would never be seen again. The Elysium Spa staff assumed that she had gone for a swim and drowned, for an abandoned beach towel had been found on the sandy shore along with a blue kerchief, although its presence could never be explained fully. Despite this tragic loss of so beautiful a woman, Dr. Bronski refused to allow sentiment to get in the way of business. Not wanting any adverse publicity to tarnish the image of his healthful kingdom—nor, indeed, to bring the light of inquiry on it—the local authorities received a hefty donation.

Thus, with the appropriate documents drawn up, Monika's husband received the unfortunate news. Within a week he took up permanently with his teenage mistress. His wife was relegated quickly to a hazy memory. Only André seemed to mourn the loss of the lovely Dane. It would take repeated consumption of Carla's spicy cinnamon wreath to make the sublime image of Monika's pale tea rose fade eventually.

However, Monika was still very much alive—as alive as she had ever been in her young life. The fishermen had taken her back to their island, where she was kept in a dilapidated shack the three of them shared. Here she remained under lock and key, her body always unclothed and her openings always ready, her need for subjugation obliged easily by the continuous presence of ropes at her ankles and wrists. These were attached to a long lead tied securely to a rotting wooden ceiling beam, thus preventing her from escaping. So complete was Monika's new confinement that she could not even go outside to use the privy without somebody's accompanying her. Yet these coarse bindings would never be removed—not even for a bath. Her captors never knew when they might come in handy.

Indeed, they found it highly pleasurable to truss their exotic slave into positions best suited for even the most aberrant of orchestrations, often inviting their friends to amuse themselves with the immobilized prisoner. Monika's one remaining kerchief made a reappearance during these get-togethers, for her inability to see how many lusty young penises she was attending to or to whom they belonged proved extremely arousing for both herself and the eager participants. She would make a game of it by attempting to distinguish one from another, making an educated guess as to whether the penis that had just been in her mouth was now firmly ensconced within her bottom, or if the former occupant of her vagina had returned for yet another engagement in the very same location. However, the odds usually went against her, for there seemed to be far too many players to keep track of.

As the oldest, Theo was usually the most inventive. Hence, for his cousin's birthday, the Dane was suspended from the old ceiling beam, the main rope tied around her waist and looped behind her knees so that as she clutched the securing line with both hands to stay upright, she hung in a pronounced squat. The extremeness of her situation severely distorted the normally graceful contours of her lower half; the pulpy lips of her labia distended in the lewdest of kisses, her buttocks two halves of a juicy melon breaking apart in a generous split—and all of this hovering over the flushed faces of her young admirers! A sturdy oak table was placed strategically directly below these womanly treats so that each young man awaiting his turn could shimmy beneath Monika to penetrate the opening of his choice and, like the rotors of a propeller, spin her legs around and around

## Elysian Days and Nights

so that his immersed penis received a vigorous burnishing within the heavenly whirlpool of vagina or rectum. On this particular occasion, Theo's greedy cousin sampled both; later he returned for more heady encounters with the female carousel whenever his plaintive pleas managed to move his elder cousin's heart.

However, Theo's tastes had matured to a significantly higher level than those of his younger comrades. Unbeknownst to them, he indulged himself in private with the fair-skinned beauty. Although he continued to partake of her amiable orifices with his penis, the succulent mysteries between her thighs held a curious fascination for him, especially the supple tongue that always grew so pink and plump. Perhaps always being the one to whom all the others looked for guidance and protection had instilled in Theo a wisdom beyond his years, for he knew that this silken flap surely held a purpose other than as an object of play—an object to be pinched and pulled at by a team of rowdy young men. Oh, how his lips yearned to encircle it!

And finally they would. One morning Theo dispatched his two friends to the village on a bogus errand, knowing the wild-goose chase he had sent them on would take up at least an hour. Monika's nude form had already been prepared for the day's events. She hung blindly from the ceiling beam, her trussed lower half awaiting the inevitable onslaught of hearty penises that comprised a normal day. Theo spent several minutes studying the distorted display that her unnatural position had created. The flirtatious nodule of flesh sensed his eyes upon it and surged out from between the splayed puffs surrounding it until finally he could wait no more. He dropped to his knees and took it into his mouth, drawing upon it shyly until he became more familiar with the foreign flavor and feel of the ripe little projectile. Its fragility astounded him—so much so that it awakened in him a sadistic urge to bite. And this he did, albeit gently at first and then with slightly more vigor. With every nip of his sharp white teeth, Monika contracted her buttocks as if seeking to close the wide gap that her hanging position had caused, the fingers of her bound hands coiling themselves in the thick brown hair beneath her. Without the stifling presence of her gag, she could easily have cried out for Theo to stop. And yet she did not. Rather, she wriggled the provocative overhang of her rearcheeks in an urgent appeal. It was answered immediately by the rough intrusion of three fingers into her unprotected anus. Theo employed them mercilessly, digging crudely into the deepest recesses of her rectum, his tongue gaining the courage to explore some of Monika's juicier terrain before hurrying back to suckle the sweet whorls of her clitoris. Indeed, his instincts were truly those of a sexual sophisticate; for in having combined pain with pleasure, he had mastered far more skill than any man twice his age could ever hope to.

Monika's blindfold was always placed over her eyes during these secret meetings with Theo. Still, she always knew whose mouth had given her this special ecstasy. She loved him for it, for his touch—no matter how coarse—somehow reminded her of André. Once Theo had enjoyed what he considered his "appetizer," Monika would then be relegated to her usual subservient role and dispatched to the rest of the group, none of whom would be any the wiser that the surplus of lubricating wetness at her slit and anus had been fostered from the ardent ministrations of their leader's tongue.

Monika never once complained about all the gluttonous young penises she had to satisfy, nor about the conditions in which she was kept. In these primitive surroundings, she had at last found complete and total fulfillment.

The flaming-haired Carla would be the only woman for whom André ever again compromised himself. Indeed, he would never forget his very first time with her and the thrill he'd derived merely from teasing the bashful mouth of her anus with his fingertip. Yet that first heart-wrenching moment, when his skilled hands separated the shapely swells of her buttocks, changed something in him forever. He had discovered a diminutive opening of the most exquisite beauty—a beauty beyond what any mere mortal could ever hope to behold in his humble lifetime. Although different in hue from Monika's pale tea rose, this precious jewel proved every bit as enticing. The furrowed facets of elastic flesh composing the virgin perimeter possessed the color of the finest ground cinnamon, the silken filaments of hair that stippled it glinting in the sunlight like wisps of copper wire.

André was pleased to see that Carla was a natural redhead, for many of the ladies frequenting the spa seemed to be artificial, their well-laden pocketbooks allowing them the luxury of purchasing their beauty, rather than of coming upon it by way of birth. And unlike most people with her fiery hair color, Carla's creamy skin was not marred by a single freckle, save for a tiny smattering deep within the snug crease of her buttocks—and one would need to look long and hard in order to detect even these.

It became immediately clear to the masseur that Carla had never been touched in this rather unconventional location. He tested the waters by letting his fingers inch closer and closer to her secret place. Her body stiffened noticeably as he neared his intended target, but she did not voice any objections. Although disconcerted by the presence of his strong dark hands in so private an area, Carla found it quite pleasurable and began to grow extremely wet from his intimate attentions, a viscous puddle forming on the patch of white towel beneath her fiery mound. The gentle tickling of knowing fingers at her quivering anus made her giggle with delight, so André deemed it safe for him to escalate matters. As with his other clients, he started out by insinuating a well-oiled finger into Carla's rectum as he massaged, holding it quietly within her to put her at ease with the unfamiliar sensation. The hypnotic pressure of his other hand kneading her neck and shoulders served to perpetuate and even prolong the illusion that all this was simply a part of the therapy—a highly essential part, at least for André and his extortive employer. However, unlike his treatment of all the trusting ladies whose naked bodies had previously lain so compliantly upon his table, rather than drawing out the inaugural stages for two to three days, André decided

# ELYSIAN DAYS AND NIGHTS

that Carla was ready for him now. Normally he would *never* have taken such a risk during a first meeting, but years of experience had taught him well. Indeed, this charming young female appeared to have quite an appetite, for one needed only to feel how hungrily the hot walls of her rectum squeezed his immersed finger to know what she wanted. Hence André inserted the tiny nozzle of his bottle into her welcoming anus, squirting the sun-heated oil all the way inside her.

Carla trembled with this unprecedented introduction, feeling the warm, slippery liquid shooting up into her. She experienced a momentary loosening sensation somewhere deep and out of reach—a sensation familiar and yet unfamiliar at the same time. Her trembling intensified as the masseur began very slowly to press the tapered head of his penis into the prepared muscular ring. He had gauged from his earlier discreet probings and pluckings that Carla had never experienced a penetration of this magnitude, and he sighed with rapture, for what André loved best in the world was a young woman's unseasoned anus—especially one of this caliber. He grasped her ankles, pulling her down toward his amorous organ until her legs dangled freely in the air, inadvertently placing her lips directly over the aromatic puddle she had made. The gleaming cheeks of her buttocks projected out in the most immodest fashion, leaving the snug notch between them completely unprotected and placed in a position best suited for an easy invasion. André advanced forward, patiently coercing her untrained rectum into swallowing more and more of his ebony penis. The rich, fruity oil helped prevent him from giving her too much pain and although Carla did experience a slight stinging burn, she allowed herself to relax and enjoy what he was doing to her. Indeed, her excitement mounted as he gained additional headway, and she found herself lapping kittenishly at the moistened spot on the towel. Within minutes, she had propped herself up on her elbows, slamming her hips back and meeting André's bold strokes expertly, the unoccupied opening of her vagina dribbling its honeyed juices onto every available surface, including the feet of her dusky pleasurer.

The masseur came with such a force that he had to grasp the edge of the massage table to keep from collapsing onto the floor. Indeed, he hadn't achieved such ecstasy since that last fateful afternoon on the beach with Monika. Carla, too, felt a powerful explosion between her thighs, albeit not quite so liquid as her dark-skinned lover's. However, the substantially endowed pendant of her clitoris had swollen so much that even the slightest motion could set it off. Upon André's withdrawal, it rubbed against the upholstered surface of the table, sparking yet another eruption.

So great was André's affection for Carla that he kept on refusing the hundred-dollar bills she tried to thrust into his hand whenever he finished with her. He didn't mind accepting a tip from his other clients, but never would he do so from Carla, for she was his special lady.

And André was special to Carla, too. She soon began inviting him back to her bungalow in the evenings. He would always arrive with his folding massage table, knowing that it would not be needed, and yet wishing to maintain the appearance of professionalism in case he might be seen heading toward her private quarters after hours. It simply would not do for the masseur to have any clients at the spa becoming jealous, for that would affect his gratuities and possibly put him in bad standing with his employer. According to Elysium Spa policy, *every* woman had to be made to feel as if she were special—and this meant keeping them ignorant of the fact that the very same things that were being done to them were also being done to all the others. Therefore, André always acted with the utmost discretion—or at least until he was safely behind closed doors, when he could be free to indulge his erotic interests with the lady or ladies of his choice.

And Carla *was* the lady of his choice.

Normally, the only staff members who could be anywhere near a bungalow after dark without attracting suspicion were the maids. They had been instructed always to remain close at hand in the event a guest needed anything. However, for obvious reasons, the management encouraged its talented employees to orchestrate as many after-hours trysts as possible, providing a lady seemed amenable to additional lustful get-togethers after an already-busy day's worth. And the convenient presence of so many beautiful young females attired in short, skimpy uniforms provided an effortless way to stockpile still more incriminating material on an unsuspecting guest.

The prettiest of all the domestics at the Elysium Spa had been assigned to Carla's bungalow. A petite yet well-proportioned brunette, Françoise's smoldering dark eyes and lush head of equally dark hair turned many male and female heads. She had an easy time at the spa and encountered little resistance to her many charms. She had come to the island directly from Paris, abandoning her adolescent dreams of becoming a famous runway model for one of the French couture houses after too many people told her that she wasn't tall enough. Apparently, beauty was not enough of a qualification for the career Françoise desired. She decided to change her life completely, answering an advertisement in *Paris Match*. The idea of working on an exotic Greek isle sounded highly romantic after the grit and cruelty of Paris. She packed her few possessions into a battered old steamer trunk, praying that she would never again have to return to the dirty streets of that city.

After giving her a thorough physical examination, Dr. Bronski hired her on the spot, unconcerned about her lack of experience as a domestic or about her lack of stature in the clitoral department. The girl's obvious appeal outweighed even the doctor's stringent standards about what made a female desirable and what did not. A reasonable man, he realized that not everyone shared his particular tastes and besides, his new employee would be catering to women, not men. Dr. Bronski discerned instantly that the girl was of a highly agreeable nature, for she had endured his rather unorthodox medical methods without ever once questioning his motives.

Françoise had no qualms about the additional duties that would be required of her. The money she would be receiving for her services proved far too tempting to allow any misplaced sense of moral indignation to interfere in the everyday business of the spa. And as for having to deal exclusively with women, Françoise had no qualms about that, either. Given her sexual preference, the thought of having the beautiful young bodies of so many beautiful young females entirely at her disposal *and* getting paid for it...why, she would happily have agreed to work for free!

In the intimate atmosphere of the Elysium Spa, Françoise felt truly appreciated for the first time in her life. Back in the days when she had been young and naïve and hoping against all the odds to become a model, she could always be found at all the best fashion houses, ingratiating herself with the statuesque young women who made their livings strutting up and down the catwalks attired in the finest Paris had to offer. Believing they might help her get the start that she so desperately craved, Françoise did their bidding—running personal errands, massaging tired and abused feet, sewing up tears in clothing. No task was too menial for her to perform. However, she also serviced her idols in other ways: licking and sucking the fragrant, steaming folds between so many pairs of slender thighs that her knees finally developed permanent bruises on them from having to constantly kneel on cold hard floors. With so much practice, Françoise soon became quite expert in the oral arts and would frequently be called upon by the willowy young models to pleasure them—even during those hectic moments between clothing changes while everyone bustled about, including the couturiers themselves. Yet, despite her skilled tongue, Françoise received nary a thank-you, let alone that much-needed boost up into the modeling world. She was being used, a fact that turned the sweet, heady flavor of all those moist young slits sour in her mouth.

Then Françoise fell in love with a willowy American model named Virginia. Of course she dared not expect to have her feelings returned from this aloof goddess, for Virginia had become the toast of Paris, with all the best couturiers competing to drape their most expensive finery over her perfect limbs. Surely someone in her league would never even notice the lovesick little French girl. Yet one day from out of nowhere, the model invited Françoise back to her Rive Gauche apartment, her tone indicating that the purpose of this visit would be for much more than a glass or two of wine. Thrilled to the point of bursting, she arrived half an hour early, only to discover that Virginia had a husband.

A few minutes later, Françoise made another discovery. Apparently, the husband planned to watch the two women making love. Indeed, it seemed that she would have little choice but to comply with this humiliating requirement, for she might never again have another opportunity to touch and taste this exquisite creature.

Virginia was already waiting in the bedroom when her husband answered the front door. Without issuing even the most cursory of greetings to their guest, he immediately ushered Françoise into the sunny boudoir. The tall windows had been thrown open to receive the warm afternoon air, the heavy mauve velvet draperies tied back with a silken cord to allow the sun to embrace all corners of the hexagonal room. The model reclined serenely upon a large, round bed, the intense light illuminating her nudity as if she were on a stage. Françoise had never seen her completely disrobed, and she grew weak at the ethereal vision before her.

Virginia's flawless oval face was turned toward one window. The slight twisting of her neck emphasized the deep hollow in her throat and Françoise noticed a tremulous pulsing of blood beneath one dainty ear. Indeed, it made her think of the fragility of life itself and her eyes filled with love for this beautiful woman. Two gentle conical swells topped Virginia's chest, the tiny peach gems crowning them facing in opposite directions. Despite the constant breeze flowing into the room, they had not yet stiffened and, in fact, looked so delicate and childlike that such a womanly response would have seemed incongruous.

Incoming sunlight framed a carefully trimmed pubic mound. A modest dark square at the apex had been left in its natural state. It reminded Françoise of a miniature painting, so minute and lovely was its canvas. The remaining silken hairs had been cropped meticulously into a short fringe to reveal the pale labial cleavage, and the same delectable shade of peach forming Virginia's nipples repeated itself here, for the ripe fruit of her clitoris thrust out impudently from this burnished seam, eliciting a wet reaction from the French girl.

Oblivious to the silent masculine presence in the room, Françoise undressed hurriedly and joined Virginia on the bed. It was difficult to know just where to start, for there was so much of this delectable woman that she wished to explore, and she wanted so very much to please her. Hence, she decided to begin with a kiss. Virginia tasted of violets, and Françoise drank greedily of her sweet saliva, aching to drink of the sweetness she knew would be raining down from between the model's slender thighs. As she stroked the velvety surface of the other woman's tongue with her own, her hands caressed the lush softness of Virginia's breasts. Tantalized by the girlish coronets atop them, Françoise bowed her head and sucked them one at time, her lips sculpting the fragile buds into two tiny peach buttons. She soon found herself being urged still lower by an insistent pair of hands upon her bare shoulders. But the French girl needed no prompting, for *this* was the direction in which she most wanted to go.

Virginia's thighs opened wide and Françoise placed her face between them, dizzy with desire for the fragrant feminine folds and the darling little flap now being offered to her. She covered the entire area with her mouth, trying to take in as much of this moist perfection as possible. Her lips and tongue worked industriously, exploring this heavenly terrain with great care. Indeed, she wanted to memorize every uphill and downhill slope and every subtle change in flavor, knowing that this moment might never come again.

Suddenly, her intense concentration was interrupted rudely by Virginia's husband, who ordered that the women alter their position, complaining peevishly that he could not properly observe the goings-on because their guest's pageboy crop was in the way. Hence his wife quickly shimmied out from beneath Françoise, who then took her place, lying on her back with the model squatting backward above her upturned face. As much as she hated to admit it, the woman's husband had made an excellent decision, for Virginia's straddle served not only to fully expose her genitalia to Françoise, but to distend the vaginal lips and clitoris dramatically as well. She resumed her oral quest happily.

The husband made himself comfortable at Françoise's feet, thus facing the upraised cheeks of Virginia's buttocks. From his new post he could now see everything that had previously been denied him and he watched craftily through the inverted V formed by his wife's outspread thighs as the pretty young woman suckled her clitoris noisily. The fleshy tongue had grown to a size the likes of which he had never managed to make of it. A tremor of jealousy washed over him. Virginia's continual moans of pleasure and her female suitor's lusty slurping did little to appease him and his agitated penis. Oblivious to the rampant emotions in the room, Françoise continued to dote on the tasty projectile beneath the critical eye of the husband, her tongue making frequent forays into the model's savory slit and vanishing so deeply within it that he thought it had gotten stuck.

Unbeknownst to Françoise, her own clitoris had become extremely prominent and her thighs parted instinctively, falling open to show the silent spectator the dewy pink slit of her vagina. Unfortunately, he misinterpreted this as a sign that she wanted him. Not wishing to disappoint the charming creature—for he always believed in being hospitable to guests—he slid his middle finger in and out of the tiny snippet, utilizing the generous pad of his thumb to stimulate the desirous little berry above. Françoise's body stiffened immediately; in her impassioned ministrations, she had completely forgotten that the woman's husband had even been in the room with them. Although she would have preferred for him not to touch her at all, she decided that he was probably harmless and refrained from making a fuss, for she did not wish to upset Virginia at so crucial a moment. Instead, she fantasized that his fingers belonged to one of the beautiful models she had recently encountered at the Chanel boutique, her line of sight so completely taken up by the fleshly accouterments above that she could not see the glowing red bulb throbbing wetly in the man's palm.

Hence this fantasy soon met with a crushing end when Françoise felt her knees suddenly wrenched apart, something hard and cruel pushing at her unpracticed entrance. When she attempted to scream, Virginia's vulva bore down heavily on her mouth, smothering her into submissive silence as a searing beam of steel plunged into the slender thoroughfare. Trapped by the thing she most desired, Françoise could do naught else but continue licking and sucking the musky female foliage as the last quivers of orgasm finally waned.

Virginia's husband pumped enthusiastically into the fresh new opening before him, urging Françoise's knees up and out so he could penetrate to the core of her being. His wife leaned forward and placed her weight on her hands, her thighs continuing to hold the French girl's head captive between them. In modifying her position, she had significantly improved the angle of view for her spouse, and he studied the skill with which Françoise drew the elastic silken tentacle of his wife's peachy clitoris into her mouth. Perhaps he could learn something from this talented little mademoiselle, so he hitched her coltish thighs even higher and wider and, without a single lull in the wild bucking of his hips, lowered himself onto the delicate breasts below, thus placing his face directly at the fissure of Virginia's buttocks. Placing his hands upon the projecting cheeks, he pulled them apart to better inspect the oral attentions taking place. And apparently all was well, for despite the girl's initial opposition, her ardor had not waned one iota. In fact, it seemed to have intensified, for the tight passage now housing his penis had grown even hotter and wetter than before—as had Virginia. Indeed, it truly warmed his heart to see his beloved wife enjoying herself so much. The creamy dribbles from her slit served as silent testimony to the artistry of her enchanting friend. He watched in delight as Françoise's talented tongue slithered forward to collect the fruit of her labors.

The brown button of Virginia's anus beckoned to her husband from between her nethercheeks. Finding it impossible to ignore, he began to lap at it, his taste buds singing from its peppery tartness—a tartness made all the more flavorful by the overflow of piquant honey from her vagina. She nudged her hips toward her husband's mouth in encouragement, her moans becoming louder and more fervent until they eventually carried out the open window and reached the passersby on the sidewalk below. One gentleman actually stopped to listen, his dormant penis coming to immediate attention within the confines of his tailored trousers. Indeed, he could only dream of the delicious activities occurring directly above his head and he took longer than usual in arriving home to his wife and children that evening. This overheard encounter had required him to satisfy his lust by squirting his fluids into the obliging mouth of an available *fille de joie*.

The dual licking of her two holes proved far more than any woman could bear and Virginia climaxed a second time, awarding Françoise with even more of the liquid sweetness she had so wished to drink. With one more powerful plunge, her husband fed the French girl's somewhat-less-willing orifice with his own liquid donation, further amplifying his orgasm by thrusting his tongue deep into the plush chasm of Virginia's convulsing rectum.

Had the woman's husband wished to possess her orally, perhaps Françoise might not have minded so much. Indeed, the paradise of having Virginia's juicy sex in her mouth was worth virtually any price—even the price of a man's head between her thighs. But when this man violated her—and did so in obvious collusion with his wife, Françoise had been devastated. No doubt he was as handsome as his wife was beautiful. But it mattered not—she had been deceived in the worst possible way. Why, she had actually believed that Virginia loved her!

Thus, with her mouth scented with Virginia's spending and her panties soaked with Virginia's husband's semen, a disillusioned and very brokenhearted Françoise rode home on the métro. She'd had barely enough coins to pay for the fare. In her naïveté, she had assumed that she would be spending the night in the model's elegant apartment, then riding with her to work in her red sports car the next morning. Tears of anguish rolled down her still-flushed cheeks as she replayed the sordid scene over and over in her mind, the faint pulsing of her tumescent clitoris cuckolding her. In her misery, Françoise failed to notice the increasing shabbiness of the other riders as she neared her stop. Suddenly the Parisian charm of her tiny apartment no longer felt like a sanctuary to her, but rather the run-down hovel which it really was. The quaint neighborhood she lived in showed its true squalidness the moment she climbed up out of the putrid bowels of the subway, furthering her grief.

This incident served as a major turning point for Françoise. There would be no more Virginias in her life, no matter how beautiful or seductive they might be. She vowed never to fall in love again. From now on, she would use women as they had always used her.

Shortly after the taste and smell of Virginia finally began to fade from memory, Françoise left for her new job at the Elysium Spa, never looking back. However, before her final departure, she decided to do something to remake herself—something which would distinguish her in some way, no matter how minor—something which would devastate every woman she met. Although pretty in a dark, petite way, Françoise knew that she could never compete with the stunning statuesque beauties like Virginia and the other models she had known. So one lonely afternoon, without any preconceived notion of what this mysterious *something* might be, she found herself wandering the Arab quarter of the city. Ever since she had quit her job, her hours had become filled with nothing but a bleak emptiness. Indeed, even this unhappy fate seemed preferable to the humiliation of returning to the salon and seeing Virginia again—or, worse yet, seeing Virginia's husband.

As she rounded yet another corner that looked identical to the one she had just come around, a small beauty parlor came into view. Although its sign was in Arabic, Françoise immediately felt comfortable with the idea of entering the establishment. At least here she would be certain not to encounter anyone she knew. No glamorous Parisian fashion model would ever allow herself to be caught dead in such a plain-looking shop.

The moment she opened the door, Françoise knew what it was that she wanted—it had been so obvious all along, and yet she had not realized it until now. Perhaps she should be grateful to the cold-blooded and hot-clitted Virginia for at least one thing. Had it not been for their encounter, the idea might never have occurred to her. Why, Françoise could hardly believe her good fortune to have wandered right into a place that could provide her with such a unique service.

A bent old crone led her into a sectioned-off area in the rear of the shop where Françoise sat tentatively on the chewed-up ledge of a padded table. A beauty parlor in a better part of the city would surely have enclosed the space with drywall, but apparently the management preferred function over fashion. Yet, despite the worn condition of the furnishings, everything looked very clean and hygienic. However, Françoise experienced a brief prickle of concern, for the only privacy barrier between her and the rest of the shop was a flimsy Japanese screen that barely concealed her from the other customers.

A rusty hot plate rested on a chipped table in one corner. The woman hobbled over to it and began to stir the contents of a cast-iron pot with a large wooden spoon. Whatever she was in the midst of preparing gave off a sweet, wholesome aroma, reminding Françoise of the seaside carnivals she had gone to as a child. Suddenly her thoughts returned to those innocent and carefree days so long ago. She pictured her girlhood self skipping from confectioner to confectioner and filling up on chocolates and toffees and licorice until her stomach cried out for mercy. A series of erratic hand signals interrupted this bittersweet reverie. She was forced to return to the present—*and* to the reason why she had come to this strange place.

The old woman gestured to Françoise to remove her skirt and panties. She did so and lay back on the rickety table with great trepidation. Its legs creaked ominously beneath her slight weight, furthering her apprehension. Perhaps she had made a mistake. Perhaps she should have considered this matter more carefully before she had gone bounding into the shop like the pigtailed ragamuffin she had once been. But it was too late, however, for the Arab woman soon approached the table, her wooden spoon coated with a thick caramellike substance. Gnarled fingers deftly rolled it into a medium-sized amber ball. Before Françoise could fully comprehend its unusual nature, it was pressed down onto her exposed pubic mound and rolled quickly across the surface, pulling out the silken black hairs that had been with her since puberty.

The speed with which the old woman worked defied the slowness of her ancient limbs. Françoise bit her tongue to keep from screaming. The process was excruciating. Yet nothing could have prepared her for the torment of the sticky ball's brutally ripping the hairs out of her labia. And it only got worse as the aged Arab neared the delicate flesh around her slit. Indeed, Françoise thought she would faint, but just when she nearly did, she found herself being rolled onto her stomach and her rear crevice attended to. The woman made a thorough job of it, leaving the insides of the French girl's supple young buttocks as smooth and silken as her newly denuded vulva.

Françoise felt reborn. She had never believed that she could be so beautiful. Her bruised pride quickly returned to normal, joined by a new sense of self-confidence. Suddenly she wanted to show herself off—to parade naked in front of all of Paris. Oh, if Virginia could only see her now! Why, she would make the willowy American crawl to her on her hands and knees and—if Françoise were in a particularly charitable mood—perhaps grant the model a little lick of her smooth, hairless cleft.

Henceforth she made regular trips to the old Arab, finding that with each successive treatment, less and less of the unsightly hair grew in. Even the pain became tolerable eventually, although this probably stemmed more from Françoise's happiness with the results than with any measurable lessening of discomfort. Indeed, each tiny black bristle plucked from her flesh made her rejoice, for it brought her closer and closer to absolute perfection.

The old woman was on the verge of retirement, so she taught Françoise the secret of the magic depilatory. Françoise could now wax herself in private and she did so religiously, cooking up a batch of the syrupy goo the instant a dark shadow formed on her pale mound. Thus liberated from the obscuring muff of hair, she reveled in her immaculate new look, striking racy poses before the tarnished old mirror in her bedroom—poses that grew increasingly explicit, as did her arousal over what she saw reflected back to her. The fleshy puffs of her labia were dramatically striking without their usual curly coif and even Françoise herself became completely captivated by the flirtatious conspicuousness of her clitoris and, upon closer inspection, her slit and anus. Her nudity excited her so much that she would kneel in front of the mirror and masturbate, spreading her thighs wide so the ripe pout split open, allowing her to study every succulent pink detail of her newly uncovered womanhood. Sated from this intoxicating perspective, she would then turn around and admire herself from behind, pulling the cheeks of her buttocks apart and sliding a finger into the glorious café-au-lait dimple precisely at the point of orgasm.

The lovely French girl had discovered the key to her future success.

At the Elysium Spa, Françoise wore a traditional black-and-white French maid's uniform complete with apron and starched ruffles. Indeed, it was traditional in every respect save for one slight alteration: She wore nothing at all beneath the short stiff skirt. According to the spa's dress code, undergarments were expressly forbidden for domestics in her class, but she quickly became used to the erotic sensation of having her genitalia and backside exposed to the air and to the longing eyes of guests and other staff members. Françoise exalted in being so delightfully unencumbered, although despite the powerful urge to do so, she had never dared to go about the dangerous streets of Paris in such a fashion. However, the island proved to be a special haven where even the most salacious of avocations were encouraged. The new maid thrived in such an atmosphere. Having always been dwarfed by the beautiful women whom she had worshiped so faithfully, Françoise made the most of her new situation. She became quite calculating in the manner in which she both moved and spoke, her every gesture designed to seduce even the most upright. She continued to remove all traces of her pubic hair with the old Arab woman's sticky concoction—even the dainty sable ringlets encircling her compact little anus.

Despite her uniform, Françoise was not a common domestic. Indeed, the moment never arrived when she would be required to get her hands soiled from mopping or scrubbing, for the real cleaning would always be done by anonymous cleaning women who came in the mornings and left by early afternoon, their pear-shaped forms unnoticed by the paying guests.

Françoise and her ilk performed the more intimate tasks of a lady's maid, seeing to it that the guest assigned to them had everything she needed in order to make her stay at the spa as luxurious and pleasurable as possible. Such duties consisted of stocking the bungalow bathrooms with imported bath salts, expensive shampoos, and fine-milled soaps of every conceivable scent; arranging for clothing to be cleaned and pressed; and taking care of personal errands. In the evenings, the maids slipped into the bungalows and performed their most important function of all: turning down the beds. This seemingly innocuous task often provided them with the opportunity they had been waiting for.

Of all the maids at the Elysium Spa, Françoise proved to be the most successful in her duties. She earned many tips in only a short time. Although all the girls were extremely appealing in both face and figure, she seemed to have a special talent for knowing just how to inflame a woman's dormant sexual tendencies toward her own kind and bring it to the fore, making her conquests frenzied with desire for the feel and flavor of another woman's body. Like André, one of Françoise's major triumphs was Carla. Unlike André, she would not spare the redhead from the judgmental eye of the camera.

The third night that Françoise went to Carla's bungalow to turn down the bed, she discovered her sitting in a chair, reading. The first two nights they had missed each other, for upon returning from the library in the main building, Carla saw the neatly folded-back covers and plumped-up pillows and knew the maid had been there. Her intimate scent still lingered in the bedroom, making Carla shiver inexplicably. She had noticed the pretty little French girl around the compound, but had not really given her much thought. Indeed, why should she? After all, she was only a maid. Yet even though Carla and her husband had servants in their three homes, somehow it seemed different here on the island—as if these people truly wished to go out of their way to please. She had never felt completely comfortable with her own staff, for they had been put in place long before she had ever arrived on the scene. Having been hired by the first Mrs. Eberhardt, they made no effort to hide their resentment of the second Mrs. Eberhardt. And Mr. Eberhardt considered the disciplining of domestics well beneath his dignity. For what else was a wife good for if not to deal with the household help?

As Françoise busied herself with her duties, Carla offered her a polite smile. She enjoyed being catered to so well and she returned her attention to the novel she was reading—an English murder mystery—feeling that all was right with the world. Although not particularly concerned with the presence of the maid, she soon found herself so distracted by her bustling presence that she could not concentrate on her reading. Words hopped all over the pages of her book like tiny bugs, creating havoc with her eyes. She had to focus elsewhere constantly to clear her vision. Therefore she could not help noticing when Françoise leaned forward to plump up the pillows. The absence of panties beneath the overly short skirt of her uniform made Carla doubt her eyes once again.

Having frequented many elegant hotels and spas worldwide, Carla had encountered more than enough similarly uniformed maids to consider this peculiar. But maybe she had not really seen what she had thought she'd seen—or, rather, *not* seen. After all, it had been a long day what with Dr. Bronski's usual morning physical, a couple of rounds of tennis, and a hearty lunch followed by swimming and sunbathing—not to mention the extremely thorough massage André had given her afterward. Indeed, the breached mouth of her anus still glowed with his ebony presence. Hence Carla finally attributed this provocative illusion to fatigue. But whichever way she rationalized it, she could not ignore the insistent throbbing between her crossed thighs that her deluded eyes had induced. However, when the maid crouched to tuck the edges of the sheets neatly beneath the mattress, the lower curves of her buttocks came into view, destroying what little remained of Carla's already rattled composure. Françoise leaned forward while she worked, the perky half-moons protruding defiantly as the starchy hem of her skirt stood away from her thighs like the paper peeled back from around a cupcake, thus displaying even more intimate details to her astonished onlooker.

Surely this could not be! Why, the young maid did not possess a single lock of pubic hair—*anywhere*. Those places that should have been covered with the dark down were instead a burnished bronzy-pink landscape of dewy flesh, hiding nothing from Carla's curious eyes. The girl's tiny vaginal opening peeked at her, showing off its succulent nature. It appeared to beckon to her. Suddenly Carla wondered what it might be like to taste it. She had never done such a thing in her life—let alone considered it—but as the seconds dragged past with Françoise continuing to remain poised with such innocent impropriety on the floor before her, the idea did not seem so foreign at all. Nor did it seem foreign to her clitoris, for it twitched anxiously, nearly doubling in size. Of course Carla had no idea that every subtle shift of the girl's body had been calculated carefully for maximum effect.

The resplendent details of Françoise's sex became ever more apparent as she reached underneath the bed and straightened out the dust ruffle, her thighs opening from the strain of her position. A bright berry projected out from between two full satiny lips. Carla squeezed her eyes shut, attempting to obliterate the disturbing image of pressing her own lips to them in a sweet, fragrant kiss. Yet the scene insisted on playing itself out against her closed lids until she could virtually taste what it would have been like to do so. Instead, she sprang from the voyeuristic theater of her chair, fleeing to the opposite side of the bed to lie down, her face burning from her stealthy observations. How could she even consider doing such an unnatural thing? Why, she, too, was a woman—and a married one at that!

Françoise unfolded herself from off the floor and materialized at Carla's side, her hairless pudendum hovering at the unsettled woman's nose level. "Does the lady require me further?" The courtesy of her tone belied the impudence of her posture. Her alluring female scent wafted toward Carla, weakening her so much that she could not stop her trembling fingers from reaching forward to slip between the maid's thighs. Françoise arched her back, urging her naked pelvis closer to the searching digits.

The sensation of touching this exotic flesh was unlike anything the redhead had ever known. Her fingers sank into the moist softness, exploring the mysterious folds and thrusting gently upward into the heated well of Françoise's vagina. The girl's clitoris fluttered yearningly against Carla's knuckles and was so charming both in character and appearance that she felt compelled to brush her lips against it. What possible harm can there be in doing so? she argued with the silent voice of her guilt—a voice that sounded very much like her husband's. However upon contact her tongue acted entirely on reflex, darting out and licking greedily at the pliant little fruit. As if in reply, the fleshy nub surged toward her mouth, seeking to gain admittance. A moment later Françoise was straddling Carla's face and she stared down through her splayed thighs, watching her clitoris disappear between the other woman's lips.

At first Carla thought the taste was strange, but as she continued to explore Françoise with her tongue, she grew used to the unusual piquant flavor and began to draw more of it in, introducing the honeyed liquid to her inexperienced palate. The maid accommodated Carla further by lying on the bed and spreading her girlish legs as wide as they would go. Her tawny folds opened up completely, revealing the rich ripe pink usually hidden from view.

A sharp jolt went through Carla's body and she cried out as if in pain, the long-buried desire for this juicy banquet of young womanhood so overwhelming that she grew faint. Indeed, her pain was genuine, for so many years of being exclusively with a man had rendered her incapable of knowing the most supreme pleasure of all. Like a starving animal, Carla plunged her face down into the rosy flesh, allowing instinct to guide her. Her tongue took on a life of its own as it covered every dribbling nook and cranny both inside and out. She surprised herself with her aggressiveness, especially when she unrolled the plump hairless pout with her thumbs, opening the girl up to even further oral discoveries. As Carla continued to explore, the entire lower half of her face became drenched in the slippery downpour. When she raised her head to take a breath, she unknowingly stared directly into the camera lens hidden behind the vanity mirror, showing both it and Thomas in the control room her lips swollen and glossed with the maid's milky juices.

Indeed, the surveillance man had already forfeited his own juices while Carla had been nursing herself on the dangling tongue of the French girl's clitoris. What a delicious moment that had been! he mused happily, imagining that it had been equally delicious for Carla as well. Yes, Françoise was truly a good friend to him, for she frequently went out of her way to provide him with an extra-special visual treat. No doubt she had orchestrated that pose specifically with him in mind, holding her pert young buttocks up and apart so that he could see not only the redhead's desperate sucklings, but the excited contractions of the maid's rear opening as well. Oh, how perfectly his tongue would fit into it! Perhaps one day she might allow him to experience what she so freely allowed his eyes to possess....

The delectable Françoise would not be the *only* after-hours visitor to Carla's bungalow. As with Monika before her, she found that she required far more than André's obligatory daily massage. His presence in her bedroom soon rivaled that of the petite maid.

The first time Carla had been compelled to invite the masseur back to her room, she had been terrified. She had allowed the handsome islander more than enough liberties with her body already and here she was asking—no, *begging*—for more. Why, the man was little more than a servant himself. Had she lost all sense of dignity since coming to the island? For indeed, the casual atmosphere of the place tended to relax one's inhibitions...or perhaps being on her own for the first time had given Carla the chance she needed to finally learn about herself.

She lay in wait for him on the bed, her plush spa robe rumpled, as if someone had tried to rip it from her body. Of course, André had no way of knowing that in anticipation of his visit, she had spent upwards of half an hour masturbating furiously. Carla's fingers were still moist and fragrant from her self-fulfilling venture, and she kept them balled into two tight fists, ashamed that he might discover her disgraceful secret. Her climax had been difficult in coming; the masseur's impending arrival had made her anxious and guilty. Had André been inclined to investigate the reason for her disheveled state, he would have found the blushing flap of her clitoris not only burning hot to the touch, but swollen to the size of an almond.

Carla had left the front door unlocked and André entered silently, making certain that no one had seen him. From the moment he walked in, he could smell the redhead's excitement. He vowed to make himself worthy of it. Propping his portable massage table against one wall, he headed directly for the bedroom, anticipating a night of the finest anal pleasures any man could ever wish for. Although well versed about the alert buttons located at various points throughout the bungalow, unlike the more calculating and policy-abiding young maid, André would not activate them. Surely the spa compiled more than enough film from their intimate daytime encounters in the sunny courtyard, so he saw no reason for this lack of the client's privacy to continue unabated into the evening.

Unfortunately, André's concern for Carla would not matter in the long run. At that precise moment, Thomas Bronski was monitoring their every movement, his softening penis still throbbing from the orgasm he had reaped from watching the lovely redhead desperately fingering the great glistening strawberry between her thighs. Indeed, he promised himself that he would taste it before too much time had gone by.

The coolness of the bungalow provided a pleasant change from the stark sunlit warmth of their usual meeting place. Tonight André decided to vary his routine slightly, forgoing not only the use of his padded table, but his trusty bottle of massage oil as well. It seemed unnecessary, for Carla was always so wet and slippery every time they met that he felt any additional lubricant would be superfluous. Without the rich, fruity oil, André could now experience his darling Carla in her natural state, and with the thought of doing so ripe in his mind, he began to tremble. Suddenly he wanted to know her in ways so intimate that he dared not give voice to them—indeed, to know her far more intimately than he had ever known *any* woman.

Observing the large pillar that André's penis formed against the front of his khaki shorts, Carla immediately went into position, placing her weight on her knees and reaching around to part her buttocks for her lover's convenience. She held herself open, eagerly waiting for the familiar tapered knob to perform its wondrous magic. But instead the masseur dropped down behind the separated cheeks and spent several minutes admiring the vista before him—or at least it felt that long to Carla, who was by now more than ready to be filled with his obsidian maleness. André's breath further warmed the already-heated anal mouth, and he touched the tip of his tongue tentatively to the orange-brown circle. The seductive muscle nipped back at him in voluptuous encouragement, and he began to swirl his tongue around and around the elastic rim, dipping repeatedly into the dark, gaping void—a void made ever so much more hospitable from his frequent usage of it.

Carla's opening was hot and spicy. André feasted on it without the least bit of self-consciousness, finding the quivering hollow very much like its ground-cinnamon counterpart, with just the merest hint of pepper as a condiment. Indeed, his tongue would feel on fire every time he tasted it—which would be as often as possible.

The recipient of these unconventional attentions recovered rapidly from her initial awkwardness at having a man's tongue in her bottom, for the pleasures gained outweighed any silly Victorian compunctions she might have had at one time. Such divine flattery had never been hers to experience. Nearly delirious with rapture, Carla unceremoniously yanked her buttocks as far apart as they could possibly stretch so that André's appreciative tongue could reach to the farthest depths of her interior.

When he had finally sated himself with this lusty aperture, the masseur awarded his penis its well-deserved turn, for it had been weeping copious tears for a taste of what his nimble tongue had just finished. And Carla received the hungry organ with greater zeal than ever, every minute nerve in her velvety chasm primed for a rigorous invasion. And she would not be disappointed, for the head of André's penis managed to locate even the most remote of pleasure centers; his earlier ministrations had paved the way for a thunderous climax for them both.

While bidding his final good-bye of the night, a good-bye which consisted of one last loving lick of the fiery slot that had given him so much joy, André decided that he wanted a keepsake—something personal of Carla's that he could hold to his heart forever. The next evening, when he came to her bungalow, a burst of inspiration struck him. The redhead had been sitting before the vanity mirror plucking a few errant hairs from her eyebrows. She always wanted to look her absolute best for the masseur, although he scarcely noticed anything unless it was located between the shapely cheeks of her backside. Hence, when she took her usual place on the bed and aimed her naked buttocks at him, instead of feeding it his tongue or penis, André snatched up the discarded tweezers and began to pluck out the coppery hairs surrounding her anus. Carla yelped with this rather cruel denuding of her already-tender rear opening, but held still while he painstakingly pulled out every last one of the fine filaments, only to collect them carefully in a tiny cloisonné box, as if they were strands of gold.

André could not help smelling how much more powerful the scent of Carla's arousal became as he worked, for his nose was mere inches from the succulent folds producing this aromatic phenomenon. Despite his single-minded preference for the less traditional conduit of a woman—and, indeed, the occasional man—he had to admit that Carla's sex was quite becoming what with its generous gleaming copper fluff. From this angle, he could see far more detail than if viewing it from the front. He considered himself highly fortunate to be looking upon such a superior example of young womanhood. The contours of her fragrant femaleness immediately brought to mind a fruit—indeed, a fruit of the juiciest kind, for a crimson mouth shimmered wetly between two pulpy lips, its discharges beginning to dribble from it in a creamy cascade over the clitoral slope below. This meaty flesh divided and framed the bubbling sliver enticingly. André could well understand why Françoise so enjoyed burying her tongue in it.

And he would have many opportunities to watch the lusty little French girl do precisely this, for many of André's visits would be made jointly with Françoise. On these occasions, they would indulge the delicious Carla together, their tongues working simultaneously on her two hungry openings until the redhead whimpered with ecstasy. These affable partnerships provided great pleasure for all, not to mention film of the most incriminating nature imaginable. Indeed, when Carla had first squatted over Françoise's dainty pink mouth, she had never dreamed that so intimate a moment would be seen by so many men—*ruthless* men whose penises craved satisfaction by any means available. The smaller girl had lain with her lips directly beneath the redhead's brimming slit as the masseur took full oral advantage of the spicy opening between Carla's projecting buttocks, her open stance all but eliminating the usually distinct cleavage the pale halves formed.

The three would change into numerous other positions, and André's dark tapered penis would have its opportunity to sluice in and out of the redhead's moistened anus. Meanwhile Françoise continued to use her mouth, licking and sucking at Carla's clitoris as it swelled to the size and shade of a ripe strawberry, her fingers stabbing into the leaking sliver below in harmony with the masseur's long, generous strokes. The constant deep thrusting in the woman's rectum served to pull the voluminous pendant backward, challenging the French girl to hold it deeply into her mouth, her lips meeting up with the humid silken bloom of Carla's labia minora.

As the invisible hand of Thomas Bronski worked frantically on his thickset penis only a brief stroll away from the bungalow, it would become Carla's turn to drown herself in the musky fluid folds of the maid, with the skilled André not missing a single beat as she shifted position. She bent down very low so that her mouth could reach the hairless crease. Spreading the girl's slender thighs, she placed her head between them, caressing the yearning lips with her own.

Suddenly it felt as if Carla were experiencing the enchantment of her very first kiss all over again—except that this particular kiss far transcended the undistinguished lips of any man she had ever known. Wishing to fully relish the feminine puffs, she drew each one into her mouth, finally absorbing both at once. A shy fluttering made itself known and she flicked the tip of her tongue over Françoise's little berry of a clitoris, feeling it expand outward from within the polished pout. A warm, tangy liquid spilled onto Carla's chin as her tongue teased and tickled, and, turning her attention to the source, she drank from it greedily, sipping so much sweet nectar from the tiny spout that she became drunk from it.

By now Carla had all of Françoise's hairless vulva in her mouth. Yet her hunger only grew in intensity. The sleek perfection excited her so that she soon found her tongue slithering down toward the richly shaded brown crinkle hidden artfully between the French girl's buttocks. Prying the pert cheeks apart to better reach her prize, Carla licked at the little hollow until it glittered. Each exquisite crinkle of the resilient perimeter caught the dwindling sunlight coming in through the open window like the facets of a diamond. Desiring still more of this brilliant jewel, she darted her tongue inside, the secret heat of Françoise's rectum scorching the adventurous tip.

The maid wriggled with unabashed delight, bearing down enthusiastically upon the other woman's encroaching tongue. The movement served to further inflame Carla's passions. Any reserve she had initially felt vanished. Placing both thumbs against the café-au-lait fringe of Françoise's anus, she tugged it open and thrust her tongue in as far as it would reach, moving it in time with the duplicate penetration occurring within her own broadened aperture.

André observed all that transpired before him. A wide smile illuminated his handsome dark features. He was pleased that his adored Carla could derive as much enchantment from the other girl's rear entry as he did from hers. He decided to slow down his movements so that she might have an opportunity to work on Françoise more thoroughly. He knew from experience that it was best not to be rushed. As this was Carla's first encounter with another female's nether regions, she would no doubt wish to explore such exotic terrain at her leisure in order to enjoy it to the maximum. Indeed, this new relaxed pace profited André as well, for it allowed him to better contemplate the redhead's savory opening, and he kept her cheeks widely spread to better appreciate the many charms between them. The tweezers had performed their work well, for even the most minute details of Carla's anus were now exposed to the light. He sighed heavily as he planted himself deeply inside of her, thoroughly besotted by the bright shade of red the stretched rim took on from their union. It glowed like a flame against the blackness of his flesh, the vibrant color reminding him of the many delicious berries he used to pluck from the bountiful fruit trees while a boy in his native land. Suddenly nostalgic for those earlier moments, André reached out a finger and plucked at the elastic tissue fitting so snugly around his penis, finding it tightly sealed.

These private gatherings became a nightly ritual for the three—and, indeed, a nightly ritual for many of the male staff members at the Elysium Spa, all of whom gathered in Thomas Bronski's cramped surveillance quarters at the stroke of six. Each invitee was required to bring his own towel, for the amount of masculine seed spilled during these cinematic events would surely have drowned them all. However, the director of the camera did not share his wealth out of the goodness of his heart, for he had many bargains to strike.

As the erotic unions between the two women intensified in their vigor, André was soon invited to partake of Françoise's rear entrance as well. On occasion the maid had entertained herself with a healthy amount of self-stimulation in this region via the introduction of various dildo objects like those in Dr. Bronski's examination room, yet this would be the first time her anus would be meeting up with the real thing. Although a devout lover of her own sex, Françoise trusted the masseur to do well by her. Surely so many beautiful women could not be wrong!

It required a skilled piece of choreography to set up the two women so that neither would feel slighted by their tapered ebony caller. Hence Françoise and Carla would hold tightly to the iron railing of the bed, their hips pressed closely together so that André would not need to travel far from one lusty opening to the next. The women enjoyed the closeness that these moments brought as the smooth bronzed curve of Françoise's left buttock nuzzled Carla's pearly right swell in a flirtatious camaraderie. And seeing both shapely sets of bottom-cheeks uplifted and nestling against each other nearly drove André to madness, especially when the matching hairless notches winked seductively at him. Yet the masseur prided himself on his self-control. Indeed, most men would not have been able to hold back a climax under these tantalizing conditions, but André was a proven master in the anal arts. He switched back and forth expertly between the two snug sockets presented so invitingly to him, their eclipsed interiors hot and slippery with his fluids and the women's own transplanted liquid offerings. André no longer used his massage oil, preferring instead to let nature take its course, for natural lubricants flowed most generously—especially those of Carla and Françoise. His penis had no difficulty sliding in and out, the dark shaft gleaming as if it had been polished. Indeed, it had. Each woman occupied herself by reaching between the spread thighs beside her to massage the other's hungry clitoris.

Always mindful of playing fair with Carla and

Françoise—for he did not want any petty jealousies to ruin the many ecstasies they would experience together—André serviced the women in several ways. Usually he would begin by taking turns plunging in and out of their outthrust backsides, counting each stroke aloud in his rich honeyed voice to make absolutely certain that he was distributing an equal number of sallies as he alternated rapidly between the two openings. The women grasped the cold iron of the bed railing, stationing themselves firmly on their widely spaced knees and whimpering with excitement—an excitement made all the more heady by the thought that the rigid organ now stretching and straining the delicate flesh of one woman's rectal passage had just emerged moist and heated from the velvety flesh of the other. Carla was particularly affected by this delicious reality. She could hardly wait to thrust her tongue back into the young maid's recently deflowered anus. Indeed, she had developed a taste for it rivaling that of the masseur's for her own flavorful furrow.

Next André employed a much slower approach, offering both Carla and Françoise the rare opportunity to closely observe the unique coupling of penis and anus—a sight they replayed in their dreams for many years to come. With this more moderate tempo, the bed railing would no longer be necessary as a means of support; instead, each woman could position herself directly at the crux of the action, the tip of her nose virtually touching the severely dilated anus before her. Indeed, Carla would forever be haunted by the shockingly vivid image of the masseur's obsidian column stabbing juicily into the French girl's charming café-au-lait ring, the thick braids atop his handsome head swinging wildly from his labors.

Carla and Françoise would often cling tightly to each other, one pair of exquisitely sculpted breasts flattened against another, two hot, swollen clitorises rubbing violently together until the breathless women grew faint from orgasm after orgasm. Originally Françoise had initiated this useful position upon her second successful encounter with the redhead, but it later proved extremely convenient for their carnal trysts with André as well.

Embarrassed and ashamed about her reckless behavior with the attractive young maid on their first night of intimacy, Carla did not speak to the girl when she arrived the following evening to turn down the bed. Instead, she sat trembling in a chair, pretending to be absorbed in a magazine. Yet her heart pounded so hard that she was certain it could be heard all the way to the other end of the tiny island. How could she have allowed such an unwholesome thing to occur? she berated herself continually. For Carla had never been close to a woman even as a friend, let alone touched or tasted one as a lover. She was so unsettled by these events that, upon awakening that morning, she had packed her bags to leave the spa.

Uttering not a single word of greeting to the bungalow's cowering occupant, Françoise slipped off her skimpy uniform and lay down naked upon the bedsheet she had just uncovered, her bronzed thighs parting subtly. Upon first glance, one would have assumed she was preparing for a nap. However, the rapid up-and-down movement of her rib cage and the subsequent gentle rolling of her breasts gave away her excitement—as did the sharp terra-cotta points of her nipples *and*, upon further examination, the sharp terra-cotta point of her clitoris.

Carla's earlier resolve not to go anywhere near this wanton seductress of a maid began to give way, replaced swiftly by a raw animal craving as she surveyed the sleek mound curving in a graceful hill beneath the girl's flat belly. She could not stop herself from ogling the firm little berry poking out impertinently from the hairless cleavage. The longer she admired it, the more prominent it became. Saliva pooled in Carla's mouth as the desire to suckle this feminine treasure soon became impossible to ignore. As if to entice her further, the French girl raised her knees, exposing herself thoroughly to her agitated observer. The dainty slit of her vagina brimmed to overflowing with its juices and they spilled forth, shimmering like creamed honey against the rosy flesh surrounding it.

Whimpering helplessly, Carla's need to consume this tart-sweet fare overwhelmed her. Realizing the futility of fighting a battle against such silken perfection, she hurled herself between the girl's open thighs, kissing the moist netherlips reverently. They quivered as her tongue pried them apart and met up with the similarly shaped object between them, the two pliant tips fluttering against each other in a fiery dance. Suddenly tears began to stream down Carla's face, spattering the insides of Françoise's thighs. Yet they were not tears of defeat, but rather of victory, for her desire for the young maid was as pure and compelling as the sun itself.

Françoise smoothed down the wild flames of hair atop Carla's head, allowing her lover full access to her fragrant folds and crevices, marveling at how long she could nurse at them without seeming to grow either tired or sated. Indeed, the redhead did not have the wealth of experience of the French girl. But perhaps her talents came to her naturally; for a moment later, a shuddering Françoise climaxed wetly in Carla's mouth. She pulled the still-licking, still-sucking woman up to kiss her, feeding on the glossy musk coating her swollen lips.

Deeming her ready for still further adventures, Françoise removed the redhead's robe and urged her onto her back. Carla closed her eyes and lay compliantly on the bed as invisible fingertips glided over her body, tracing the graceful outlines of her breasts and moving still lower to draw gentle circles on her upper thighs and abdomen. She thrust her pelvis upward toward the teasing fingers, yet Françoise purposely avoided the twitching nucleus of crimson flesh, for she had plans for it. Suddenly she pressed her lips against Carla's ear, her hot breath singeing the elaborate whorls. "There is something special I want to do with you," she whispered huskily, her words taking on an even more erotic note from her accent.

Carla shivered, a powerful jolt electrifying her clitoris. It stood at immediate attention, rising from its nest of coppery hair and pointing directly at Françoise. The redhead had always been embarrassed by its size, believing herself unlike other women—even freakish. Not that she had ever seen another woman's genitals close up, but she knew deep down that this part of her was different and it made her want to hide from the amused scrutiny of others—especially that of her husband.

A virgin until her wedding night, Carla would never forget the disbelieving eyes of her bridegroom—not to mention his stifled giggles—after she had switched off the light hurriedly. Although fairly voluminous even in its dormant state, once aroused, her clitoris resembled a large strawberry. And the young bride had been most aroused on this very special night, for she had waited her entire life for this moment. Indeed, for as far back as she could remember, female friends and relatives had told her that her body would be the greatest gift she could ever give a man, hence she should hold tightly to her virtue until "the right man" came along. Her romantic notions were soon dashed. The expression on her husband's face confirmed her worst fears about herself. Carla would never again feel such desire for a man— especially the man she had married.

However, instead of the sallow smirking face of her husband rising in readiness to penetrate the most tender core of her womanhood, she now had the lovely Françoise poised above her. She sighed blissfully as her hips were straddled lovingly by a pair of slender brown knees. Somehow it felt right to have the nude body of this enchanting young girl on top of her and Carla let her arms fall open at her sides, offering herself as a willing sacrifice to the maid's every carnal whim.

Françoise looked down and smiled, using the fingers of one hand to open up her polished silken pout. With the other, she parted Carla's copper-haired lips expertly and lowering herself, united their two yearning clitorises in a moist, sweet kiss. Carla hoisted her legs up instinctively, wrapping them snugly around the French girl's trim waist. The women began grinding their splayed vulvae together, the fierce friction bringing on orgasm after orgasm until they grew so wet that Françoise finally slid off.

This would become the favorite position for the masseur to apply his special talents. While Carla and Françoise rubbed their lusty clitorises against one another vigorously, he would grab hold of the intertwined figures, sinking his penis into the muscular depths of one, then reemerge only to dive right back into its neighboring twin. The combined juices of the women dribbled generously onto their respective anuses, therefore making André's journey all the slicker and all the more satisfying. The close proximity of their two rear orifices also made his job easier, for he could concentrate his energy on servicing them instead of on complicated and lengthy navigations.

After he had gone, Carla and Françoise cooled their burning openings with the aid of each other's tongue. The normally tight seals were loosened sufficiently to allow the caressing appendages full entry with surprisingly little labor. Indeed, Françoise felt not the slightest bit of remorse that a hidden camera was picking up every immodest detail of Carla's long pink tongue thrusting deeply and hungrily into the yawning café-au-lait cavity that had just been stretched and punctured by the masseur's ebony organ. After all, she didn't mind that she, too, was being recorded and then viewed by any number of men at the spa. Why, she even paid an occasional visit to the surveillance room herself once all the guests had retired for the night, for she found it quite pleasurable to watch her passionate performances on film, although the desperate heat in Thomas Bronski's dark eyes often made her nervous—as did the urgent stiffness in his trousers. Despite their symbiotic relationship, Françoise made it a point never to dally too long lest he take the established limits of their friendship too far.

The young maid genuinely loved her job and performed it freely. And why shouldn't she? Not a single guest had ever once lodged a complaint against her. She left these women well satisfied, and that alone was a reward in itself. There could be no place in Françoise's new world for guilt—not even when it came to the magnificently clitted Carla. Indeed, judging by the lack of coercion required to make her perform the most indelicate of acts, the redhead appeared to be enjoying herself tremendously. Later, when she would be made aware of the reels and reels of highly explicit film taken of her, she would no doubt consider *any* price worth paying for the exquisite pleasures she had experienced during her stay at the Elysium Spa.

Less callous than Françoise, André was not quite so comfortable with his complicity. Yet there seemed to be little he could do about it, so he tried to give Carla as much pleasure as possible, hoping that in some small way this could make up for the pain and humiliation she would later suffer when Dr. Bronski revealed the true character of the spa. Hence the masseur spent more time with her than with any other guest. His every waking moment—even those spent plunging in and out of the hot rectums of the other charming young ladies, soon became occupied with how best to satisfy her every desire—even desires she did not as yet know that she had.

Indeed, what with so much lustful activity taking place, it was no wonder that upon his every examination of Carla, the doctor unwrapped a clitoris even grander than it had been the morning before. How gloriously it filled his hungry mouth! He would nourish himself upon it long after the second round of his ejaculate had dried to a white powder on the floor—until finally his assistant had to announce from behind the locked door that his next appointment was waiting.

André often thought about Carla's husband, conjuring him up as a balding aging captain of high finance with sickly spotty white flesh that never met up with the sun. No doubt the man hadn't the faintest notion of what his fiery young wife wanted, nor the creativity necessary to give it to her. The masseur knew well of this type, for the women who graced his massage table had traded away their youth to these men.

In his romantic fantasies, André envisioned himself and Carla running away together. Surely she could get enough money out of her wealthy husband for the two of them to live the rest of their days in fine fashion. Perhaps he might even take her back home to sunny Barbados, where they would run naked on the beach like a couple of carefree children and he could have access to her spicy rear opening any time of the day or night. And perhaps one day he might even find Monika again. What a paradise their lives would be! Indeed, Carla would find the luscious Dane's pale tea rose quite pleasing to her tongue.

Because of his obsession with the back entrance to the body, the masseur wondered about the powerful impulses motivating his penis toward this somewhat-unorthodox target. Indeed, the moist pink sliver between a woman's thighs did not particularly move him. Not that he found it unappealing—it was simply that he felt such an indomitable draw toward the snug tawny hollow nestling between a pair of womanly buttocks. To test himself, André indulged in the occasional frolic with those of his own sex, all of whom were firm and beautiful—the absolute perfection of fine young manhood. Yet their brawnier backsides did not afford him quite the same rapture as the more seductive rear of a woman. A certain velvety softness was lacking—something so intrinsically feminine that André knew he could never take up with males as a regular habit. Not that he ruled it out entirely, however, for his encounters with men only made his encounters with women all the sweeter and more magical.

Whenever business at the spa was slow—something that happened during the peak of the Mediterranean summer heat—André sought out the muscular Paolo for sexual solace. His Latin temperament provided a dramatic foil for André's West Indian tranquillity, adding a great deal of zest to their infrequent escapades. The Italian tennis instructor's superb command of his body earned through many years of sports conditioning had a major advantage that proved irresistible to the masseur—the muscles in Paolo's rectum could squeeze a man's penis to orgasm without its even having to move. Indeed, such prowess would always leave André completely drained of strength, semen, and feeling, as if he had just stuck his organ into a superhuman vise.

Since he was lazy and unambitious by nature, the island life suited Paolo perfectly. Although he had won a few tournaments in his day, he did not relish spending the remaining years of his youth chasing after a tennis ball—especially when it was so much easier to simply stand around and tell others how to do it—those others being the attractive young female guests who solicited his expertise on the court. Paolo possessed a natural talent for giving orders to women, particularly when he benefited from the results of his unusual brand of coaching...

...For after tennis, Paolo had yet one more game on the schedule and he never lacked a partner for it. As with the other male staff members with highly visible positions, the Italian was handsomely endowed in every respect. Yet he continually confounded the women he gave his time to, for once they had gotten a taste of what he had to offer, they invariably wanted more. Yet no matter how much they begged and pleaded, Paolo refused to give them more. Instead, he walked away chuckling from their crumpled bodies, knowing that the spoiled rich ladies—indeed, they were all the same to him—would return to the seclusion of their bungalows and rub themselves red and raw in their frustration.

The curly-haired tennis instructor preferred his

women one way and one way only: kneeling before him with the wide girth of his penis filling their desperately seeking mouths. He had no particular need for their supple, scented bodies and, in fact, rarely ever touched them except to entwine his fingers in their hair as they worked on him from below. How he loved seeing their eyes widen upon the moment of his rapture when his semen shot into their awaiting mouths. Not that Paolo took a woman completely by surprise; the quickening of his breath and the accumulation of his secretions on her industrious tongue no doubt alerted her that he was on the verge of coming. However, not even the most experienced fellatrice could have anticipated the amount of hot thick liquid that would shoot into the back of her throat. And Paolo made absolutely certain that these charming ladies swallowed every drop, forcing their lips to hold him tight until his last shudders subsided, his reservoir depleted.

Paolo had always suspected he was unusual in this respect. Hence he decided to perform a scientific experiment to determine exactly *how* unusual he actually was by masturbating into a drinking glass and measuring the amount of semen he ejaculated. His research yielded some surprising results, for indeed, the quantity stunned him; he had filled half the glass with the white froth. No wonder the women who had been awarded the privilege of having his penis in their mouths always looked as if their eyes were about to pop out, he mused. Why, if given the opportunity, he could probably feed the starving masses.

Instead, Paolo managed to content himself by feeding

the starving masses at the Elysium Spa, thereby also feeding the blackmailing eye of the hidden camera—occasionally providing his muscular backside to his dusky coworker whenever boredom got the better of him. Being the recipient of André's elegantly tapered penis did not shake the Italian's confidence in his own masculinity in any way; like a friendly game of tennis, such activities were merely for recreational purposes and were not to be taken seriously. Besides, these sodomistic couplings would often be held in conjunction with the fawning genuflection of a young female stationed at Paolo's penis. And there never seemed to be a shortage of them; for if the tennis court lacked a player, a fellow staff member would just as easily suffice.

Young Melissa had been on the island for only a short while. Rather homely in face and figure, she was given a menial position requiring none of the specialized skills of the spa's more comely employees. Melissa gave towels to every guest who came to sun herself on one of the chaise longues surrounding the swimming pool—and she performed this task day in and day out, handing out freshly laundered beach towels to each new arrival, only to collect them later for the laundry. Although not the most exciting of jobs, anything seemed better than the small Irish village and its cast of ruddy-cheeked busybodies Melissa had fled. On the day she turned eighteen, she bade farewell to this part of the world, packing her few modest possessions into a secondhand carpetbag and taking the first plane ride of her life to Athens, her one-way ticket paid for by the Elysium Spa.

## Elysian Days and Nights

It did not take long for the girl to develop a crush on the handsome Italian tennis instructor. The courts were located near the swimming pool, and several times a day, Paolo passed by the cabana where Melissa spent her hours sorting and folding towels. He looked so dark and mysterious—so unlike the bland-faced boys from back home—and indeed, so unlike *any* man she had ever imagined even in her dreams. She would find herself counting the minutes between the times Paolo walked by, hoping to engage him in conversation. Not that she really had anything to say to him—or to any man, for that matter. In school, Melissa's teachers had always considered her a shy mouse of a girl and her new career dispensing towels appeared unlikely to change that. Her mirror told her that she was just as plain as the boys she had so often turned away from in disgust, yet she held out a faint hope that maybe—just maybe—Paolo might notice her.

And one day he finally did. The mounting desire in Melissa's young body led her to spy on Paolo one sunny afternoon. He had just finished coaching a guest on her backhand, and their two figures stood beneath the striped canopy of the shed where the tennis equipment was stored. Their discussion looked quite animated. Melissa settled herself on her belly in the shade of a nearby tree, where she could both see and hear the couple, yet not be seen nor heard by them. However, their voices proved far too low for her to make out what was said, although there could be no mistaking the raw passion in the woman's hushed tones.

Paolo's tennis pupil possessed an ethereal sort of

beauty the ruddy-complexioned girl instantly admired—and just as instantly resented. Melissa stared enviously at the ivory oval of the young woman's face...at the golden hair wound into one long continuous silky braid shimmering elegantly down her back...at the long, slender arms and legs...at the perfectly rounded hips and breasts. The simple white tennis dress she wore complimented the honeyed glow of her skin, made all the more intense by the generous Mediterranean sunshine. How Melissa wanted to weep with the injustice of it all!

The woman dropped abruptly onto her bare knees in front of Paolo. With her view slightly obscured by the scrubby dry grass, Melissa raised herself up on her haunches, thinking that the lovely creature probably just needed to retie her shoe, for she had been running most vigorously on the court this afternoon. Yet this proved not to be the case at all. From her improved vantage point, Melissa could determine that the laces were indeed still intact. Rather than checking her shoes, the lovely sports enthusiast unclasped the jeweled clip from her hair, shaking out the lustrous waves. Paolo's fingers grabbed them up in great hunks, forcing her angelic face toward the front of his tennis shorts.

Melissa watched in confusion as the fair head began to bob forward and back in a strange rhythm. The white flash of the woman's wristband moved frantically between her parted thighs, its cadence as incomprehensible to the unworldly young girl as the continually dancing head above. Could this be some sort of prayer—or perhaps a pagan ritual? Judging by its primitive nature, the practice could conceivably be native to the island. Melissa decided to ask Dr. Bronski about it; surely he would be pleased that she took such an interest in the local history of the region. Why, he might even consider her worthy of a higher position. Suddenly Melissa envisioned her graceless little form in a maid's uniform, her lackluster self transformed instantly by the neat black silhouette with its starched white apron. Oh, she would be so pretty!

A low animal groan broke into Melissa's fantasy. The Italian threw his dark curls back, his mouth falling open and the primal noises issuing from deep in his throat frightening the spying girl. She scuttled from her hiding place out into the open, her only thought being to protect her beloved Paolo. She did not care that she might also be putting herself at risk—she had to save him! But when she saw the thick, fleshy stalk projecting out of his body and being swallowed up by the kneeling woman, Melissa cried out sharply, a pain such as she had never known piercing her gut.

Because of her noisy sucklings on the hot masculine muscle in her mouth, the woman did not hear the girl's anguish. However, Paolo swung his head to the side, his complacent brown eyes meeting the stunned Irish girl's innocent blue ones. Melissa's first thought was to run. But she could not move; she was trapped by the Italian's knowing stare. Smiling lazily, he continued to lock onto the servant girl's flushed face and remained so until the final spurts of his orgasm emptied into the obliging mouth before him, overflowing in creamy rivulets down the woman's finely chiseled chin and staining the white bodice of her dress. Even as she swallowed, he could not remember her name.

Melissa gagged on the phantom semen in her mouth, unable to believe what she had just witnessed. A woman taking a man's penis into her mouth! Why, she had never even heard of such an unnatural thing. And when this appealing young female's tongue darted out to collect the spilled froth from her chin, Melissa shuddered in revulsion. Yet as distasteful as it seemed to her, she felt an urgent pulsing between her thighs. She realized that she, too, wanted to do this to the handsome tennis instructor.

The next day Paolo stopped by the cabana and, not finding Melissa there, went inside out of the hot sun to wait. She soon returned, her gangly arms laden with a heap of clean towels that required folding and stacking on the shelves. However, the moment she saw him lounging against the counter, the fluffy white towels dropped to the floor, as did she. "Oh, Paolo!" Melissa cried miserably, kneeling before him in supplication. "Let me do to you what that woman did."

The Italian did not answer. Instead, he inched his tennis shorts down over his muscular brown thighs, teasing the desperate girl with the deliberate slowness of his movements. He wore nothing at all beneath his shorts, and his sturdy organ pointed at the ceiling as it wobbled indecently with its own cumbersome weight. Melissa stared transfixed at this amazing spectacle standing away from his body like an exotic root shooting up from a garden of glossy black curls, leaving behind the pendulous bulbs of his testicles. Almost as long as the rolling pin back home in her mother's kitchen and about as thick, the bronze skin of his penis was webbed with a series of delicate blue lines. She could feel the warmth radiating off it, and it further heated the already deep flush on her cheeks. Yet what seemed to compel her the most was the large pulsating knob at the end. Melissa followed the satiny ridge with the tips of her fingers, encircling it several times before eventually gaining the courage to explore the summit. Unlike the rest of the shaft, it blazed with a rich rosy color. She marveled at how smooth it felt—indeed, as smooth as if it had just been polished by the softest and most luxurious chamois cloth.

A slippery wetness anointed the pads of Melissa's fingers. When she tried to ascertain the source of this phenomenon, she noticed a tiny pinhole at the crest leaking out a fluid much like clear honey. Somehow she knew that these viscous tears would be just as sweet, and she leaned forward to shyly flick her tongue over the convulsing spout. Paolo pushed himself against her unacquainted lips, urging them apart, and she gratefully accepted the body of his penis into her mouth.

The tennis instructor tasted both sweet and bitter at the same time. Melissa grasped him firmly at the base, consuming him with all the unquenched desire of her innocent young love, praising him with her tongue and gagging when he thrust into the depths of her untrodden throat. However, she was determined to master the technique, for she wanted to prove her worthiness to him—to outshine the golden-haired woman whose lovely mouth had been here previously and she willed her throat to widen for her beloved Paolo. Without her even being aware of its consequences, she cupped the silken pouch below in her hand and caressed it reverently, unknowingly speeding up the mysterious lustful process.

The fluttery sensations in Melissa's groin compelled her to lick and suck this strange instrument with even more zealousness. She swallowed as much of its unruly bulk as physically possible, sensing this would please him. Paolo began to make the same animal sounds as before and she sealed her lips around him, the pulsing between her thighs becoming stronger and more insistent until she finally had to lodge her hand there in order to quell it. Rather than alleviating this peculiar affliction, her manipulations seemed only to aggravate it. Melissa rubbed herself fiercely against her fist, concentrating her movements so that the little bud nestling within her most private place received the full brunt of the friction.

Suddenly it felt as if something down there had sparked and caught fire. She found herself being lifted high into the air, then falling back down in a whirling free fall. Before Melissa could check whether she had somehow damaged herself with her hand, Paolo let out an anguished roar. A never-ending gush of hot, briny fluid brought tears to Melissa's eyes. She held the Italian's wildly jerking penis in her mouth, wanting to drink every last drop of what he had to feed her. As with those who had gone before, this would prove impossible. Some of his come spilled from her lips and dribbled down her neck, accumulating in a warm, foamy puddle in her brassiere. Yet Melissa managed to salvage even this by reaching into her blouse and scooping it out with her fingers, licking Paolo's errant seed off them until her ravenous thirst had at last been quenched.

Now that she had been fully initiated into performing the one and only act that Paolo would allow any female to perform no matter how beautiful or sensual she might be, as a trusted coworker, Melissa was next invited to participate in the tennis instructor's occasional dalliances with André. Paolo knew he could trust the girl, for she had become so addicted to his grand organ that she would have agreed to anything he asked of her.

In her naïveté, Melissa did not consider it particularly unusual that Paolo required her to administer the very same procedure while simultaneously allowing André to work his ebony instrument in and out of his projecting backside. Indeed, she knew virtually nothing about the ways of man and woman, let alone man and man. Her pious parents had preferred to keep their daughter in total ignorance about such sinful matters. And except for what she had recently learned on her knees, Melissa still knew virtually nothing. So she happily took Paolo's magnificent flesh into her mouth on demand, her eyes brimming with tears at being allowed such an honor, her fingers slipping stealthily up her skirt to rub the flexible node beneath the dampened gusset of her panties. Somehow the act of touching herself felt shameful to her, yet she so much wanted to experience that wondrous soaring sensation again. For the rest of her life, Melissa would always need a man's penis in her mouth in order to come.

This served as a most equitable arrangement for all concerned. Safely beyond the intrusive reach of Thomas

Bronski's hidden cameras, the two men could allow themselves to unleash their primitive impulses, secure in the knowledge that their disgrace would remain a secret, the slavish presence of the plain little Irish girl making the tennis instructor far more amenable to André's sodomistic attentions—not to mention their frequency. Thus, as the masseur pumped Paolo's hot, muscular passage, the Italian in turn pumped Melissa's hot, young mouth, and *everyone* got what he or she most wanted.

Even before joining the staff at the Elysium Spa, Paolo had always known he was special. Indeed, he was not just some common Italian who spent his evenings loitering around the Spanish Steps waiting to be picked up by any ruttish man or woman with a few lire to spend. He was destined for far greater things than what awaited him on the ancient streets of Rome. So leaving behind his tennis racquets, Paolo traveled to New York City, where he found many who were willing to take him under their wing and teach him what would later be the key to his future success. And he learned the ways of this vast modern land rapidly, and acquired many of these modern ways himself.

Wanting to be more like his American counterparts, Paolo had himself circumcised at the ripe old age of twenty-six. Although initially shocked by the refurbished contours of his favorite body part, he knew deep in his heart that he had made the right decision. Ever since the loss of his foreskin, his magnificent penis never lacked the plush accommodations of an attractive young woman's eager mouth. Oh, he'd had plenty of offers from eager young men as well, and would occasionally do a bit of slumming in that direction—strictly for practice, of course. For the young Italian, however, nothing could ever be as intoxicating as a prostrate female kneeling before him and receiving her seminal communion directly from its holy source.

In New York City, he easily collected willing devotees. Perhaps it was his good looks and charming accent that opened the mouths and pocketbooks of these jaded city ladies, for Paolo found himself well entertained during his stay in America. Not one lira from his precious savings had to be squandered on a rooming house—nor, for that matter, on meals. He had seen the insides of so many Park Avenue penthouses that they soon began to look identical to him, as did the red-lipsticked mouths encircling his newly trimmed penis. Hence the time had finally come for Paolo to return home to Europe. Only Rome and the yearly grind of competing in the Italian Open now seemed stale to him. He needed a change— and that change took the form of the Elysium Spa.

Unlike in America, on Dr. Bronski's tiny Greek isle, no longer would Paolo become bored with the proliferation of red lipsticked mouths hungering for his penis. Indeed, this new atmosphere felt charged with electricity, born from the dormant lust of beautiful young females whose carnal desires had been too long denied. As with tennis, Paolo made a game of it, choosing whom to satisfy and whom not to according to his fancy, using the skills once reserved for winning tournaments to provoke and inflame, only to thwart afterward. He would often deny the most needy of the women, keeping her at bay until she fell weeping to the ground, begging for a taste of what he offered the other guests so freely. Only then would he finally nudge the waistband of his shorts down over his firm muscled hips, relinquishing his wet rigid organ to the overwrought woman's devouring attentions. These episodes always brought the most powerful and liquescent climaxes for Paolo and he provided his beneficiary with a bountiful meal she would never again encounter in her lifetime. Indeed, the handsome young Italian always came out the winner.

Oddly enough, these highly fortunate ladies never seemed satisfied with his generosity. Perhaps too much wealth and privilege had altered their ability to be humble, for they would constantly implore him to employ his penis for other more conventional pursuits. Paolo simply could not comprehend why anyone should wish to squander his creamy donation in a less-cultivated orifice—indeed, in any orifice without the ability to savor so flavorful a libation. He could not know that these women's anomalous encounters with Dr. Bronski and André and the pretty young maids had awakened in them a long-forgotten craving to have a real live penis thrusting into their vaginas. However, such pleasures went far beyond the scope of his work. No matter how urgent the plea or how much money exchanged hands, he simply refused to compromise. Paolo was nothing if not a man of principle!

When their passions grew heated enough from their courtside repast, these frustrated females would seek out

# ELYSIAN DAYS AND NIGHTS

Manuel's company. In his own subtle way, he had become somewhat of a savior to those requiring attentions of a more traditional nature. His position as chief of spa security provided him with a good deal of freedom, for due to the size and remoteness of the island, he was not kept very busy. As a general rule, he would make only a few brief rounds of the compound. Then he could spend the majority of his time keeping a watchful eye on the voluptuous activities flourishing all around him. And the young Spaniard was more than willing to take up any slack left over by a fellow staffer—especially Paolo, toward whom he harbored an unspoken rivalry.

As with the Italian, Manuel had been hired for his good looks and for the generous length and width of his penis, the latter having gone unappreciated for far too long. No doubt, here among these sophisticated women of the world, his manly asset would be given the respect it deserved. Manuel planned to stay in peak condition so that his new career would last well into middle age, and maybe even beyond. He had discovered the promised land and vowed never again to return to the backward provincialism of his home.

Indeed, the girth of Manuel's penis had so intimidated the pretty seon so that his new career would last well into middle age, and maybe even beyond. He had discovered the promised land and vowed never again to return to the backward provincialism of his hish conquest would need to use two hands in order to hold him. However, if Manuel even dared suggest that she take it into her pretty, rouged mouth, his words would

123

be met immediately by a stinging slap across the cheek. He would be left standing like a fool, his erect penis sticking angrily out of his trousers. What can you expect from a bunch of peasants? he would grumble, hastily stuffing his rejected penis back where it had come from—only to bring it right back out again within the sanctity of his bedroom and finish what had begun in the fetid alleyway. Well, no longer would he need to suffer such needless humiliation. Here at the spa, he would be among women of culture and breeding—women who knew quality when they saw it. He had so much lost time to make up for.

In his capacity as chief security officer, Manuel had located the best spots on the island for observation duty. He could usually be found concealing himself within the leafy bushes surrounding the swimming pool. Here he could view the ladies at his leisure, amusing himself by comparing and contrasting their most intimate features. Dr. Bronski had insisted that all his patients allow the healthful life-giving rays of the sun to nourish their ailing bodies without hindrance, so Manuel could always count on seeing at least a handful of beautiful young females lying naked around the pool, their tanning limbs sprawling carelessly as they dozed and—depending on where he was situated, letting him see the succulent pink the sun never touches, which reminded him of two slices of the juiciest rare filet. How his mouth watered at the sight!

Conversations would rarely be initiated among these sunbathers. Each worried that a careless slip about a forbidden tryst with a staff member could set off an explosion, thus endangering not only that person's employment, but the ardent participant's reputation as well. To avoid any possibility of social contact, the ladies turned their chaise longues away from the pool and consequently away from each other, facing toward the outlying shrubbery to ensure a maximum of privacy—and unknowingly providing Manuel with a lush landscape of unobstructed viewing pleasure.

Such covert access to the guests meant that he could determine ahead of time which of them he would most like to enjoy. Not that he wouldn't have taken on every last one if given the opportunity. However, Manuel preferred women with some type of extraordinary physical feature—whether abnormally large breasts and nipples or a pair of wide buttocks that, because of their spread, completely unveiled the wrinkly little disc between them. Even if covered over by skirt or slacks, one could usually recognize such a provocative attribute by the distinct heart shape of the woman's backside. In fact, Manuel had developed a foolproof method for detecting this most distinguished characteristic, for in observing from behind a woman walking, the two cheeks appeared to move away from each other as if being pulled apart. Fortunately, at the Elysium Spa, such unique qualities were not all that difficult to find. Manuel would enjoy them to the utmost. The swimming pool served as his own personal hunting ground.

Not a week had gone by in his employment when Manuel came across a lady very much to his taste. As with his future conquests, the Spaniard had discovered Talia's charms while hiding in the bushes facing her chaise longue. Her well-cleft buttocks and the graceful opening between them provided an irresistible vista—as did the fleshy sandwich her netherlips formed as she lay on her side with her thighs pulled up against the wine-tipped cones of her breasts. Manuel could see the deep red gash of her vagina weeping its honeyed tears. He fought the impulse to leap from the shrubbery and stab it with his penis. This was hardly the place, what with all the other guests sunning themselves only a few feet away. Not that he would have minded an audience; ever since coming to the spa, he took great pride in showing off his penis. Why, a woman needed only to look at it and she would surrender herself to his every desire.

Talia had been at the Elysium Spa for two weeks by the time the security chief arrived on the scene. Frenzied with excitement thanks to Paolo, the twice-daily sessions with the masseur did little to assuage her voracious appetites. Manuel presumed she would be unlikely to refuse his advances. His assumption was indeed correct, for Talia quickly revealed herself to be a very cooperative and enthusiastic partner, allowing the Spaniard to pose and manipulate her in the most unseemly ways imaginable. He even dared to take her by the swimming pool when no one was around, forcing her to straddle her chaise longue so that her already-divided buttocks thrust out over the edge. The division between the cheeks became so exaggerated that her anus stretched into a socket big enough to fit his fist into. The threat of a sunbather's unexpected return added a delicious element of danger to the meeting, and

Manuel perversely hoped that they would get caught. Perhaps then he might manage to introduce yet another lovely young guest to his penis, or—his fondest desire of all—to possess two women at the same time.

For the time being, Manuel managed to satisfy himself with Talia. The possibility of their interludes growing boring was too remote for him to fret about. This slim, earthy brunette had more than enough charms to keep the security chief interested. What made their couplings so fiery was that every time he penetrated her from the back, he would not need to spread her buttocks to watch his penis sluicing in and out of her ripe little slit. Every molten detail of their connection became fully visible to his eyes—and, indeed, the eye of Thomas Bronski's camera. Not a man for secrets, Manuel preferred such feminine details to remain exposed at all times. Indeed, if he had his way, every female would be clean-shaven from pubic mound to tailbone.

Beneath the blazing afternoon sun, Manuel bucked his way in and out of Talia's vagina, the sweltering heat fueling his sexual energy and consequently fueling the womanly scents of his partner. His aggressive thrusts made her slide up and down along the surface of the chaise longue, and her clitoris rubbed repeatedly against the hot vinyl slats, often getting stuck between them. Rather than freeing herself, Talia would reach under the chaise and pull the pliant little appendage completely through the narrow space. Gripping it firmly with her thumb and index finger so it could not slip back out, she squeezed the offending strips of plastic together, pinching and thoroughly entrapping the sensitive flesh. Thus with the Spaniard's every movement, her clitoris fought to escape from its vinyl fetters, stretching and straining and swelling until giving her the results she wanted—and only then did she finally release it.

The exceptional elastic quality of Talia's clitoris had made her a much-favored patient of Dr. Bronski, who spent many an hour manipulating it into various shapes until it scarcely resembled its original form. During his entire career as a physician, never had he seen anything like it. Indeed, it had the consistency of chewing gum! The longer he worked it, the more malleable it became. No doubt this remarkable specimen was a case for the medical textbooks.

And thanks to Talia's naturally splayed bottomcheeks, Manuel could also entertain himself with the bizarre spectacle of the reddened flap being pulled and punished beyond its capacity. Yet there would be other advantages as well, for he could keep his hands free for more specialized pursuits, such as plugging up the yawning mouth of her anus which, thanks to the well-honed skills of the masseur, had become highly accommodating to virtually any form of ingress. Although not particularly a rear-entry man, the security chief could not help sampling it as well. He appreciated the fact that it had already been opened up and used on a regular basis; such spirited repetition primed it to stay open at all times. To Manuel, this endowed Talia's anus with a special beauty; for as long as he could remember, he had always been attracted to unusually large attributes on a female. However, Talia would only be the first of many remarkably featured young ladies who visited the Elysium Spa.

What with the variety of women Manuel encountered on a daily basis at his new job, every day seemed like Christmas. Indeed, there were so many lovely packages for him to unwrap and so many tasty treats to sample. Despite his pleasurable dalliances with Talia's hospitable hind opening, most of all, the Spaniard enjoyed the sight, smell, and sensation of a woman's genitals. He found himself continually on the prowl for a thickly lipped vulva and—if good fortune chose to shine upon him that day—an extremely well-developed clitoris to garnish it. Thanks to Dr. Bronski's meticulous screening process, stemming from his own personal preference for the fine silken tongue, Manuel did not have far to go in order to locate precisely what he wanted. Yet never in his life had he dreamed of meeting up with an extremity of such noble proportions as Carla's glorious beacon; indeed, the very instant he laid eyes on it, he knew he had to have her at any cost.

The security chief had barely managed to conceal himself in the shrubbery when Carla emerged from out of the twinkling rectangle of the swimming pool. Her rosy skin shimmered with water, the droplets glittering like blue diamonds in the coppery fire of her pubic thatch. His heart slammed against his rib cage as he watched her walking slowly toward her chaise longue, moving as fluidly as if she had been a creature of the water instead of merely a visitor to it. The high globes of her breasts swayed gently, the breeze coercing the nipples to harden into two pieces of cinnamon candy.

Several of the ladies peeked stealthily at her as she passed, their lips stretching into bemused smirks as they focused on the fleshy orange-brown tip protruding from the mass of curls crowning Carla's vulva. However, there was also a feverish gleam in their eyes—a gleam one would never expect to see on a woman as she gazed on another of her sex—a gleam particularly evident in the usually tranquil aquamarine eyes of the young lady next to her.

Not entirely oblivious to this attention, Carla inched her chaise nearer to the outlying bushes to escape the disquieting scrutiny of her fellow guests and settled herself hastily on the white towel draped over it, inadvertently placing what had earlier been such an object of curiosity just inches from Manuel. He could hardly believe his luck. He, too, settled in for what would no doubt be some excellent sightseeing. And he would not be disappointed. As the sensual heat from the sun warmed and dried Carla's goose-pimpled flesh, a unique presence began to make itself known between her casually parted thighs. In his excitement, Manuel almost gave himself away from his hiding place. He held his breath to quiet his excitement, staring in awe as the redhead's clitoris rose up from the flames and, when her thighs fell completely open in sleep, spread its glossy strawberry-colored wings as if to take flight.

That a woman such as this would surely attain many an orgasm from the rigorous thrusting of a penis into the little puncture below was Manuel's first thought, and he could hardly wait to prove his theory. For now, however, he had a more immediate need to attend to.

With a trembling hand, he reached inside the khaki trousers of his uniform and extracted his throbbing organ from the dampened cloth encasing it. More unruly than ever, it seemed to want to pull away from his palm and, like a divining rod ferreting out a source of moisture, pointed in the direction it most wanted to go...the ripe peeled fruit between Carla's opened thighs. The dribbling knob had swollen to a bright purple, glowing like a searchlight in the dense foliage. With a couple of swift tugs, Manuel sprayed the shaded pavement beneath her feet, the hot, foamy liquid hitting the cool cobblestones with an audible sizzle.

As the heat of the day intensified, the other guests around the pool started to gather up their possessions before leaving. Manuel found himself treated to the charming extravaganza of several sunbaked pairs of naked buttocks bouncing jauntily beneath the modest cloak of a beach towel as the ladies receded into the distance. Nevertheless, this visual pleasure rapidly gave way to physical discomfort as sweat soaked into every fiber of the Spaniard's clothing. In his lethargy, he hadn't even bothered to return his depleted penis to his trousers. It drooped miserably against his cotton-covered thigh, bearing little resemblance to the majestic pillar it had been only moments ago. What he needed was a nice, refreshing swim. He knew his favorite strip of beach would be empty. Ever since Monika's unsolved disappearance, no one went down there. So Manuel waited patiently, hoping that the rising temperature would soon awaken Carla and the woman on the next chair over from her, the only remaining sunbathers. The minutes crawled past and he kept checking his wristwatch, discovering that time had moved along far more rapidly than he had originally thought. Perhaps he should toss a pebble at the ladies to disrupt their siesta. Indeed, this was getting ridiculous. Manuel had important work to do—he couldn't hang about in the bushes all day!

Suddenly he realized that the other woman was not actually asleep at all. In fact, she had been lying on her side observing Carla for nearly as long as he had—only now she was a lot less discreet about it. Stretching and bending her elegant legs as if to relieve a cramp, she held the left one crooked and placed her hand within the wide V of her thighs. To Manuel's delight, she began to move it around and around in slow purposeful circles, all the while continuing to concentrate on the redhead's slumbering form. Although not quite as near to him as Carla, the security chief could see that she was a woman of great beauty, with her dazzling green eyes and long shapely limbs and glossy sable hair—a brilliant black that reappeared in a somewhat shorter and curlier version in the region of his interest. His drained organ twitched instantly with renewed life.

The wife of a foreign diplomat, she answered only to "Souci," as in *sans souci*. Yet according to staff gossip, she did not live up to her hedonistic nickname. Apparently, none of the comely young maids had achieved any headway with the woman—not even the multitalented Françoise. And the same went for Paolo and André. It made one wonder exactly what she did to occupy her time at the spa, for Manuel had even overheard Dr. Bronski remark that perhaps this particular guest preferred dinner parties over pleasure. Yet seeing her now with her legs flung apart and her fingers oscillating so lovingly between them, the Spaniard knew this to be untrue.

Souci was indeed a stunning young woman—so much so, in fact, that the trivial inconveniences of heat and sweat no longer mattered to Manuel. The unexpected bonus of her leisurely masturbation more than made up for any amount of discomfort he suffered. And soon there would be even greater performances worthy of his wholehearted applause as she abandoned her self-stimulation and rose from her chair, flinging over one shoulder the rumpled towel she had been lying on. Souci walked on tiptoe, as if to create the least amount of disturbance possible, and came to an abrupt halt beside Carla, standing so close that her knees grazed the vinyl-wrapped frame of the chaise longue. As she gazed down at the sleeping woman, her pink tongue danced over her lips with a lasciviousness that shocked even Manuel—for Carla's legs still remained immodestly sprawled and Souci appeared to be staring directly at the voluptuous blossom between them. Indeed, her own lustrous bud stood out quite prominently from her sable thatch. The Spaniard found himself licking his lips in a lewd parody as he studied her in profile, for the tip of her clitoris blazed with the same livid purple as the tip of his penis. She began to finger it, making it flush and protrude all the more.

A symphony of emotions played across the lovely face of Carla's admirer, her serene features eventually settling into an expression of such raw lust that Manuel's already-fully-erect penis grew another inch. Ever so carefully, Souci lowered herself until she was level with Carla's thighs, placing her hands gently on the armrest of the chaise so as to keep her balance. Her body trembled with the strain of her squat and indeed, with fear and excitement as she leaned forward so that her eyes, nose, and mouth hovered directly above the unfolded display of feminine flesh below. She was so focused on her mission that she failed to notice her bare knees dipping into the warm spume that Manuel had delivered only a few moments earlier. She probably would not have noticed even if the entire staff of the Elysium Spa had gathered poolside to cheer her on, let alone notice the one lonely spectator lurking in the shrubbery beside her—nor indeed, the ever-vigilant camera mounted on the roof of the cabana just across the way, recording her every move.

Souci knew she would need to proceed with extreme caution, for these next few seconds would determine either her success or her failure. Hence, with a touch as light as the air itself, she draped her beach towel over Carla's face. Although Souci found the woman extremely appealing both in face and figure, under no circumstances could she afford to be recognized—especially were her actions to be met with protest—in which case she would hurl herself into the bushes and crawl out on the other side where, fortunately, her bungalow was located. Although Souci had never committed such a sin as the one she now sought to perpetrate upon the sleeping woman, the penalty in her social circle would have been just as severe as if she had made a regular habit out of preying upon unsuspecting young females. For she was the wife of an ambassador and as such had to act with decorum.

Indeed, Carla was not entirely a stranger to her; they had once been introduced at an embassy luncheon. At the time, Souci considered the redhead rather dull. However, her opinion quickly changed after several afternoons' worth of communal sunbathing and several evenings' worth of dreams about the strawberry-colored pendulum jutting out from the redhead's fiery pubic fluff—dreams that were accompanied by a stream of wetness between Souci's thighs and on the sheet beneath her. She would always awaken with her fingers enveloped by the sopping folds. She could think of nothing else but this fleshly aberration. Though she snickered and sneered like all the other sunbathers who caught a glimpse of it, she was fascinated by this distinctively female feature. Suddenly Souci found herself waiting behind the cabana for Carla to arrive, only to race across the hot cobblestones to claim the chaise longue beside her. She would spend the next two hours peering surreptitiously at Carla's clitoris and daydreaming about the feel, flavor, and fragrance of it. Indeed, the extent of her lechery appalled her.

But at last Souci's fantasies were about to become a reality. She lowered her mouth over Carla's upstanding clitoris. A violent tremor shook her as she absorbed the silken bulk in its entirety. The unrelenting heat of the afternoon had made the lusty tongue moister and muskier than ever, triggering an immediate orgasm in the hungering woman. She squeezed her thighs together, continuing to gorge on this exotic delicacy and continuing to come over and over again—as did the ever-watchful Manuel from his leafy burrow a couple of feet away. How wrong her first impression of the redhead had been. She was anything but boring!

Carla sensed something closing over her head and clitoris and stirred fitfully, her hands reaching up to wrest the covering from her face. Yet someone held it wrapped firmly around her. Although this proved frightening in itself, the pleasure she began to experience from the impassioned sucking on her tumescent extremity soon overrode any initial concern for her safety. Judging by the warm welcoming mouth, surely this person meant her no harm. She was certain that it had to be a woman, for the lips and tongue possessed a softness unlike any man's. Indeed, only another female could know so intuitively how to create such exquisite sensations. As Carla allowed the unwieldy flap of her clitoris to be wooed by this invisible stranger, she felt herself peaking.

The Spaniard could not help envying the dark-haired woman. The rapture on her face told him that not only was Carla's distinguished endowment visually spectacular, but it was delicious as well. From his conveniently located vantage point, not only could he see Souci's rouged lips wrapped gluttonously around Carla's clitoris, but he could hear the aggressive slurping of her mouth. No doubt a woman of experience would have had a far more refined technique, yet this unintentional crudeness only heightened the thrill for Manuel—as did the image of the woman's tongue slithering into the redhead's juicy slit to receive its first baptism.

Such sweltering poolside entertainment provoked the security chief to want Carla more than ever. Like Souci, he found himself increasingly haunted by the abnormal growth between her thighs. How he wanted to capture this wild lump of flesh—only to tame it with the length and width of his penis, thereby forcing it to submit to the wiles of his manly scepter. He would make the wanton projectile understand who was *really* the boss; with him in charge, there would be no tongues or fingers.

Unfortunately, Manuel would need to wait a lot longer than he'd expected. Carla proved a most difficult conquest. Sensing his unwholesome interest in her, she adroitly managed to avoid him at every turn. Indeed, he made her as uncomfortable as the leering Italian and she often went out of her way to avoid the both of them, thus spending even more time in her bungalow with André and Françoise. Instead, the security chief occupied himself with Paolo's castoffs—which kept his days and nights extremely busy. As much as he hated to admit it, the man certainly knew how to charge up the ladies, for they would impale themselves on Manuel's penis before he even got his trousers down. But from what he could discern, Carla seemed to be the only woman from this latest group of guests who had not succumbed to the tennis instructor's courtside games and Manuel attributed this to the first-rate talents of young Françoise, for perhaps the redhead now preferred the flavor of her own gender to the brackish fluids of a man. However, this did not overly concern him. He derived personal satisfaction in the fact that the conceited Italian would not be making this exceptional female one of his many triumphs.

Hence Manuel waited patiently for his opportunity, meanwhile taking full advantage of the scores of overheated vaginas that came his way. Many arrived directly from the tennis court, with traces of the frothy milk shake they had just drunk still wet on their lips. The Spaniard happily volunteered his services no matter where he was or what he was doing, often taking a woman in the shade of a tree or on the beach or—if circumstances permitted—at the swimming pool, where fiery memories of Talia still lingered vividly in his mind. If a lady proved particularly to his liking, Manuel would make house calls—or, in this case, bungalow calls—his departure often within minutes of André's arrival. It never occurred to him to consolidate his resources with the dusky islander, even though André might very well have agreed. For, unlike the tennis instructor, Manuel found André to be quite an amiable fellow. Indeed, he had a great deal of respect for the masseur's fine work; only a man of tremendous talent and ability could motivate all those shapely young buttocks to rise up in desire for his ebony penis.

So the Spaniard often wished that he could remain behind to observe the masseur in action instead of having to slink out of a guest's bungalow like a common thief, but pride prevented him from doing so. Hence when André appeared only moments later, he would always be puzzled as to the significant puddle flooding the entrance he had come to penetrate. Unaware of Manuel's earlier visit, he attributed this liquid phenomenon to the woman's excitement over having her rectum so thoroughly filled by an expert.

The security chief became totally obsessed with the idea of watching his colleague, and he finally decided to do something about it. Because of his position at the spa, his presence in the control room at various times throughout the day and evening did not seem unusual. Despite Thomas Bronski's peculiar nature, Manuel even became quite friendly with him. Indeed, he could certainly put on the charm when he wanted something—and he definitely wanted something from the doctor's brother. The surveillance man frequently invited his new comrade into the stale little room to enjoy events as they unfolded. These private meetings—for they were not in the same vein as the evening staff get-togethers—provided Manuel with additional insight into the guests. This would be how he first learned that despite all the daily sexual activities at the Elysium Spa, the needs of one particular orifice were not being met. It devastated him to think that not one of these beautiful ladies had had a live penis inside her vagina during the entire time of her stay. Certain he must be mistaken, he asked Thomas, who spent many hours monitoring the guests. With suspicions duly confirmed, Manuel knew what he had to do. He became a man with a mission, taking meticulous mental notes on which of the ladies had the greatest need for his services, in order subsequently to fulfill it.

Continuous entry to Thomas Bronski's control room had a price. However, considering the vast benefits he derived from his new friendship, Manuel considered it cheap and was more than willing to pay it. It didn't seem much of an inconvenience to allow the strange little fellow to sniff and lick his fingers after they had just finished exploring the moist, fragrant terrain between a woman's legs. But when Thomas upped his price, the security chief became anxious. Being a Spaniard, he did not take kindly to the idea of another man putting his hands on him. But when the younger Bronski's insistent pleas turned to threats that might have resulted in the loss of employment, Manuel knew he had no recourse but to oblige him.

From this point on, the security chief had become duty-bound to run to the dank little surveillance chamber after each juicy session of coitus, whereupon Thomas would lick his still-damp and sticky penis until not a speck of feminine dribbles remained anywhere on the bronzed flesh—not even on the taut brown sacs of Manuel's testicles. Although rigidly secure in his masculinity, the Spaniard grew understandably concerned when his drooping organ began to show renewed signs of life beneath the other man's tongue. He would immediately stuff it back inside his trousers and flee from the control room, leaving a dreamy-eyed Thomas to lick the final piquant residue from his lips.

Manuel's closest rival insinuated himself into more and more of the private gatherings at the spa, extending his territory far beyond his kingdom of the tennis court. Aside from so much off-court activity, Paolo's dalliances with André and the plain-faced and plain-figured Irish girl had begun to bore him. Deciding that he required a change of pace, he quickly put a stop to them. However, this change of pace did not necessarily preclude the handsome islander, who had grown rather fond of the tennis instructor's muscular rear passage and would have done anything to maintain continued access to it.

The Italian knew well how terribly he frustrated the ladies with his indifference to their bodies and thought it might prove amusing to raise their agitation to an all-new level. Although he preferred to include Carla in his plans, this time Paolo became the frustrated one; unlike the other guests, the redhead apparently had not the slightest interest in tasting the magnificent delights of his trimmed organ. But Paolo was not deterred. Determined to have at least one go at her before she left, he realized that he would need to seek out André's assistance, for the masseur evidently had a powerful influence over the woman.

Therefore Paolo set his trap, offering himself once again to the rejected masseur. No doubt the powerful vise of his rectum would be hard to resist—even with the ready availability of so many females. A trusting André played right into his hands. However, this time Paolo made it absolutely clear that he would be willing to award his backside to the masseur's ebony penis only if one of the lovely guests was present and participating—and that lovely guest had to be Carla.

This unethical proposition was difficult for André to accept. Although he kept blissfully busy with his daily servicing of the ladies, he could not bear to miss out on the rare delight of having the gifted Italian—and doing so with the participation of his adored Carla gave him a mighty convincing incentive to deceive her. He did not believe it would make a real difference in the long run, for had he not been deceiving her ever since she arrived by his intentional failure to inform her about the hidden cameras recording every voluptuous move of her naked body? Although André occasionally experienced guilt from all this treachery, he refused to let it overwhelm him. He had an important job to do—and the pleasures he reaped in benefits made everything worth it. If a little personal blackmail became necessary for him to accomplish his goal, so be it! If Paolo could threaten to withhold his special favors, then so indeed would André.

The next day, after Carla returned from a lazy afternoon of sunbathing by the pool and receiving the unexpected ecstasy of Souci's impassioned mouth, she discovered both André and Paolo waiting in her bungalow. They had let themselves in with a master key to disable the hidden camera in the bedroom before she arrived. The Italian had no wish for his occasional divertissement with André to become the evening's entertainment. Although crime had never been a problem on the tiny island, the habits Carla had acquired from spending a lifetime living in large American cities could not easily be undone. She had locked the front door, which only made the presence of these two intruders all the more of a surprise.

Carla had planned to indulge herself beneath a long cool shower to take the edge off the blazing heat of the sun on her skin—not to mention the blazing heat of Souci's lips on her clitoris. She still did not know the identity of her mysterious suitor and though she suspected the attractive aquamarine-eyed woman on the neighboring chaise longue, she could not be entirely certain. Whoever it was moved too quickly to be caught in the act. Indeed, Carla would either be sound asleep when the towel came down over her face and the first warm caress of human breath cascaded across her vulva or in the last shudders of orgasm when the shrubbery at her feet rustled and snapped with the sounds of a hasty escape. By the time she had regained her wits, the only sign remaining that she hadn't imagined the entire episode was the slight undulation of the foliage.

The unexpected appearance of her male guests made it clear that Carla would need to alter her itinerary for the evening and she found herself somewhat miffed at the prospect, for she had arranged a special after-dinner engagement with Françoise. The maid had hinted at the presence of a third party—another comely young domestic or possibly even one of the guests. Carla had hoped it would be the latter—perhaps her furtive poolside lover hungering for a dessert far sweeter than those usually served in the spa dining room. And how exquisite it would be to reciprocate—to finally steal a taste of the honeyed folds that had heretofore been kept away from her. Would this other woman possess the same piquant sweetness as Françoise?

The three were to converge on the beach shortly before dusk for a nude swim and whatever other frolic that might result afterward. As Carla stepped into the shadowy coolness of her bungalow, she could think of nothing else. The rush of blood to her clitoris stubbornly refused to recede. At this rate she would never last through dinner! She hurried toward the bedroom, her fingers already beneath the hem of her towel busily spinning the lustful tongue in dizzying circles.

And then Carla happened upon André and Paolo—and, indeed, they happened upon her. Their two faces beamed with lascivious delight when she entered the bedroom. Her hand froze, her face and neck burning with shame—especially when she saw whom the masseur had brought with him. Carla did not appreciate the Italian's arrogant demeanor and she appreciated it even less as a shirtless Paolo lolled casually on her bed, having made a complete jumble of the clean sheets and blanket that had been arranged so artfully by one of the maids only that morning. Wishing to recapture her lost dignity, her mouth opened to issue a severe upbraiding. Yet the all-too-intimate scene of his bronzed flesh against the bright white of the bedclothes turned Carla's words into a helpless squawk. She looked helplessly toward her dark lover for an explanation. Rather than providing one, André pulled at the towel she had wrapped so carefully around her and it dropped to a fluffy white heap at her feet, revealing the tumescent evidence of her recent activities.

Carla stood in the center of the room, her rosy flesh misted with a fine perspiration. The diffuse light from the window made her body shimmer with an ethereal luminescence that reached from the whites of her eyes all the way down to the protruding strawberry of her clitoris. The shock of what the masseur had just done left her dazed. In her confusion, Carla did not know whether to retrieve the lost towel and cover her nudity or remain on display before this uninvited audience. She trembled with the uncertainty of what was about to transpire, her nerve endings prickling with a new awareness of her surroundings. Suddenly every sound seemed amplified, especially the masculine breathing coming from the bed. Soon she could hear nothing but Paolo's measured respiration as it grew faster and faster, drowning out her own ragged breathing.

Inexplicably, Carla's intense dislike of the tennis instructor excited her. A sudden spurt of wetness bathed the insides of her damp thighs. She began to reach for the fallen towel, hoping to hide her womanly response to the presumptuous Italian before he took notice of it. Her limbs moved painfully slowly, defying her feeble attempt at modesty. She felt as if she were trying to run in the ocean, yet everyone else around her appeared to be flying—indeed, soaring through the air. André took her fluttering hand and led her toward the bed, where Paolo continued to lounge on his side, his dark eyes coolly appraising her body and taking in the obvious signs of her arousal. Carla had never in her life been scrutinized with such an apparent lack of emotion, not even by the emotionless man she had married. Yet perhaps this cold-blooded appraisal had started up the production of her juices, for not even the tight clenching of her vaginal muscles could stop the lubricious flow.

However, when Paolo's gaze fell upon the tumid growth projecting unabashedly from the coppery nest of

Carla's pubic mound, something resembling humor flickered in his eyes. Souci's earlier praise had left it in a state of extreme disarray, for the tip had split into two distinct fragments of glowing pink flesh, making it seem as if there were a pair of clitorises instead of one, the two pointed defiantly in opposite directions. Making no effort to conceal his amusement, the Italian pulled her down on top of him, so that her face hovered just above his muscular thighs. His rapid breaths gusted through the flames of her hair, scalding the paler skin beneath. "I have something far more impressive that I know you will enjoy," he replied with a crafty smile, tweaking Carla's clitoris to make absolutely certain she comprehended his implication. A sharp cry told Paolo that his message had indeed been understood. He shrugged off his constricted tennis shorts, gathering up a fistful of her hair so that she could not flee from the fate he had orchestrated for her.

Carla's eyes widened with astonishment as his now-unfettered penis rose up to greet her. Since she had thus far escaped the submissive position of the many ladies who had eagerly gone to their knees before him, this would be the first time she ever saw Paolo without his proper tennis garb—much less without any clothing at all. To help her fully appreciate what he had to offer, he held her face close, teasing her with his bouncing organ. Carla could smell the maleness of him along with a lingering hint of soap from his morning shower. This erotic fusion frightened her, as did the size and extremely ready condition of his penis. She found herself both fascinated and repulsed at the same time.

Never had she encountered anything so huge; indeed, it looked almost obscene as it stood out from a wreath of silky black ringlets, virtually dwarfing the small, shiny globes below. Indeed, Paolo's penis looked as if it had been sculpted from the hardest marble on earth; although, unlike the cold, unyielding substance it resembled, this masculine monument radiated an urgent heat that refused to be ignored.

The smooth rosy head bumped insistently against Carla's lips, anointing them with a syrupy fluid and she turned her face away in disgust from the leaking pinhole. How could all those women desire such a monstrous thing in their mouths? she wondered with a shudder. Suddenly the obvious parallels between the tennis instructor's penis and her own overgrown appendage came to mind. However, before she could make any additional comparisons, André grasped the back of her neck, pressing her mouth down hard against the moist, throbbing bulb. The wetness from her lips seeped into her mouth and onto her tongue. Carla wanted to spit the substance out. But every time she tried, she ended up by taking in even more of the Italian's tangy droplets.

André knew what Paolo wanted and had promised to deliver it. And he would never go back on his word, for he had too much to lose. The masseur had prepared himself for the possibility that Carla might never forgive him. But guests would come and go—even the most enchanting ones. Monika had taught him this painful lesson, and it would be one he'd never forget. Hence, as he placed the redhead's mouth at the mercy of Paolo's insatiable organ, André realized that his dreams of running away with her were, indeed, only dreams. How could he ever expect to hold on to such an exquisite woman? One needed only to see the avaricious gleam in the Italian's dark eyes to know that Carla was and always would be the object of desire for every man who met her—and every woman as well. The Elysium Spa had become the islander's reality, and that reality included Paolo. Despite the tennis instructor's capricious temperament, at least he would still be there the next day…and the next one after that. For, like André, he was unlikely to leave this paradise of Dr. Bronski's creation.

Positioning Carla so that she straddled Paolo's lower legs, André adjusted her knees to their maximum spread and placed himself behind her unprotected buttocks. With her head in the Italian's lap, her cheeks were uplifted. They split apart to flaunt every intimate detail within the satiny orange fissure. So wide a stance had also compelled the copper-haired lips of her labia to unroll, thus exposing her delicate vaginal sliver as it dripped profusely onto the dangling strawberry, drowning it with its sweet cream.

The expression of bliss on the masseur's face did not escape Paolo's notice. Suddenly the man whose greatest desire had been to spurt the bountiful sap of his climax into the redhead's hot mouth surprised himself by his envy of André's view. He, too, wished to feast his eyes on what would surely be a most delicious landscape. He turned his head, managing to catch a brief glimpse of the bifurcated tongue before Carla's fiery tresses blocked it from his view.

No matter which way she moved, Carla was trapped. And, thanks to the masseur, she saw no way to avoid performing the disgraceful deed Paolo evidently required of her. But just as she experienced the first prickly pangs of rage toward the man who had up till now given her so much pleasure, André's strong fingers clamped over her projecting buttocks, spreading them so wide that she cried out. Her immediate reaction was to reach back and check for blood, for it felt as if he had torn the puckered opening between them. Yet when she brought her fingers back, the only wetness she had collected from her wounded anus was the wetness that had spilled onto it from the dripping orifice directly adjacent to it.

Indeed, once again, Carla's anus demonstrated its astounding resiliency as André forced the cinnamon ring to expand beyond its limits, showing him the carnelian secrets beyond. He never seemed to tire of its raw exotic beauty and he pressed his lips against it, paying homage by licking at the sultry hollow. The twitching halo of muscle tasted salty and humid, which provoked André to lick all the more greedily at the dilated entry. Then his tongue knifed in to the root, ferreting out the secret spice of Carla's interior. Her hips began to roll in rhythm with his oral lovemaking, her impassioned sighs resounding throughout the room. Paolo stared into her face, relishing the brazen spectacle of her pleasure and knowing that he too would very soon be experiencing his own.

Suddenly Carla understood why both of these men had come to her today. Perhaps this moment had been inevitable from the very start—from the day of her arrival, when Dr. Bronski had accompanied her on a grand tour of the spa compound, all the while speaking encouragingly of the many healthful activities available to her. They had stopped briefly at the tennis court, where Paolo had just finished slamming a ball across the net to some poor frazzled guest totally incapable of returning it. His chiseled body vibrated with self-assurance. As Carla stood uncertainly beneath the striped canopy that had on so many occasions sheltered him and the kneeling figures of countless females from the sun, she found herself being scrutinized by a pair of the darkest, most piercing eyes she had ever seen. She felt stripped naked, her every intimate part spread open for the sheer amusement of it. Carla knew then that she would never take up the racquet no matter how supposedly beneficial it might be. Yet she could not hide herself entirely from the heated stare of the tennis instructor.

She had felt Paolo observing her whenever she passed by the tennis court—observing her as if he were biding his time for something. And finally she had discovered what that *something* would be—only because of her distaste for the man, Carla was determined not to give it to him. However, when the scorching knob of André's penis began to probe her well-primed anus, it seemed so natural to simply open her mouth and take the weighty beam of pulsing flesh inside. Paolo's voluptuous groan of pure ecstasy made her realize that she had indeed, done the right thing.

The Italian wound his fingers in the flaming mane bobbing above his groin, triumph surging throughout his body. Yes, he would feed the aloof redhead a fine meal tonight, he mused, hoisting himself deeper into Carla's receptive mouth, the sharp edges of her teeth scraping the overstretched flesh of his penis as it charged down her throat. Her emerald eyes squeezed themselves shut, for she could not bear to look upon the hated object she now sucked so worshipfully. Yet even this minor concession to modesty would be denied her.

"Open your eyes!" Paolo hissed, jerking cruelly at her hair. "I want you to appreciate your good fortune."

There was something frightening about the tennis instructor—something calculating and ruthless that belied the playful dark curls atop his handsome head. Carla immediately did as he ordered. As her eyelids unlocked themselves from their stubborn seal, a vista of even darker curls came into view from which sprouted a thick fleshy root whose bulk could not be ascertained, for it remained buried inside her mouth too deeply. Even so, its great width could still be gauged and Carla opened her mouth wide until her lips cracked in her struggle to contain it, her jaw aching from the unnatural strain. As with so many others before her, it proved impossible *not* to be impressed by so miraculous a male specimen. To her shame and dismay, she sensed her resistance weakening.

A viscous fluid leaked continually from the throbbing bulb in her throat. Carla allowed the entire shaft of Paolo's penis to slip out so she could wipe up the tangy-sweet droplets with the tip of her tongue. She sensed that this would please him immensely. His lack of a foreskin prompted her to concentrate her efforts on the susceptible crest. To justify her actions, she convinced herself that she had no recourse but to cooperate, for such a reluctant complicity would no doubt bring matters to a rapid close—and that would likely be the end of it with the presumptuous Italian. Yet, rather than accelerating the act, Carla took a leisurely oral tour of the glowing limb before her, savoring every contour and ridge of Paolo's maleness, unwilling to acknowledge her mounting excitement at the combination of his silken penis in her mouth and André's silken penis in her rectum.

Carla felt empty when André pulled out of her. She was certain that he hadn't come, for her highly sensitized passage could always feel the powerful barrage of liquid fire that signaled the masseur's climax. As if in collusion with André, Paolo removed himself from the welcoming hearth of her mouth, leaving her doubly empty. Bewilderment and disappointment showed on Carla's pretty face. She lifted her head from the Italian's lap, gazing up at him with undisguised hope in her eyes. Her lower lip trembled as an unexpected eagerness to endure still more of what he had to offer rendered her mute. Paolo could not resist her plea. He pushed her onto her back and climbed onto her. Just when Carla expected him to penetrate her in the traditional way and opened her legs in readiness, he stationed himself with his naked buttocks almost sitting on her breasts. Squatting above her upturned face, he thrust his weighty organ down into the depths of her throat.

Carla's hands came up as if to ward off a blow, but instead they grasped the thick base, attempting to regain control over the cumbersome object. Paolo aided her by leaning forward over her head, thereby centering his weight on his elbows instead of on his pelvis. This shift in balance served him well; his hips gained complete mobility. Hence he could pump the redhead's luscious mouth to his heart's content—pumping it as she had no doubt expected him to pump the juicy little slit that, by parting her thighs, she had placed at his disposal. Well, he was very sorry to disappoint her, but he had not as yet consummated *this* particular relationship. Indeed, Paolo wished to conquer every last millimeter of the woman's throat—to fill her mouth with so much of his elixir that it dripped from her eyes.

Despite the devious nature of her two gentleman callers, Carla had assumed that she was the center of this unwholesome gathering—which only made what followed all that much more difficult to accept. Never could she have anticipated André's next move. Had her mouth been uninhabited, she probably would have let out a horrified shriek. Instead, her tongue was brought into quiet submission by the fleshy burden rubbing against it—a rubbing that grew increasingly more aggressive when the muscular opening between the Italian's buttocks was corked by an ebony stopper that still sizzled with the heat from Carla's sumptuous interior.

So profound was this dual seduction that Paolo believed he would die. He thrust roughly into the hot cavern of Carla's mouth just as his own was thrust into. Raising his buttocks high, he invited André to go as deeply as he pleased, moaning in delirium as the secret male gland halfway inside his rectal canal was thrust against repeatedly. The masseur seemed to aim the narrow head of his penis directly at it. Suddenly Paolo felt himself letting go, overcome by an ecstasy so sublime that he wept as his semen gushed forth into the solicitous mouth below and André's boiling liquids shot into him from behind.

The muscles of Carla's graceful throat worked industriously as she attempted to swallow what had been given her. Much of the bountiful froth spilled from her lips. To Paolo's surprise and delight, her pink tongue slithered out and collected the errant dribbles like a hungry kitten in pursuit of the last drop of sweet cream. The twin emeralds of her eyes gleamed in the waning light. Indeed, he could almost hear her purring. His penis erupted with yet another dose of its liquid passion—which he squirted joyfully into her open mouth and she consumed gleefully.

Although he had at last fulfilled his desire to take Carla in the way she most wanted *not* to be taken, the tennis instructor did not appear in any particular hurry to leave the battleground of his victory. The bronzed monolith jutting out from his body was still hungry. It twitched and undulated against his muscled belly. The still-tumescent head glittered provocatively with Carla's saliva, serving as a powerful testimony to her capitulation. Paolo felt the heat of her eyes upon it as he lay where he had collapsed after his triumphant moment of pleasure. He chuckled quietly to himself, marveling that the redhead could still be thirsty. Suddenly his previous trysts with the homely little Irish girl and the many female guests so willing to fall to their knees for him now seemed like mere children's games compared to the fiery sensuality of this woman. Indeed, Paolo imagined Carla as a match: One needed to know the correct way to strike it in order to get it to light.

The masseur maintained a wide berth between himself and his two love partners. He extricated himself from Paolo's herculean vise before Carla had gotten out from under him. Perhaps it was only a matter of masculine pride, but he simply could not bear the thought of her watching him slide his penis out from Paolo's anus. Although he would have preferred that she had never learned of his dependency upon the handsome young Italian, Carla's lovely presence had amplified his excitement far more than he wished to admit. The shame of having manipulated her for his own selfish goals rendered André incapable of meeting the arresting green of her eyes. Nevertheless, he managed a furtive glance at her prone figure, expecting to be met with a look of sheer hatred.

But Carla did not seem in the least way damaged by her forced oral encounter with Paolo. She rested comfortably on her side, her face and neck flushed with the strain of pleasuring the Italian, her clitoris more prominent than ever as it bulged out from between her compressed labia. Her quiet compliance during the act indicated that she had not attained orgasm, and André decided to reward her for her generosity toward his friend. More than anything he wanted to hear that breathless cry of climax spring from Carla's penis-swollen lips, so he approached her side of the bed tentatively, waiting for the attack that was sure to come.

But her eyes did not see him; instead, they remained fixed on Paolo's organ, which flourished noticeably from her admiration. At that moment, either of the men could have done anything they desired to her, for thanks to the tennis instructor, Carla had reached the ultimate stage of surrender. However, André had only one desire. He rolled her over onto her belly, spreading the reddened cheeks of her buttocks. The loosened notch between them still glistened with his lubricating fluids, inviting him to finish what he had started. Waves of luxurious heat shimmered upward from the well-breached opening. Just gazing on it reactivated André's spent organ instantly.

Paolo materialized at his side, eager to discover what occupied so much of the darker man's attention. The normally indifferent Italian had never looked upon this part of a woman—let alone investigated its erotic potential—but suddenly he understood the masseur's unshakable obsession for the pursed little portal. As it swallowed up André's obsidian knob with a juicy smack, Paolo's own passage began to burn once again for the presence of the tapered shaft. Yet he also burned to introduce his own significantly thicker version into Carla's accommodating entrance.

When Paolo finally resolved to try the cinnamon wreath for himself, the masseur resumed his earlier posture behind him. The three became connected like links in a chain—with André plugging himself into the Italian who, in turn, plugged himself into Carla. Had she not been sufficiently stretched and exercised by so much daily practice, she would probably have been left torn and bleeding from such an oversized guest. Even so, Carla suffered a tremendous stress on the mouth of her anus and the walls of her interior unlike anything she had experienced with André—or experienced with some of the more substantial objects Françoise liked to use on her. Yet it felt exhilarating to have a man at least three times the girth of her island lover digging so deeply and savagely into her. Balancing on well-parted knees, Carla reached back to spread herself wide for the incoming invasion, her eyes closing to block out everything except for the sensations created by Paolo's penis.

Carla's scalding rectum vibrated against the Italian's immersed flesh. The anxious contractions of her overstretched anus squeezed him to tears. He could hardly blame André for making this his exclusive port of entry, for the supreme ecstasy such a penetration provided would coerce *any* man into abandoning a woman's more established openings. Indeed, Paolo seemed to rejoice in distorting her every contour. Wishing to appropriate even more of Carla, he reached between her thighs to locate the voluminous tongue of silken flesh and pinched it hard, stretching and pulling at it until it stuck out from her body like a miniature penis. He knew that such intentional coarseness would not be well received, which was precisely why he continued tormenting the lusty flap. Carla surprised him by placing her hand over his and rearranging his fingers, moving them so they wiggled the upstanding protuberance back and forth and around and around depending on her particular fancy. Since he still had a free hand remaining, Paolo decided to further amuse himself by inserting some of his fingers into the sopping spout below. He plunged them in and out, unaware that he did so in harmony with the masseur's penis in his backside.

The molten softness against the Italian's skin made him remember days long past. He tried hard to recall the last time he had taken a woman here, the image of a plumpish young girl in a red-and-white–striped swimsuit too vague to bring into focus. Yet, despite the fragrant plushness of a vagina, Paolo did not particularly miss the conventional methods of lovemaking, for both he and his noble organ preferred to have total command over a woman. This meant stuffing her mouth with his penis—or, on a rare occasion like this, stuffing the mouth of her anus. Yes, such encroachments could bring even the most unruly female into submission.

Carla whimpered from the pleasurable anguish of having her bottom packed so full of hot male flesh. She urged the fingers between her thighs to move faster. Her clitoris had ballooned up so large and gotten so slippery with the continual stream of wetness from her slit that Paolo could hardly keep hold of it and had to add yet another finger to harness the irrepressible mass. By this time, his entire hand had become engaged in the battle. Every sinew seemed to scream for mercy. However, any attempts to regain his cramped hand were met by a determined pressure against his wrist, telling Paolo that he would not be released until his work had been completed successfully. The fingers of his other hand still remained lodged deeply within Carla's vagina, and his wrist began to ache from its contorted status. Surely the demanding woman didn't expect him to stimulate her forever?

A feline cry followed by a violent bucking against his bespattered pelvis granted Paolo his freedom. Carla had finally reached the summit. He let his captive hands relax in the pulpy folds, returning his attention to the dual pleasure of being both the giver and the receiver. The precision of the masseur's thrusts in and out of his backside pushed his own penis farther up Carla's rectum. She groaned in agony each time he rammed her to the hilt, the stinging burn incapable of blotting out her second orgasm.

Just when he had gone as far as physically possible, Paolo exploded, his unstoppable fluids gushing against the final barrier of her interior. André then seized the Italian's heaving buttocks and wrenched them apart, shoving himself in as deeply as Paolo had just done to Carla, and spraying his insides almost as generously.

Many days passed before Carla was completely free of Paolo's generous liquid offerings. However, the loss made little impact for the regular injections of the masseur's special serum kept Carla constantly filled. Yet she did not mind in the least. The delicious rapture she derived made up for any minor inconveniences, She soon found herself wishing for another opportunity to meet up with the narcissistic Italian's strapping appendage.

Indeed, half of Carla's wish would be granted, for she would be receiving yet another similarly endowed guest.

Only this time it would not be Paolo.

Owing to the Italian's success with the seemingly aloof Carla, Manuel decided that the time had come for him to take some action as well. It would no longer do for him to sit back passively and watch, courtesy of Thomas, all the voluptuous activities taking place in the redhead's bungalow. Something had to be done. Carla appeared to be heating up to a variety of carnal combinations—her enthusiastic obliging of Paolo's prodigious penis in her mouth and rectum serving as the most convincing evidence. Had it not been for the queer little surveillance man's ingenuity, he might never have learned of his rival's coup de grâce. In his prurient wisdom, young Bronski had seen fit to equip the bedroom of Carla's bungalow with yet a second camera, in case of any unforeseen mechanical difficulties with the first. Indeed, the extra bonus of witnessing the cocky Italian getting his own backside none-too-daintily reamed gave Manuel much laughter. He vowed to use this information toward his own ends.

Carla's final acquiescence to Paolo's demands did not make the security chief's task any easier. He turned up wherever she went in hopes of attracting her attention. He even tapered his uniform's trousers to make them fit more snugly, thereby accentuating the very ample contours of his penis. Since the redhead had so eagerly sampled the Italian's grand specimen, Manuel assumed that she would just as eagerly wish to sample his. Yet he quickly realized that no matter what he did or how he did it, he would never have Carla on his own terms. So, taking an example from his detested rival, he altered his strategy.

Manuel well knew Carla's preference for André's glossy black penis in her bottom and the maid's juicy, hairless folds on her tongue. Perhaps he would add the final spice to Carla's sexual stew if he could somehow manage to enlist the aid of his two attractive coworkers. However, unlike the Italian, he refused to sacrifice his own backside to coerce the masseur. It was bad enough to have been forced into using his penis as a bartering tool to gain admittance to the surveillance room; Manuel feared he would lose himself completely if the situation demanded anything more. Hence, when he finally approached André with his proposal, he did so with trepidation and with the promise of a substantial cash inducement. Neither was necessary.

Indeed, André and Françoise seemed quite interested in the prospect of the three of them taking on the lovely redhead together, although the young maid made it clear that she would not tolerate any gratuitous physical contact on Manuel's part. But she needn't have worried. The Spaniard's only desire was to possess the sumptuous body he had up till now unhappily merely observed from a distance.

On the last night of her stay at the Elysium Spa, Carla sprawled restlessly across the bed that had been the scene of so much libidinous abandon, her bare skin prickling with expectation. She had taken the initiative of undressing, although whether André and Françoise would even be visiting her remained uncertain. Perhaps they were as saddened by her imminent departure as she. The thought of leaving tomorrow morning had tainted the perfect sunny day with a murky pall. How would she ever return to her dull domestic life after the erotic heaven of these past weeks? Indeed, Carla had grown extremely fond of her lusty companions, not to mention dear Dr. Bronski and his odd little contraption. She would have happily extended her stay another week or more—especially with the latest turn of events, but her husband had already dispatched several curt cablegrams to the spa, demanding she return to her wifely duties forthwith. Thankfully, the lack of a reliable telephone system had spared her from his direct scolding.

Every word of the advertisement in the glossy fashion magazine had been true—the Elysium Spa *was* a woman's paradise. For on this tiny Greek isle, Carla had been adored, her physical uniqueness prized and worshiped, and consequently ravished. Why, even the disagreeable Italian had come to admire what her own husband had scorned. So much adulation had given Carla a chance to explore the full realm of sexual possibility, yet there was still much for her to study. However, she had but one regret: she had been unable to conclusively put a face to the mouth that had bewitched her twice already, although in her fantasies it always belonged to the sable-haired enchantress with the brilliant aquamarine eyes.

Unbeknownst to Carla, this evening would provide her with an all-new lesson in the body's infinite capability to give and receive pleasure. When the door to her bungalow opened and the figures of her two friends stepped inside, they were followed by a third. Believing it to be Paolo, Carla's heart began to flutter, as did her clitoris. She shivered at the delicious memory of him thrusting his tremendous organ down her throat and up her rectum. She had never felt so completely plundered. The dormant tongue between her thighs stretched its way out from its labial confines, displaying itself proudly to her three visitors. Indeed, no longer would Carla clench her thighs together in embarrassment; now she opened them wide so that her fleshy attribute could be all the more conspicuous and celebrated. Like the depilated Françoise, perhaps she too might one day sweep away the obscuring locks of hair so that every silken detail of her true beauty would be fully visible.

Carla's emerald eyes went wide when she saw the persistent Spaniard in Paolo's stead. And when he shucked off his clothing, her eyes went even wider. The resemblance between his penis and the Italian's gargantuan member compounded her excitement. Had she been wrong to have dismissed him so quickly?

Manuel joined his fellow staff members, who had already stripped and were busy positioning the redhead for their mutual pursuits. This was the first time the Spaniard had her warm, fragrant body at his fingertips, so he went slowly, memorizing every enchanting curve and crease as Carla knelt unashamedly on her hands and knees. Her rosy breasts swayed gently beneath her and Françoise slid beneath them, taking each orange-brown nipple into her mouth and molding them into spikes, her own terra-cotta versions pointing out jauntily from her more modest swells.

André's dusky fingers spread Carla's buttocks, offering the security chief an opportunity to examine the fine cinnamon crinkles encircling the darker chink of her anus. The opening proved somewhat larger than he had anticipated. No doubt its elasticity had finally succumbed to the rigorous daily forays provided by

André and, more recently, the tennis instructor. Yet this exaggerated circumference did not detract one iota from its uncanny ability to charm and delight. Manuel fell under its spell instantly.

As he continued admiring Carla's rear orbit, the masseur began to encircle the yawning rim with the tip of his tongue, eventually eclipsing the flawless disk by thrusting inside. His long tongue disappeared completely within the dark passage. Suddenly the young Spaniard found himself considering Carla's rear entrance. Now that he was so near to one of such obvious appeal, he could definitely appreciate the merits this action would offer—as did his penis, which dribbled its impassioned droplets onto Carla's leg without letup. The fact that his Italian adversary had already partaken of it only further tempted the security chief and he resolved to do the man one better.

As Carla stretched her knees farther apart, Manuel observed just how tumescent her clitoris had gotten. It had achieved quite a reputation around the spa, but viewing it this close up and in so excited a state proved a dazzling sight indeed. Despite the soothing cream bathing it continually, the ripened kernel glowed hotly in its copper nest, lengthening out by a succession of furious twitches similar to a man's erection. Manuel thought of his own lusty organ and its present condition. Indeed, the redhead's clitoris seemed to beckon to him, demanding to be molested by his ruthless fingers. But before he could clamp it with his thumb and index finger, the French girl shimmied her petite form down toward Carla's pelvis and placed her mouth directly beneath the dangling appendage. Despite having these two carnally charged males for an audience, she began to suck on it, her lips deliberately drawing the bright pink wings of flesh out from the puffy sheaths. Suddenly everything in the world vanished from Françoise's perspective; all that existed was the sweet, velvety flap in her mouth. She worked on it with all the intensity of a nun in prayer, savoring what would probably be her last taste of this distinctive morsel.

Although Manuel had paid dearly for the privilege of watching the women together on the screens in Thomas's office, nothing could have prepared him for this lustful reality. The enthusiastic slurping of Françoise's mouth on the redhead's bulging clitoris made the semen boil in his testicles. As the room became scented with the arousal of the two women, he could hardly hold back from hoisting his penis into Carla's bubbling sliver. For the first time, he appreciated his rarely exploited ability to delay his climax. Otherwise he might have lost it right then, not only embarrassing himself, but ruining everyone's carefully crafted plans.

Carla shook with orgasm, her tiny slit filling up with still more of the creamy fluid. Indeed, this seemed to be what the pretty young maid had been waiting for. She allowed the surplus to drip down into her open mouth, only to diligently lick the rest away, the expression on her face one of divine bliss. Yet another generous dose instantly replenished what she had already consumed, but just as her tongue darted forth to swab it up, André dipped the head of his penis into the molten current and used it to lubricate Carla's quivering anus. He had more than enough left over to lather the rest of his shaft. The viscous discharges glistened whitely against his obsidian skin, amplifying their forbidden relationship.

Françoise moved out from between her female lover's thighs, permitting the still-shuddering woman to be shifted into a position more favorable for a rear penetration. Manuel stood by while the experts took charge, flicking his tongue across his lips like a man readying himself for a meal he had waited an entire lifetime to eat. Yet Carla's extreme exposure proved far too intoxicating for him to remain idle. He dropped behind her outthrust buttocks to ogle the priapic piece of flesh he was determined to master. The redhead's clitoris dangled from her as if a weight hung from it. Françoise's mouth had pursued it vigorously, and the security chief's hot breath gusted over the wet projectile, reactivating its distinctive perfume. Inspired, he pressed his nose to it, drawing the musky fragrance deep into his lungs. Every luxuriant inch of Carla's body flushed from this lewd attention—especially the object that had provoked it. Suddenly Manuel feared she would object to his presence. But she remained silent, docilely allowing her limbs to be manipulated like those of a helpless doll. The Spaniard's nose continued its ungentlemanly trespass.

When André had finished, Carla rested on her side and he adopted the same position behind her, fitting himself into the graceful curve of her back. The narrow bulb of his penis bobbed expectantly against the savory hole awaiting him. Manuel interpreted this as his cue and went onto his side as well. He faced her, the significantly broader bulb of his own organ instinctively sniffing out the orifice he had chosen. Carla's emerald eyes stared into his, making him giddy. He wondered what could possibly be going through her head at this moment. Surely she must have realized what he and the masseur were setting out to do.

Any questions in Carla's mind were answered promptly. Manuel gripped Carla behind one knee and raised it high, holding her leg aloft. The seductive cleavage of her buttocks and labia became far less pronounced from this induced splay, augmenting the dramatic split from her tailbone to the inflated tip of her clitoris and improving the accessibility of the neighboring openings between her thighs. Indeed, nearly two inches of André's penis had vanished effortlessly inside the redhead's anus just from the Spaniard's clever arrangement of her legs. Yet the masseur would not be the only one to benefit; Manuel's thick organ arced out from his belly, further severing the copper-haired puffs as it sought out the entrance it had waited so long to penetrate. The hot nugget of Carla's clitoris twitched wetly against the pulsating flesh of his penis. He looked down between their closely pressed bodies and discovered that the famous extremity had completely cloaked its spongy tip.

At André's instruction, Manuel began to slide into the velvety softness of her vagina. His bulk fit in quite easily. Upon reaching the halfway point, the masseur started pushing in from behind, grasping the base of his penis firmly to better command it. This muscular entry often posed difficulties even under normal circumstances—and these were definitely not normal circumstances. If only he could have counted the number of times he had been ejected from this heavenly vise!

The security chief could feel André's penis pressing through the thin membrane separating the two chambers. It proved both exhilarating and disturbing—indeed, almost incestuous. On impulse, he closed his mouth over Carla's, sucking hard on her ripe lower lip. Suddenly he recalled being in Thomas Bronski's surveillance room watching her doing something quite similar to the pretty young maid. But it had been with another type of lip—albeit a lip just as ripe and plump and delicious as the one he now had clamped between his teeth. Indeed, if Manuel had not viewed such tantalizing scenes, he might very well still have been stagnating in that stifling little office instead of becoming an active participant in Carla's erotic tableaux.

While André continued to make additional headway, the Spaniard felt himself being nudged out. He struggled to maintain his stronghold, buoyed onward by a fierce determination to subdue the redhead as Paolo had done. To show her just how wrong she had been to ignore him, Manuel lifted her knee even more, opening her tight slit dramatically and force-feeding it the swollen purple knob of his penis. With several inches of unsatisfied flesh still to go, the two men fought to infiltrate Carla's crowded passages completely, the buried heads of their massive organs rubbing against each other as they progressed. She whimpered from the stress this double impalement placed upon these delicate tubes; she felt like the victim of a medieval torture rack. Yet, instead of pleading for clemency, she thrust her buttocks out to help André fit into the more constricted thoroughfare of her rectum. He grabbed the topmost cheek, wrenching it away from its twin until her anus distended like a hungry mouth to suck him in.

At last André and Manuel won their struggle. They allowed themselves a brief respite, their battle-weary penises soaking in the luxuriant territory they had finally managed to conquer. Up till now, Françoise had kept out of the way, although not the slightest detail of her friend's double penetration had escaped her watchful eye. The normally discreet little berry of her clitoris sprouted boldly from the sleek seam of her labia, and her arousal became even more apparent when she squatted backward over Carla's face. The hairless folds had grown extremely fluid and fragrant. The redhead tongued them greedily, anointing her fingers in the downpour so that she could slide them easily in and out of the café-au-lait ring of Françoise's pert bottom. Carla's licking gained in its ferocity as the maid's intoxicating smell intensified. Her muffled moans turned ever more desperate as the men began pumping into her, their penises slamming juicily against her well-dilated openings.

Manuel could hardly believe his good fortune. Not only was he embraced by the smoldering conduit of Carla's vagina, but he found himself enjoying a bird's-eye view of her lusty pink tongue slithering between the unbearded lips of Françoise's labia, which the girl held conveniently spread with her fingers. His alert ears picked up all the subtle nuances of the redhead's eager lapping and sucking. He stared enraptured as she strained to penetrate the wet, musky sliver with her tongue. The security chief was so near that he could have licked the maid's piquant cream from Carla's lips. In fact, he very much wanted to do so, but he suspected that she would not have welcomed such a kiss from his sex. But before he had any time to regret this lost opportunity, Françoise leaned forward and parted her buttocks. The light from the bedside lamp shined brightly on the burnished stripe between them, illuminating the twinkling little star of her anus. For a brief moment, Manuel imagined that this explicit display had been intended specifically for him—especially when the maid's fingers traveled toward the delicately creased perimeter and plucked it open. However, Carla's fervid tongue immediately plunged into the enlarged hollow, terminating his brief—but pleasant—fantasy.

The tension built as the men thrust in and out of the redhead's two openings. Yet, despite the overwhelming passion of their penises, they continued to sustain the synchronization of their strokes with a skill born to those regularly practiced in such cooperative endeavors. Indeed, the more they took from the woman imprisoned between their bodies, the more they wanted to take. Hence, while André continued to isolate Carla's already-well-breached buttocks from each other, Manuel slid his hand down toward the coppery fire between her scattered thighs and captured the hot lump of wanton flesh that he wished to command. Now he could implement the next stage of his desire. He started out by kneading it slowly and deliberately between his thumb and index finger, observing that her forays into the French girl's rear outlet grew ever more ravenous as he did so. In spite of the slippery condition of Carla's clitoris, the Spaniard had no trouble keeping hold of it, for its ample bulk could not easily escape from his determined fingers. Thus he increased the pressure at steady intervals, the wild choreography of her tongue indicating that his labors were having the desired effect.

Manuel knew that Carla disliked him, and this only made him want to humble her all the more. He would force her into such a state of excitement that she would perform before him the ultimate of forbidden acts and, for his crowning achievement, to make her come. No matter how hard she tried to wriggle away from his unrelenting hand, he would stimulate her to a full and frenzied orgasm. Yet with so much other libidinous activity happening simultaneously, how could he ever be entirely certain he deserved all the credit when that decisive moment finally arrived? If only Carla hadn't been so stubborn! Why, he could have met with her alone, taking her in the missionary style, as he had originally intended. Then her enormous clitoris would have been forced to accept the constant friction of his penis. Indeed, the fiery redhead would then have had to concede that *Manuel* had been the sole catalyst for her pleasure!

Carla's passages reacted violently to the dual presence of her male intruders. Her climaxing walls squeezed the two penises lodged within her until they, too, gave up the fight. Their boiling fizz squirted from them in rapturous surrender and doused both of her interiors. Françoise trembled from her own private ecstasy, crushing the loving mouth below with her sopping vulva until the last droplets of her orgasm had been tasted and then swallowed. Only then did she allow the shuddering redhead to breathe air that was not scented with her pungent female folds. The men stayed happily ensconced within the saturated vises until their dwindling organs slipped out on their own. Then they released Carla from the moist clutch of their bodies. Still quaking from his pleasure, Manuel clamped his mouth over her well-glossed lips in a proprietary kiss, thrusting his tongue deep into her mouth. To his astonishment, Carla's tongue snaked forward to meet his in a piquant entanglement, sharing with him the ambrosial flavors of the pretty French girl.

The four lay in scattered disarray upon the bed, their senses still finely attuned to one another. They seemed to know unconsciously that the events of the past few minutes would not become the finale of the evening, for indeed, their hunger for the redhead and hers for them could not be assuaged by simply one coupling—regardless of its complexity. A matter of detumescence would hold the men temporarily at the sidelines.

Carla and Françoise wanted more. The fleshy indicators of their desire billowed outward from their pouty female lips with even more fervor now that they had experienced their first orgasms. Words were superfluous. The women moved closer together and began to kiss, their fingers exploring each other's flushed and fragrant bodies gently. As Manuel and André looked on, these explorations grew ever more passionate. Suddenly the maid rolled on top of Carla, fitting her sun-browned thighs into the slender contours of the redhead's waist. Bowing her dark head, Françoise flicked her tongue across the stiff coppery points of Carla's nipples, her ardent attentions prompting them to turn bright orange. Carla brought the maid's face up to meet hers, seizing the teasing tongue with her lips and sucking on it like a cherry lollipop. Further emboldened, she wrapped her arms and legs around the young maid, drawing her knees up high to embrace and entrap her small body. Her excited breathing alerted Manuel that something climactic was about to occur.

He was not disappointed. Both women unrolled the pulpy puffs of their sex, bringing into full view two very florid and very wet clitorises. Although an exhilarating enough sight in itself, apparently Françoise had far more in mind than merely showing off this feminine attribute to her three friends. She nudged Carla's upstanding clitoris with her own. This provocative caress looked to their enamored male observers like one tongue licking another. The striking contrast between the two pennants of flesh made the scene even more erotic in Manuel's eyes, for the redhead's imposing strawberry appendage completely dwarfed the maid's diminutive little berry. Yet both were equally charming and brought a renewed throbbing to his spent penis.

Françoise brought her pelvis down, grinding her denuded vulva into the redhead's sublime mount. Her bottom jutted out from her gyrations. Their jackknifed positioning displayed each woman's set of lusty openings. Manuel placed himself directly behind the intertwined figures, intending not to miss a salacious second of their sapphic lovemaking. The young domestic's syrupy wetness trickled down and mixed with Carla's contributions, which also contained some of his own. Eventually this delicious brew pooled around the yawning cinnamon orbit below. The Spaniard's mouth grew wet in sympathy. He found himself reflecting upon this particular orifice and its phenomenal capacity to receive a man's gluttonous organ. Indeed, it had already swallowed so many miles of male flesh that Manuel decided he, too, would gain entry to this unorthodox alleyway; he had seen André do it often enough—now it was *his* turn to feed the hungry mouth of Carla's lovely backside.

The perspiring women finally ceased their complex maneuvers. With pleasures taken and slits overflowing, they fell away from each other, panting, their moist fingertips still touching as if not wanting to break the contact. The security chief used this intermission to whisper discreetly into André's ear, proclaiming his desire to infringe on what had—at least up until the arrival of Paolo's insatiable penis—been the masseur's sole territory. He feared his humble request would be refused, for everybody on the staff knew that a strong emotion had developed between the two—one needed only to behold the hopeless love on André's handsome dark face every time he plunged his ebony organ into the redhead's anus. Perhaps the fellow already regretted giving the Italian a sampling of what he cherished so dearly. And just because Carla had been willing to forfeit André's exclusive right to her rear entrance did not mean she would do so again.

Yet even from that first breathtaking moment when he had parted the pale swells of her buttocks, the masseur had known that these impassioned encounters were only temporary. He had prepared himself for the eventuality that another man might one day wish to possess his adored Carla in the fiery paradise between her buttocks. Meanwhile, the object of the Spaniard's illicit desire crawled obediently to the foot of the bed and grabbed hold of the iron railing, apparently more than willing to submit to whatever her last night at the Elysium Spa brought her. Françoise took her place by her side, ready to do whatever would be necessary to make Carla happy.

Since Manuel was still a novice, André gave him the lead. He positioned his dribbling organ at the plumbed dimple the masseur had vacated. It distended outward, as if to kiss the spongy purple tip, offering a sweet taste of the velvety delights that could be found inside. With a little coaching from the spa's resident expert, the Spaniard fitted the broad head of his penis into the moistened rim of Carla's anus. Regardless of all the activity it had recently endured, the muscular furrow still managed to grip him snugly—indeed, with a special snugness that not even the most talented vagina could ever hope to duplicate. His brief poolside tinkerings with Talia's generous rear opening proved no match for this exquisite niche; it might as well have been his first time taking a woman in this unsanctioned manner. As with Paolo before him, Manuel suddenly understood why the masseur had chosen this particular harbor as his sole port of entry. As Carla thrust her shapely backside out to welcome him, he slid deeper and deeper into the mysterious chasm of her rectum, certain that he would never be the same again...

...*nor* would any woman who met up with him. For from this day on, the Spaniard would demand both front and rear access to a woman. And if she refused to comply...well, he would just see about that!

When the oversized knob of Manuel's penis could reach no farther into this unfamiliar opening, he went into immediate action, employing movements similar to what he had used at Carla's more yielding front entrance. Sharing her with André had trained him for the unremitting struggle to keep himself securely implanted in this more reluctant passage. His enthusiasm prompted the security chief to adopt more aggressive tactics. He delivered rough strokes, ramming the tender flesh of the redhead's well-utilized fundament with impunity.

Carla cried out each time the Spaniard's long organ knifed into her. The tensed fingers of her hands seemed to throttle the iron railing she continued to clutch. But once again she did not utter a single word of complaint against her brutal attacker. Having been penetrated previously by André and showered subsequently with the foamy fruit of his labors made Manuel's ravishings far easier to endure. Save for a slight variation in the rhythm of his thrusts, it could just as well have been the similarly endowed Italian behind her. Nevertheless, Carla's dislike for the security chief equaled hers for the arrogant Paolo. Yet having Manuel's herculean organ digging so roughly and deeply into her rectum gave her a pleasure of the most sublime nature. She shut her eyes, imagining that the two men she had once shunned were taking turns driving their hot, thick penises through the once-chaste slot of her anus.

Discerning that his prodigy could cope well enough on his own, André crouched behind Françoise. With one good shove, he buried his less monumental organ in her slender backside. As he worked his obsidian shaft in and out, she held the iron railing stoically, concentrating intently on the savory scent of Carla's sex and on the financial bonus she would receive after this recent group of guests had finally departed from the island. It was certain to be a lot of money, especially if the divine creature groaning and bucking alongside her paid up—which the maid fully expected her to do. Yes, she had definitely gone out of her way for the spicy young redhead—much further than she would have gone for any woman. But every once in awhile, someone truly special came along. After all, Françoise *was* only human.

Just when Manuel thought he would have Carla's juicy bottom all to himself, the masseur tapped his shoulder and indicated that they should change places. Although disappointed, one quick glance at the maid's reddened gouge glittering wetly and enticingly in the lamplight and he went at it like a seasoned professional—so much so that Françoise had to plead with him to moderate his technique. As she reminded him bluntly, she was not as practiced in anal entry as her friend.

Seeing the Spaniard's eager assault on the petite French girl, André initiated yet another switch. Before his penis even had time to dry off, Manuel found himself once again happily ensconced inside of Carla's more generous hind passage. Despite being accustomed to the masseur's artistry, she gave no indication that she minded the Spaniard's somewhat unrefined style—which was just as well, for tonight he vowed to outdo both the masseur and his Italian rival in one go. Indeed, by the time he finished with the redhead, she would not even remember that the other two men possessed a penis, let alone that they had stuck them well up her amorous rectum.

Manuel reached around to stroke Carla's clitoris. He found it an unwieldy handful that had already partaken of several orgasms. Françoise attended to her own needs, for she did not wish to escalate her contact with a man any more than necessary. Ever since her violation at the hands of her beloved Virginia's husband, she had had little use for men. Why, had it not been for Carla, she would never have consented to the disgrace of being sodomized—especially by a man she considered a common Latin hustler. The only recreation this part of her body indulged in would be from another woman's delicately probing fingers and tongue, or the odd visit from the small vibrating massager she had purloined from Dr. Bronski's examining room. Even that had taken quite a bit of getting used to—not to mention a fair amount of lubricant—before she could fully appreciate its stimulating merits. Indeed, Françoise would experience the most intense orgasms whenever it was lodged in her rectum and switched on at full speed. And she would not be the only one to benefit from this unique instrument. Every time she used it on Carla, the woman went into a fit, thrashing and moaning like a crazed animal as the maid rammed it in and out of the redhead's cinnamon opening while sucking simultaneously upon the colossal tongue of her clitoris. The French girl derived a particular thrill from administering the largest of the doctor's special instruments into her friend's well-greased anus, marveling at how the diameter of the resilient perimeter could widen to such an extravagant degree.

Yes, Françoise had enjoyed some fine adventures with Carla. Some had included the expectant moments just before the scheduled arrival of the masseur and his mystery guest. In order to prepare for what would inevitably be a rigorous rear encounter, the women indulged in a lustful game of erotic cleansing in the oversized white marble bathtub in Carla's bungalow. Keeping her knees spread so that her feminine attributes could be seen and admired fully, the redhead squatted on widely spaced feet facing the maid, the erect strawberry between her thighs twitching noticeably. Although she hadn't the slightest notion why Françoise had coaxed her into a bath that did not contain a single drop of water in it, she went along with this fanciful whim anyway, certain she would not regret it. For when had she *ever* regretted any of her interludes with the delicious young French woman?

Françoise utilized the spa's rich herbal shampoo to moisten three of her fingers and reached behind her lovely companion to fondle the splendid spheres of her buttocks. As expected, the redhead's stance had more than enhanced the ready accessibility of the fiery gap within the divided cleft, and she inserted her fingers all the way into Carla's rectum. Carla gasped with surprise at this abrupt intrusion, yet she held her bottom poised cooperatively for its purification, as ever so slowly and meticulously Françoise urged her slippery digits in and out of the smoldering cavity, eliciting many impassioned sighs from this subtle penetration. The steady convulsing of Carla's clitoris grew ever more frantic with these tender ministrations—as did the desire to reciprocate so delightful a service. Hence the saucy maid's slimmer rear entry received a thorough cleansing from Carla's nimble fingers. For several minutes, each woman reveled in the pleasure of the other's deep probings, their tongues weaving together in a hungry kiss as their fingers continued to slide in and out of the slickened conduits, the overstimulated walls of their interiors squeezing one another's fingers in a flirtatious and, indeed, shameless embrace.

For the convenience of the guests, a handheld sprayer had been attached by hose next to the hot and cold water spigots. However, the ever-creative Françoise had developed a far more sophisticated purpose for this ordinary device. Once the water had reached the desired degree of warmth, she inserted the black plastic nozzle just inside the elastic ring of the redhead's anus and depressed the control lever to the halfway point, allowing an intoxicating rush of water to flood the soapy chamber beyond.

Growing light-headed from the increasing pressure, Carla's hands reached out and grasped the sides of the tub. Never had she experienced so peculiarly erotic a sensation. She closed her eyes in rapture as the maid continued to pump her full of warm water. Françoise depressed the lever completely so the redhead would receive the full force of the cleansing deluge. Upon determining that Carla's rectum had at last reached its limit, she whipped out the nozzle and directed the powerful jet of water at the voluminous flap of ripe pink flesh projecting from Carla's labia, the force of the water flattening the great bulk to one side.

Suddenly, a substance normally taken for granted had suddenly become a power to be reckoned with as Carla battled to hold the unruly water inside her. The intense roiling in her abdomen combined with the insistent liquid current against her clitoris brought on the beginnings of a faint. But just when she thought she would finally succumb to blackness, she startled herself out of it with a loud cry. It felt as if she were soaring and filling all at the same time as her body quaked with a violent and prolonged climax. The water shot out of her with even more energy than when it had gone in, taking with it André's semen from earlier that morning. Carla sucked desperately on the sweet tip of Françoise's tongue, her moans losing themselves in the girl's throat.

But Carla would be granted little time to recover from her ordeal of watery ecstasy, for Françoise could barely wait to undergo the cleansing merits of the spray herself and she thrust out her bottom, parting the pert young cheeks in eager readiness to accept as much of the water as Carla deemed appropriate. She found the procedure quite stimulating, especially with the redhead at the helm. And her charming protégée showed herself to be utterly relentless in her application of the nozzle, filling the maid until she whimpered—and still she refused to let up on the handle. Françoise would be on the verge of orgasm by the time the mighty stream was aimed at the stiffened little berry of her clitoris. Then she lost all control over the circle of muscle between her buttocks. Water gushed from the café-au-lait opening with the force of a stormy ocean wave. Indeed, Carla came a second time just by watching the water being purged from the French girl. It splashed provocatively against her bare toes. She hastened toward the fount, opening her mouth to drink of the hot liquid spurting from the distended rim. Afterward the two women clung together as their last shudders waned, their lips and tongues still feeding ravenously on each other. For a brief instant, Françoise actually forgot that a camera had been recording every intimate detail of their heady passion.

Recalling their earlier bathtub frolic, Françoise decided to do something extra special for this engaging guest on her final night at the spa and reclaimed her sore backside from the masseur's plundering penis. André retreated from her in bewilderment; his tapered shaft wavered uncertainly against his belly. Yet it would not be idle for long, for the maid unlocked Carla from the iron railing and turned her so that she would have to lean forward on her hands and knees. Neither man could find any fault with this new pose. If anything, it improved not only the visual presentation of the redhead's obvious charms, but their accessibility. Not wanting to miss a tasty second inside of Carla's sweltering rear hollow, Manuel slowed down his movements, adjusting himself so that the entire length of his penis could remain within the voluptuous haven it had entered only moments before. Unfortunately, his fingers soon lost their grip on the voluminous clitoral flesh. However, he needn't have worried that it would be neglected. Françoise flipped onto her back and shimmied her petite form up toward the blazing coppery fire of Carla's pubic thatch until her mouth was centered directly below the dangling pendulum. With teasing little pecks, she began to kiss the insides of the trembling thighs encasing her, urging them farther apart so that the fragrant folds above would be easier to reach. When the redhead's knees were fully extended, she peeled back the swollen labia with her thumbs, thus completely exposing the silken extremity between them. So much attention had caused it to separate into what looked to the prurient Spaniard like two delicate slices of rare beef. Françoise's mouth closed over it hungrily, making him ache with envy.

Seeing that all was well with the ladies, Manuel resumed his previous pace. His excitement was enhanced by the hearty sucklings coming from below. His aggressive thrusts helped drive Carla's vulva down even lower until the French girl could reach it more easily. Indeed, rather than Françoise straining to reach the delicious morsel she sought, it had come to her. She absorbed the fluttering mass in its entirety, licking the surrounding pink of the tangy inner sheaths lovingly. Her legs remained sprawled carelessly between the redhead's splayed hands, consequently putting her depilated vagina and backside at the mercy of anyone with a mind to using them. Tiring of being a bystander, André hoisted the maid's sun-browned knees up and away from each other and penetrated her anus from this direction. Much to Françoise's consternation and the masseur's delight, he could reach far deeper at this angle than he ever had when approaching from the rear, and he decided to penetrate this way frequently in the future. The two men now faced one another above the flushed, perspiring bodies of the women they were sodomizing and they smiled, a special bond forming between them.

Carla reacted much the same as she had when the maid had utilized the talents of her mouth in combination with the battery-charged talents of the vibrator. She thrashed and shuddered beneath Manuel's weight. The pleasure was almost too great to bear. The juicy harvest between Françoise's thighs beckoned. She lowered her mouth to the plump, hairless lips that unfurled like a spring blossom. Drawing the erect little button into her mouth, she sucked it in concert with the ardent nursings upon her own significantly more substantial sprout, all the while keeping her eyes wide open, for she enjoyed looking upon the other woman's sleek feminine beauty. She became thoroughly captivated by the explicit drama of Françoise's diminutive anal opening being repeatedly stretched and punctured by the masseur's ebony column. Indeed, Carla knew that her lusty lover was also closely observing all the indelicate particulars of her own cinnamon-shaded garland receiving a rude goring by the Spaniard. Soon their tongues were traveling everywhere, splashing merrily into each other's slits and even posting themselves at each other's overstrained anuses to lick these moistened intruders thrusting in and out.

Orgasms would be wet and plentiful that evening, especially for the women. Finally Carla and Françoise collapsed from this lively tangle. Their burning rectums were glutted with male fluids, their thirsty mouths with female fluids. For days afterward, their tongues tasted those savory treats. Many more days passed before the semen from their gentleman partners emptied out of them completely, so deeply and copiously had it been deposited.

Thomas will certainly enjoy a fine meal tonight, Manuel thought with a bemused smirk as the bungalow faded into the darkness behind him. His body still hummed with the ecstasies it had indulged in when he opened the door to the dank cubbyhole that passed for the younger Bronski's office. Although he would have preferred to relish his mastery over the redhead for a while longer, he knew that Thomas could not be dismissed so recklessly—particularly after what he had no doubt just witnessed on his surveillance monitor. Upon entering the room, not only did Manuel step into a fresh puddle of froth, but the technician dropped to his knees and took the entirety of the Spaniard's spent penis into his mouth, sucking upon it with such force that it exploded with its third climax of the night, leaving both men more confused than ever about their symbiotic relationship.

Perhaps the delicious image of the women's soapy fingers seducing each other's lusty rear portals was what had finally sent the surveillance man over the edge.

Thomas Bronski had very nearly gone reeling out of his stale office that evening, determined to possess the redhead even if he had to do so in front of the maid. Let the clean-shaven little tart see his poor excuse for a penis! Indeed, what did it matter? Carla would be gone soon, and along with her any opportunity there would have been for him to ravish the lush landscape of her nakedness. Yet Thomas's delirious dark eyes had been unable to leave the viewing screen. Instead, he had wept hot, sticky tears into his trousers. The later appearance of the handsome Spaniard and his well-dipped organ only intensified his fever for his brother's most favored guest.

Early the next morning, Thomas gathered the extensive collection of film he had amassed of Carla and hid it in his private quarters for safekeeping. The plane that would carry her back to her old life was scheduled to leave the island around noon. However, just before boarding, she would be presented not only with her bill, but receive an escort to Dr. Bronski's elegantly appointed screening room for a free preview of her erotic escapades. In the entire history of the Elysium Spa, not one guest had failed to agree to the financial terms set forth upon departure. And the doctor showed himself to be extremely flexible regarding payment. No woman would renege on her financial obligations, for she had too much to lose if the true circumstances of her therapeutic holiday ever became known. Yet Thomas had taken quite a fancy to the distinctive redhead. Her obvious physical attributes provoked him to risk not only his job, but the wrath of his older brother. So, on this warm, sunny morning, he had a special proposal for her.

A light rapping awoke Carla from a deep sensual sleep. She had been dreaming of the sweet cream between Françoise's thighs and how delicious it had tasted, especially when the girl's charming rear opening was simultaneously put into service. The feminine confection seemed to flow all the more generously during anal stimulation. Carla's body still quivered from these succulent pleasures. She wrapped the wrinkled bedsheet around her and shuffled sleepily to the door, cracking it open barely enough to peer out. A young man hovered anxiously on the front step. He held his hands behind him, as if concealing a small object. One eyebrow twitched unchecked, giving him an expression that had a jarring effect to the onlooker. Carla took a step back. Although attractive in a quirky sort of way, there was a strange aura about the fellow—a certain something in the liquid brown of his eyes that could be described only as predatory. Suddenly Carla thought he was a trespasser to the island. Just as she moved to slam the door, he lodged his foot in the space and introduced himself as Dr. Bronski's assistant. The urgency in his tone roused her. Assuming that he brought some unfortunate news from home, she opened the door.

Without waiting for a further invitation, Thomas strolled into the bungalow as if he belonged there. To Carla's shock, he went into the private dominion of her bedroom and sat down on the rumpled stage of the previous night's orgy. The passionate scents of a few hours ago still lingered heavily in the air and on the bedclothes, and her face flushed to an embarrassed scarlet, certain he, too, would be able to recognize the potent smell of sex. The surveillance man noticed several discolored areas on the sheet and trailed the tips of his fingers over them in a seductive caress, his sly smile informing Carla that he knew precisely what had gone on.

Carla could never have guessed his depth of knowledge on her doings so she found no reason to doubt him when he explained his unusual function at the spa. And when Thomas reached into his jacket pocket to produce the stills he had made from the miles of film Carla had starred in unwittingly, she knew that her foolishness had placed her entirely at the mercy of Dr. Bronski's villainous brother. Indeed, there could be no denying that those were *her* eager hands pulling apart the cheeks of her buttocks to welcome into the yawning orange slot between them the full ebony length of the masseur's penis—nor could anyone possibly dispute the owner of the gluttonous pair of lips fastened so hungrily over the maid's lustrous little berry. Carla could not bear to look at the other photos of her with Paolo and Manuel. The obscene nature of these couplings brought tears of humiliation to her eyes. Surely the kind doctor could not have been a party to such treachery! Nevertheless, the thorough invasiveness of Thomas's cameras did, in fact, remind her of the thorough invasiveness of his brother's daily physical examinations. Suddenly Carla realized that the dreadful words this strange young man had spoken could not be lies. She would either have to give him what he wanted or pay for her recklessness the rest of her life. However, she had no money of her own; it would always be doled out parsimoniously by her husband—and *only* if she could prove a legitimate need for it. It would take her years to pay off the amount Thomas had put forth—indeed, far more years than she had left on this earth. "But how do I know I can trust you?" was all Carla could manage before her throat closed up completely.

"You'll just have to take my word for it," came the smug reply.

It seemed she would have little choice. Hence, with their bargain signed and sealed, Carla disrobed and performed the first of many tasks demanded of her. It was still early in the morning, and the surveillance man had been saving up his fantasies for a very long time. She fell to her knees and took his stumpy organ into her mouth, finding it rather disagreeable after the pretty maid's aromatic flesh. Yet she forced herself to treat it with enthusiasm, rolling her tongue reverently around the retreating ridge of foreskin and up over the exposed vermilion head, licking away the syrupy droplets that continued to replenish themselves in ever-greater quantities as if to spite her.

Thrusting his pelvis forward, Thomas urged himself deeper into Carla's mouth. She accepted him as far down as she could endure. His fluids left a warm viscous trail upon the velvety surface of her tongue. His penis grew larger as he pumped her slender throat aggressively. He pinched the upstanding prongs of her nipples until they glowed a bright orange-red against his acquisitive fingertips. It did not take long for Thomas to come. It was as if he had been saving up for this as well, for he continued to spasm wildly in Carla's mouth, spewing out so much hot thick semen that she needed to keep swallowing and swallowing as she had done with the Italian—and *still* the glutinous liquid would not stop gushing onto her exhausted tongue.

When his reservoir had finally depleted itself, Thomas sank heavily onto the bed, his chest heaving with the power of his climax. Carla spat out the last dribbles from his discharging organ and wiped the stickiness from her lips on a loose fold of sheet, her belly bloated from the frothy fare she had been forced to imbibe. When the surveillance man closed his eyes and appeared to be dozing, Carla naïvely assumed that the carnal worship of her mouth had been all he'd really wanted, especially since he now seemed incapable of initiating any further priapic activity.

But Thomas would not lie still for long. He wished to make the most of these precious few moments with the tantalizing redhead. Grabbing her wrists, he pulled her down onto the bed beside him and kissed her mouth, licking the pink pillows of her lips ravenously. They had puffed up considerably with her earlier devotion to Françoise's juicy feminine folds, and their lustful condition was further enhanced by the more challenging consumption of Thomas's organ. Suddenly he imagined that he could taste the piquant essence of the French girl on them, and his tongue began to search out new territory in hope of additional pleasure. Carla lay completely still as he ran his burning tongue down the slope of her neck and up along the damp hollows beneath her arms, their tangy muskiness hauntingly similar to the womanly scents lower down. Thomas licked the concave curves with deliberate slowness, taking up the light drizzle of perspiration that had formed from Carla's previous oral labors. The sensation of his tongue gliding over these ticklish nooks made her squirm with a combination of excitement and annoyance and, fearing she would try to get away, he pinned her wrists high above her head until he had swabbed up every last salty-sweet droplet from her armpits. Such unswerving loyalty to the task prompted an eruption of liquid honey to spurt forth from the tender sliver of Carla's vagina, and she clenched her thighs together instinctively. Her breasts swelled with the surveillance man's attentions. He cupped the tender globes in his palms, bringing them up to his mouth and sucking hard on the pliant nibs, opening wider to absorb the surrounding areolae. Indeed, within moments, Thomas discovered that the buds his lips now encircled were the exact same shade of cinnamon as that tinting the fragrant ring of the redhead's anus.

While he was sampling more and more of Carla's savory flesh, it became apparent to Thomas that she both tasted and smelled of that secret part of a woman that he had been deprived of far too often. Having observed from the private watchtower of his surveillance office the libidinous activities of the evening before, he knew that the richly scented bodies of Françoise, André, and Manuel had left their moist tracings upon Carla, marking an intoxicating trail for his nose and tongue to traverse. Determined that none of this enticing territory should elude him, Thomas allowed his hands to explore the redhead more fully, prodding both of her sore openings until they eventually gave way, their dewy status inviting his fingers to burrow defiantly into them. Assigning one hand to each inlet, he lodged his fingers in Carla's vagina and rectum, embarking upon what he hoped would be a thorough investigation of these parts. All those hours of spying on young women in various stages of sexual intimacy had made the surveillance man more inquisitive than ever. He pulled at the resilient perimeters of both portals to peer into the humid darkness, as his brother had done so often. However, without Dr. Bronski's instruments, Thomas had little success. He cursed himself for his lack of planning. Indeed, the doctor's equipment was probably sitting in a drawer going to waste when all this time he could have been putting it to good use.

Despite the marauding presence of her sunrise caller's hands, Carla continued to clamp her thighs together, the muscles tensing and bulging with the strain of maintaining what little remained of her dignity. More than anything, she wished to keep the flamboyant details of these parts to herself; her wetness was shameful enough, yet she simply could not bear for this dreadful little man to behold her in such full bloom. Suddenly the embarrassment she had once experienced whenever anyone went near her clitoris returned with a vengeance, driving Carla to shelter the fleshy extremity from prying eyes and fingertips. In its normal state, the russet tip stuck out considerably; after all the ardent attention from the previous evening, much of the florid strawberry beneath the darkly shaded hood flared into view, causing the lusty pendant to resemble the top of a man's thumb. Indeed, even with her legs braced, the brazen tongue still managed to defy her by jutting out from her tightly compressed thighs, parading itself before Thomas Bronski's ogling eyes.

Like his older brother, he had already become hopelessly ensnared by the uniqueness of this particular fragment of flesh. He grasped Carla's knees, pushing them outward to expose the succulent tidbit. Her womanly dribbles stippled the pale insides of her thighs. He bowed his head to clean away the fragrant residue with his tongue, eliciting a series of flustered shudders from the redhead. The copper-haired pout above had separated from the exaggerated sprawl of her legs. For the first time, the surveillance man could appreciate firsthand a woman's intricate secrets. The silken flap of Carla's clitoris blazed a fiery red, pointing out at him like a bidding finger. The spectacular appendage becoming even more spectacular when he opened the seam of her labia completely. Thomas came closer, his hot breath fanning across the distended button. To his enchantment, it began to flicker. The orange-brown tip branching into two delicate petals and revealed the whorled complexity of its structure. He could only gasp in helpless admiration. Viewing it through the impersonal glass of a monitor could not compare with the imposing presence now before him and he fancied it growing even larger under inspection.

It was not entirely his imagination. Despite Carla's dislike of the surveillance man and everything he represented, she could not remain immune from his unwelcome attentions. Her clitoris twitched and stretched beneath the feverish dark eyes of her examiner;

her florid sliver below pooled with warm, creamy honey. Thomas did not wish to miss out on so fluid a bonus and tasted her love-juice. The titillating reality that much of this condition stemmed from her earlier activities only heightened the pleasure for Thomas, for the redhead had not had time to wash off her passions.

The surveillance man's penis reactivated itself immediately as he explored the yielding contours never before bestowed upon him. His tongue swabbed up moisture from the redhead's steamy folds, sponging up any leftover traces of the maid and the security chief as well. Nothing would be left untasted—not even the peppery spice of the redhead's rear hollow which, sampling it secondhand, proved even more delectable as it accepted Thomas's tongue. He spread the cheeks of Carla's buttocks, straining to reach the innermost core of her being. Indeed, so welcoming was the loosened notch that he decided to save his penetration of it to the very last.

Bronski's inexperienced but enthusiastic tongue swirling frantically around and within the exterior and interior of Carla's vagina and anus interspersed with his deep sucklings upon the erect projectile of her clitoris made her come with an anguished wail, the fragrant button jerking between his enthusiastic lips. She bucked frantically against his mouth, offering him even more of her tangy nectar to drink. He thrust his tongue into the quivering slit, feeling the heady palpitations of her receding orgasm, the storm from above raining its sappy droplets onto his chin.

Carla lay dazed on the chaotic jumble of the

bedsheets, trying to recover from the ecstasy and humiliation of orgasm at the instigation of the doctor's abominable brother. Yet Thomas would not grant her any rest. Next he ordered her to masturbate for him—while looking directly into his eyes. He had observed the redhead numerous times within the ostensible privacy of her bungalow and found the elaborate series of hand motions quite entertaining, not to mention the succulent visual spectacle of her unmasked female foliage as she opened her thighs wide in a rhapsodic prelude. And this morning Carla did not disappoint him. Her fingertips virtually flew over the tumid strawberry, quickly resulting in a second bout of wild bucking. Her skilled fingers slipped fondly into the sopping hole below—where they remained until Thomas pulled them back out, only to lick the glossy coating from them, his dark eyes burning as brightly as the coppery fire of her pubic mound.

With taste buds temporary satisfied and in full form for penetration, Thomas extended Carla's perspiring thighs and aimed the famished head of his penis at the bubbling crimson entrance. Like a man jumping into uncharted seas, he plunged into Carla's humid canal, finding himself sinking blissfully deeper and deeper until he finally reached bottom. Her inner passage still sore from the rugged pounding it had sustained from Manuel's overgrown organ, even the surveillance man's considerably more modest girth pained Carla. She moaned wretchedly with his every sweeping stroke. Not entirely indifferent to her tender condition, Thomas relaxed the wishbone he had made of her legs and leaned his pelvis into hers, the short repetitive motions of his slickened shaft lovingly stroking the bulging hump of clitoral flesh and bringing with them renewed pleasure and diminished discomfort. Soon the redhead's moans of distress became moans of desire. He reached around to cup her contracting buttocks, lifting her up into him, his fingers slipping past the moist chink of her anus and into the secluded chasm beyond. The surveillance man's cry of pleasure could be heard several bungalows down, for it felt as if he had just stuck his fingers into a ring of fire. Suddenly his penis erupted, issuing several rapid-fire bursts of hot semen into the thirsty conduit of Carla's vagina.

She remained pinned beneath Thomas' limp body, believing that this time he had finally finished with her. However, instead of relief, Carla experienced an incompleteness—as if she wanted still more from this strange and demanding visitor. Although she felt no affection toward the younger Bronski, she had to acknowledge that the past half-hour had not been unpleasant. The fellow appeared to harbor a desperate sort of passion for her that she could only find flattering despite its occasional savage bent. Indeed, the rubbing of his thickset organ against her clitoris had inflamed Carla nearly to another climax, but the sublime summit somehow managed to elude her. Another minute of such primal friction and she might have been there—had Thomas not overstimulated himself by the introduction of his fingers into her bottom.

Only since her arrival on the island had Carla found herself the focus of so much lustful attention. Regardless of the sordid truth behind the sexual interludes at the Elysium Spa, she did not regret a single delicious moment—not even those that had just passed. Perhaps the other staff members' sexual motives might have been coupled with financial ones, but at least the man lying on top of her did not want any money. In fact, the only thing he seemed to want was *her*. But what would Carla do once the island had receded to a microscopic speck in the center of a vast blue glittering sea, her plane rising higher and higher and leaving behind the treasures of André and Françoise for the next lucky guest to enjoy? Or what about the treasure of Dr. Bronski and his queer little contraption that so effectively unveiled the needy tongue of flesh between her thighs? How would she ever again cope with the dullness of marital life now that she had experienced so much ecstasy—*and* in so many uncommon ways? Carla considered throwing herself on the doctor's mercy and begging him to let her stay on. Why, he wouldn't even have to pay her! She would do *anything*—any job he required of her, no matter how lowly or illicit in nature.

The heaviness on Carla's body began to shift, interrupting her hopeless fancies. However, the sense of incompleteness nagging at her would soon be remedied, for Thomas rolled her over and hoisted her buttocks high into the air, his seeking fingers unlocking the anxiously braced crease between them. The satiny orange stripe previously concealed by the presence of the two shapely spheres gleamed in the early morning sunlight, the fine coppery hairs damp with perspiration and female discharges. Yet not a single hair sprouted forth from the uncurtained environs of the redhead's anus, which now lured Thomas. With a scholar's intensity he studied the moist cinnamon band, finding its plucked conspicuousness doubly compelling. Just below this twitching portal, his semen had mixed with Carla's juices and dripped out of her plundered slit in a creamy rivulet, catching on the large glittering ruby below. Indeed, it dangled as if from a chain, no longer ashamed of its size. Already radiant with the surveillance man's saliva, the bifurcated flesh grew even larger from this extra polishing. He tickled it with his pinkie, and received an encouraging wink from the as-yet-unplumbed dimple above.

Unable to resist her excited contractions, Thomas pressed the tips of his thumbs against the elastic mouth of Carla's anus, exposing the stygian depths. To his astonishment, he discovered that the interior had always been in shadow. Further examination revealed the true peach tincture beyond the enlarged aperture—a peach that made his tongue flutter hungrily in expectation of another life-giving taste. Suddenly Thomas moored his lips to it, letting his tongue slice into the magnified socket, his thumbs stretching the puckered rim even farther and ironing out the delicate little crinkles that composed the resilient perimeter. Carla answered the surveillance man's adoring stabs by thrusting her splayed buttocks backward against his enraptured face, squeezing his tongue with her sphincter muscles until tears of joy coursed down his blushing cheeks.

When Thomas finally fitted the bulging head of his insatiable organ into the redhead's anus, he found it wet and open, delighted to receive him. He slid in all the way up to his overburdened testicles. With every stalwart throb, he filled out the walls of Carla's rear passage, his penis nourishing itself on the lush surroundings and growing longer and thicker than ever before. Indeed, it now bore little resemblance to the stumpy specimen it had once been. It was a suitable rival to those who had gone before. Thomas pumped the smoldering sanctum with renewed pride and vigor, imagining he could go on forever.

Carla felt her interior expanding and held her buttocks high, swallowing every scourging inch of this new violator, at last complete as her smarting backside entertained its third visitor since sundown the previous evening.

The following week, as a new batch of arrivals touched down on the island's tiny airstrip, the Elysium Spa welcomed the newest member of its multitalented staff. This latest hire proved every bit as appealing as the finest of her male and female coworkers, possessing as she did a certain uniqueness which would make her immensely popular with the guests.

Attired in a scanty maid's costume, Carla learned her duties under the expert tutelage of Françoise: the subtleties of turning down beds, arranging toiletries—even walking, bending, and—more importantly—how to display her breasts to their maximum advantage within her snug, crisply starched uniform. Most surprising of all, she also needed to master an entirely new way of standing. Like the statuesque Paris fashion models

Françoise had once yearned for, Carla had to locate the center of her weight and shift it backward, thus pushing her pelvis forward, which lifted her overly short skirt so that the lustful tip of her clitoris would show. Since she was already significantly endowed in this respect, it would be unnecessary for her to remove any obscuring locks of hair. Even with all her sparkling copper pubic hair, the orange-brown hood stuck out like a signpost. Never had Carla imagined that there would be so much to the job, nor that the French girl's alluring mannerisms were, in fact, carefully calculated.

Very soon Carla began to work on her own, enticing the women she had been instructed to serve into committing acts previously unknown to them. Many requests for personal favors were forthcoming immediately. She tried her best to accommodate every last one, for the ladies were all so sweet and lovely that it seemed terribly selfish to refuse them. Nor could *they* refuse the irresistible display of Carla's tumescent clitoris thrusting brazenly out from the abbreviated black skirt. Indeed, it would be in a constant state of arousal, fostered not only by the absence of undergarments beneath her uniform, but by the salacious conditions of her employment at the spa. Even the most difficult of guests could not abstain from taking a nice lavish suck upon the redhead's famous extremity—all of which would, of course, be transmitted onto film for future use.

Within days, Carla was assigned to a guest who had extended the length of her stay for several weeks. By all reports, this particular lady had not as yet succumbed to any of the maids; not even Françoise's engaging face and figure could move her. Hence the redhead was dispatched as soon as her mentor deemed her ready for such a challenge. Yet, unbeknownst to Carla, she had already gotten a head start. On the first evening when she entered the bungalow to turn down the bed, she discovered the seemingly stubborn occupant to be none other than the sable-haired woman from the swimming pool.

The two stood staring at one another for several minutes. Their mutual shock was so palpable that it vibrated through the air, instantly energizing the female indicators of their desire. There would be no need for words, for both sets of green eyes spoke of the furtive moments previously enjoyed and their repetition long yearned for. With a desperate wail, the brunette fell to the floor in total surrender, gazing hungrily at the spectacular apparition above. She hoisted up the inadequate hem of Carla's uniform until it exposed the savory delicacy she sought and, with trembling thumbs, rolled back the pouting lips of fiery hair encasing it. A plump strawberry burst forth, and she sealed it with her mouth, climaxing instantly.

Souci knew that the redhead had recognized her, but suddenly her wish to remain anonymous had lost its importance. Now her only wish was to feed on the moist, fleshy object fluttering in her mouth. She gripped it between her lips as Carla lowered herself to the floor, her thighs opening wide so her poolside lover could consume her completely. Yet this had been her desire as well. She urged Souci onto her back, pivoting around so that the woman could continue on uninterrupted with her oral lovemaking. She still wore the towel from her afternoon sunbathing, and Carla wrenched it from her fragrant body, burying her mouth within the soft, wet cleft she had waited endless weeks to taste.

No longer did Carla find herself the recipient of amused snickers, but instead the recipient of appreciative *oohs* and *aahs* from scores of the world's most beautiful women—women like Souci—women who were helpless to resist taking her to their beds and were thrilled to indulge in the basest of practices—only to go to their knees and beg for more of the same. From now on, Carla's days and nights would be filled with the sublime pleasures of André and Françoise, plus any woman who captured her fancy and—if she could manage to fit them into her busy schedule—Paolo and Manuel, and perhaps even the quirky little surveillance man.

Carla had indeed found the paradise the magazine advertisements promised.

# MASQUERADE

**AMERICA'S FASTEST GROWING EROTIC MAGAZINE**

## SPECIAL OFFER
### RECEIVE THE NEXT TWO ISSUES FOR ONLY $5.00—A 50% SAVINGS!

A bi-monthly magazine packed with the very best the world of erotica has to offer. Each issue of *Masquerade* contains today's most provocative, cutting-edge fiction, sizzling pictorials from the masters of modern fetish photography, scintillating and illuminating exposés of the worldwide sex-biz written by longtime industry insiders, and probing reviews of the many books and videos that cater specifically to your lifestyle.

*Masquerade* presents radical sex uncensored—from homegrown American kink to the fantastical fashions of Europe. Never before have the many permutations of the erotic imagination been represented in one publication.

## THE ONLY MAGAZINE THAT CATERS TO YOUR LIFESTYLE

---

Masquerade/Direct • 801 Second Avenue • New York, NY 10017 • FAX: 212.986.7355
E-Mail: MasqBks@aol.com • MC/VISA orders can be placed by calling our toll-free number: 800.375.2356

☐ 2 ISSUES $10 *SPECIAL* $5!

☐ 6 ISSUES (1 YEAR) FOR $30 *SPECIAL* $15!

☐ 12 ISSUES (2 YEARS) FOR $60 *SPECIAL* $25!

NAME _____

ADDRESS _____

CITY _____ STATE _____ ZIP _____

E-MAIL _____

PAYMENT: ☐ CHECK  ☐ MONEY ORDER  ☐ VISA  ☐ MC

CARD # _____ EXP. DATE _____

No C.O.D. orders. Please make all checks payable to Masquerade/Direct. Payable in U.S. currency only.

# MASQUERADE BOOKS

## MASQUERADE

### ROBERT SEWALL
**THE DEVIL'S ADVOCATE**
$6.95/553-0
The return of an erotic masterpiece! The first erotic novel written and published in America, Clara Reeves appeals to Conrad Garnett, a New York district attorney, for help in tracking down her missing sister, Rita. To Clara's distress, Conrad suspects that Rita has disappeared into an unsavory underworld dominated by an illicit sex ring. Clara soon finds herself being "persuaded" to accompany Conrad on his descent into this modern-day hell, where unspeakable pleasures await....

### OLIVIA M. RAVENSWORTH
**THE DESIRES OF REBECCA**
$6.50/532-2
A swashbuckling tale of lesbian desire in Merrie Olde England. Beautiful Rebecca follows her passions from the simple love of the girl next door to the relentless lechery of London's most notorious brothel, hoping for the ultimate thrill. Finally, she casts her lot with a crew of sapphic buccaneers, each of whom is more than capable of matching Rebecca lust for lust....

**THE MISTRESS OF CASTLE ROHMENSTADT**
$5.95/372-4
Lovely Katherine inherits a secluded European castle from a mysterious relative. Upon arrival she discovers, much to her delight, that the castle is a haven of sensual pleasure. Katherine learns to shed her inhibitions and enjoy her new home's many delights. Soon, Castle Rohmenstadt is the home of every perversion known to man—and under the iron grip of an extraordinary woman.

### ATAULLAH MARDAAN
**KAMA HOURI/DEVA DASI**
$7.95/512-3
"...memorable for the author's ability to evoke India present and past.... Mardaan excels in crowding her pages with the sights and smells of India, and her erotic descriptions are convincingly realistic."
—Michael Perkins,
*The Secret Record: Modern Erotic Literature*
Two legendary tales of the East in one spectacular volume. *Kama Houri* details the life of a sheltered Western woman who finds herself living within the confines of a harem—where she discovers herself thrilled with the extent of her servitude. *Deva Dasi* is a tale dedicated to the cult of the Dasis—the sacred women of India who devoted their lives to the fulfillment of the senses—while revealing the sexual rites of Shiva. A special double volume.

### GERALD GREY
**LONDON GIRLS**
$6.50/531-X
In 1875, Samuel Brown arrived in London, determined to take the glorious city by storm. And sure enough, Samuel quickly distinguishes himself as one of the city's most notorious rakehells. Young Mr. Brown knows well the many ways of making a lady weak at the knees—and uses them not only to his delight, but to his enormous profit! A rollicking tale of cosmopolitan lust.

### J. P. KANSAS
**ANDREA AT THE CENTER**
$6.50/498-4
Kidnapped! Lithe and lovely young Andrea is whisked away to a distant retreat. Gradually, she is introduced to the ways of the Center, and soon becomes quite friendly with its other inhabitants—all of whom are learning to abandon restraint in their pursuit of the deepest sexual satisfaction. Soon, Andrea takes her place as one of the Center's greatest success stories—a submissive seductress who answers to any and all! A nationally bestselling title, and one of modern erotica's true classics.

### VISCOUNT LADYWOOD
**GYNECOCRACY**
$9.95/511-5
Julian, whose parents feel he shows just a bit too much spunk, is sent to a very special private school, in hopes that he will learn to discipline his wayward soul. Once there, Julian discovers that his program of study has been devised by the deliciously stern Mademoiselle de Chambonnard. In no time, Julian is learning the many ways of pleasure and pain—under the firm hand of this beautifully demanding headmistress.

### CHARLOTTE ROSE, EDITOR
**THE 50 BEST PLAYGIRL FANTASIES**
$6.50/460-7
A steamy selection of women's fantasies straight from the pages of *Playgirl*—the leading magazine of sexy entertainment for women. These tales of seduction—specially selected by no less an authority than Charlotte Rose, author of such bestselling women's erotica as *Women at Work* and *The Doctor is In*—are sure to set your pulse racing.

**A DANGEROUS DAY**
$5.95/293-0
A new volume from the best-selling author who brought you the sensational *Women at Work* and *The Doctor Is In*. And if you thought the high-powered entanglements of her previous books were risky, wait until Rose takes you on a journey through the thrills of one dangerous day—the ultimate day off.

# MASQUERADE BOOKS

## N. T. MORLEY

**THE LIMOUSINE**
$6.95/555-7
Brenda was enthralled with her roommate Kristi's illicit sex life: a never ending parade of men who satisfied Kristi's desire to be dominated. While barely admitting she shared these desires, Brenda issued herself the ultimate challenge—a trip into submission, beginning in the long, white limousine where Kristi first met the Master. Following in the footsteps of her lascivious roommate, Brenda embarks on the erotic journey of her life....

**THE CASTLE**
$6.95/530-1
A pulse-pounding peek at the ultimate vacation paradise. Tess Roberts is held captive by a crew of disciplinarians intent on making all her dreams come true—even those she'd never admitted to herself. While anyone can arrange for a stay at the Castle, Tess proves herself one of the most gifted applicants yet....

**THE PARLOR**
$6.50/496-8
Lovely Kathryn gives in to the ultimate temptation. The mysterious John and Sarah ask her to be their slave—an idea that turns Kathryn on so much that she can't refuse! But who are these two mysterious strangers? Little by little, Kathryn not only learns to serve, but comes to know the inner secrets of her stunning keepers.

## J. A. GUERRA, EDITOR

**COME QUICKLY:**
**For Couples on the Go**
$6.50/461-5
The increasing pace of daily life is no reason to forgo a little carnal pleasure whenever the mood strikes. Here are over sixty of the hottest fantasies around—all designed to get you going in less time than it takes to dial 976. A super-hot volume designed especially for modern couples on a hectic schedule.

## ERICA BRONTE

**LUST, INC.**
$6.50/467-4
Lust, Inc. explores the extremes of passion that lurk beneath even the coldest, most businesslike exteriors. Join in the sexy escapades of a group of high-powered professionals whose idea of office decorum is like nothing you've ever encountered! Business attire is decidedly *not* required for this unflinching look at high-powered sexual negotiations!

## VANESSA DURIÈS

**THE TIES THAT BIND**
$6.50/510-7
The incredible confessions of a thrillingly unconventional woman. From the first page, this chronicle of dominance and submission will keep you gasping with its vivid depictions of sensual abandon. At the hand of Masters Georges, Patrick, Pierre and others, this submissive seductress experiences pleasures she never knew existed.... One of modern erotica's best-selling accounts of real-life dominance and submission.

## M. S. VALENTINE

**ELYSIAN DAYS AND NIGHTS**
$6.95/536-0
From around the world, the most beautiful—and wealthy—neglected young wives arrive at the Elysium Spa intent on receiving a little heavy-duty pampering. Luckily for them, the spa's proprietor is a true devotee of the female form—and has dedicated himself and his staff to the pure pleasure of every lovely lady who steps foot across Elysium's threshold....

**THE CAPTIVITY OF CELIA**
$6.50/453-4
Beautiful Celia's lover, Colin, is considered the prime suspect in a murder, forcing him to seek refuge with his cousin, Sir Jason Hardwicke. In exchange for Colin's safety, Jason demands Celia's unquestioning submission.... Sexual extortion guarantees her lover's safety—as well as provide Celia with ever mor exciting sensual delights. Soon, she finds herself entranced by the demands of her captor....

## AMANDA WARE

**BINDING CONTRACT**
$6.50/491-7
Louise was responsible for bringing many prestigious clients into Claremont's salon—so he was more than willing to have her miss a little work in order to pleasure one of his most important customers. But Eleanor Cavendish had her mind set on something more rigorous than a simple wash and set. Sexual slavery!

**BOUND TO THE PAST**
$6.50/452-6
Anne accepts a research assignment in a Tudor mansion. Upon arriving, she finds herself aroused by James, a descendant of the mansion's owners. Together they uncover the perverse desires of the mansion's long-dead master—desires that bind Anne inexorably to the past—not to mention the bedpost!

**BUY ANY 4 BOOKS & CHOOSE 1 ADDITIONAL BOOK, OF EQUAL OR LESSER VALUE, AS YOUR FREE GIFT**

# MASQUERADE BOOKS

## SACHI MIZUNO
**SHINJUKU NIGHTS**
$6.50/493-3
A tour through the lives and libidos of the seductive East. No one is better that Sachi Mizuno at weaving an intricate web of sensual desire, wherein many characters are ensnared and enraptured by the demands of their carnal natures.

**PASSION IN TOKYO**
$6.50/454-2
Tokyo—one of Asia's most historic and seductive cities. Come behind the closed doors of its citizens, and witness the many pleasures that await. Lusty men and women from every stratum of society free themselves of all inhibitions....

## MARTINE GLOWINSKI
**POINT OF VIEW**
$6.50/433-X
The story of one woman's extraordinary erotic awakening. With the assistance of her new, unexpectedly kinky lover, she discovers and explores her exhibitionist tendencies—until there is virtually nothing she won't do before the horny audiences her man arranges!

## RICHARD McGOWAN
**A HARLOT OF VENUS**
$6.50/425-9
A highly fanciful, epic tale of lust on Mars! Cavortia—the most famous and sought-after courtesan in the cosmopolitan city of Venus—finds love and much more during her adventures with some of the most remarkable characters in recent erotic fiction.

## M. ORLANDO
**THE ARCHITECTURE OF DESIRE**
Introduction by Richard Manton.
$6.50/490-9
Two novels in one special volume! In *The Hotel Justine*, an elite clientele is afforded the opportunity to have any and all desires satisfied. *The Villa Sin* is inherited by a beautiful woman who soon realizes that the legacy of the ancestral estate includes bizarre erotic ceremonies.

## CHET ROTHWELL
**KISS ME, KATHERINE**
$5.95/410-0
Husband or slave? Beautiful Katherine can hardly believe her luck. Not only is she married to the charming and oh-so-agreeable Nelson, she's free to live out all her erotic fantasies with other men. Katherine's desires are more than any one man can handle—luckily there are always plenty of men on hand, ready and willing to fulfill her many needs!

## MARCO VASSI
**THE STONED APOCALYPSE**
$5.95/401-1/mass market
"Marco Vassi is our champion sexual energist." —VLS

During his lifetime, Marco Vassi's groundbreaking erotic writing was praised by writers as diverse as Gore Vidal and Norman Mailer, and his reputation as an indefatigable champion of sexual experimentation was worldwide. *The Stoned Apocalypse* is Vassi's autobiography; chronicling a cross-country trip on America's erotic byways, it offers a rare glimpse of a generation's sexual imagination.

## ROBIN WILDE
**TABITHA'S TICKLE**
$6.50/468-2
Tabitha's back! The story of this vicious vixen didn't end with *Tabitha's Tease*. Once again, men fall under the spell of scrumptious co-eds and find themselves enslaved to demands and desires they never dreamed existed. Think it's a man's world? Guess again. With Tabitha around, no man gets what he wants until she's completely satisfied—and, maybe, not even then....

## ERICA BRONTE
**PIRATE'S SLAVE**
$5.95/376-7
Lovely young Erica is stranded in a country where lust knows no bounds. Desperate to escape, she finds herself trading her firm, luscious body to any and all men willing and able to help her. Her adventure has its ups and downs, ins and outs—all to the pleasure of the increasingly lusty Erica!

## CHARLES G. WOOD
**HELLFIRE**
$5.95/358-9
A vicious murderer is running amok in New York's sexual underground—and Nick O'Shay, a virile detective with the NYPD, plunges deep into the case. He soon becomes embroiled in an elusive world of fleshly extremes, hunting a madman seeking to purge America with fire and blood sacrifices. Set in New York's infamous sexual underground and peopled with thrillingly unconventional characters.

## CLAIRE BAEDER, EDITOR
**LA DOMME: A Dominatrix Anthology**
$5.95/366-X
A steamy smorgasbord of female domination! Erotic literature has long been filled with heart-stopping portraits of domineering women, and now the most memorable have been brought together in one beautifully brutal volume. A must for all fans of BD/SM fiction.

# MASQUERADE BOOKS

## CHARISSE VAN DER LYN
### SEX ON THE NET
$5.95/399-6

Electrifying erotica from one of the Internet's hottest authors. Encounters of all kinds—straight, lesbian, dominant/submissive and all sorts of extreme passions—are explored in thrilling detail.

## STANLEY CARTEN
### NAUGHTY MESSAGE
$5.95/333-3

Wesley Arthur discovers a lascivious message on his answering machine. Aroused beyond his wildest dreams by the acts described, he becomes obsessed with tracking down the woman behind the seductive voice. His search takes him through strip clubs, sex parlors and no-tell motels—before finally leading him to his randy reward....

## AKBAR DEL PIOMBO
### THE FETISH CROWD
$6.95/556-5

A triple treat! A full-fledged trilogy presented as a special volume guaranteed to appeal to the modern sophisticate. Separately, *Paula the Piquôse*, the infamous *Duke Cosimo*, and *The Double-Bellied Companion* are rightly considered masterpieces, rife with wit, intelligence, and stunning eye for sensuous detail.

### DUKE COSIMO
$4.95/3052-0

A kinky romp played out against the boudoirs, bathrooms and ballrooms of the European nobility, who seem to do nothing all day except each other. The lifestyles of the rich and licentious are revealed in all their glory.

### A CRUMBLING FAÇADE
$4.95/3043-1

The return of that incorrigible rogue, Henry Pike, who continues his pursuit of sex, fair or otherwise, in the most elegant homes of the most debauched aristocrats. Ultimately, every woman succumbs to Pike's charms—and submits to his whims!

## CAROLE REMY
### FANTASY IMPROMPTU
$6.50/513-1

Kidnapped and held in a remote island retreat, Chantal—a renowned erotic writer—finds herself catering to every sexual whim of the mysterious and arousing Bran. Bran is determined to bring Chantal to a full embracing of her sensual nature, even while revealing himself to be something far more than human....

### BEAUTY OF THE BEAST
$5.95/332-5

A shocking tell-all, written from the point-of-view of a prize-winning reporter. And what reporting she does! All the secrets of an uninhibited life are revealed, and each lusty tableau is painted in glowing colors.

## DAVID AARON CLARK
### THE MARQUIS DE SADE'S JULIETTE
$4.95/240-X

The Marquis de Sade's infamous Juliette returns—and emerges as the most perverse and destructive nightstalker modern New York will ever know. Her insatiable hungers come to dominate Manhattan's underground, and one by one, the innocent are drawn in by Juliette's empty promise of immortality, only to fall prey to her deadly lusts.

## ANONYMOUS
### LOVE'S ILLUSION
$6.95/549-2

Elizabeth Renard yearned for the body of rich and successful Dan Harrington. Then she discovered Harrington's secret weakness: a need to be humiliated and punished. She makes him her slave, and together they commence a thrilling journey into depravity that leaves nothing to the imagination!

### NADIA
$5.95/267-1

Follow the delicious but neglected Nadia as she works to wring every drop of pleasure out of life—despite an unhappy marriage. A classic title providing a peek into the secret sexual lives of another time and place.

## NIGEL McPARR
### THE TRANSFORMATION OF EMILY
$6.50/519-0

The shocking story of Emily Johnson, live-in domestic. Without warning, Emily finds herself dismissed by her mistress, and sent to serve at Lilac Row—the home of Charles and Harriet Godwin. In no time, Harriet has Emily doing things she'd never dreamed would be required of her—all involving shocking erotic discipline.

### THE STORY OF A VICTORIAN MAID
$5.95/241-8

What were the Victorians really like? Chances are, no one believes they were as stuffy as their Queen, but who would have imagined such unbridled libertines! Nigel McParr now lays bare everything we thought we'd never know. One maid is followed from exploit to smutty exploit, as all secrets are finally revealed!

---

**BUY ANY 4 BOOKS & CHOOSE 1 ADDITIONAL BOOK, OF EQUAL OR LESSER VALUE, AS YOUR FREE GIFT**

# MASQUERADE BOOKS

## TITIAN BERESFORD

### CHIDEWELL HOUSE AND OTHER STORIES
$6.95/554-9

What are the deliciously dastardly delights that keep Cecil a virtual, if willing, prisoner of Chidewell House? One man has been sent to investigate the sexy situation—and reports back with tales of such depravity that no expense is spared in attempting Cecil's rescue. But what man would possibly desire release from the breathtakingly corrupt Elizabeth?

### CINDERELLA
$6.50/500-X

Beresford triumphs again with this intoxicating tale, filled with castle dungeons and tightly corseted ladies-in-waiting, naughty viscounts and impossibly cruel masturbatrixes—nearly every conceivable method of erotic torture is explored and described in lush, vivid detail.

### JUDITH BOSTON
$6.50/525-5

Edward would have been lucky to get the stodgy companion he thought his parents had hired for him. But an exquisite woman arrives at his door, and Edward finds his lewd behavior never goes unpunished by the unflinchingly severe Judith Boston

### THE WICKED HAND
$5.95/399-6

With a special Introduction by *Leg Show*'s Dian Hanson.

A collection of fanciful fetishistic tales featuring the absolute subjugation of men by lovely, domineering women. From Japan and Germany to the American heartland—these stories uncover the other side of the "weaker sex."

### NINA FOXTON
$5.95/443-7

An aristocrat finds herself bored by the run-of-the-mill amusements deemed appropriate for "ladies of good breeding." Instead of taking tea with proper gentlemen, naughty Nina "milks" them of their most private essences. No man ever says "No" to Nina!

## TINY ALICE

### THE GEEK
$5.95/341-4

A notorious—and uproarious—cult classic. *The Geek* is told from the point of view of, well, a chicken who reports on the various perversities he witnesses as part of a traveling carnival. When a gang of renegade lesbians kidnaps Chicken and his geek, all hell breaks loose. A strange but highly arousing tale, filled with outrageous erotic oddities, that finally returns to print after years of infamy.

## P. N. DEDEAUX

### THE NOTHING THINGS
$5.95/404-6

Beta Beta Rho has taken on a new group of pledges. The five women will be put through the most grueling of ordeals, and punished severely for any shortcomings. Before long, all Beta pledges come to crave their punishments!

## LYN DAVENPORT

### THE GUARDIAN II
$6.50/505-0

The tale of submissive Felicia Brookes continues in this volume of sensual surprises. No sooner has Felicia come to love Rodney than she discovers that she must now accustom herself to the guardianship of the debauched Duke of Smithton. Surely Rodney will rescue her from the domination of this stranger. Won't he?

### DOVER ISLAND
$5.95/384-8

On an island off the west coast, Dr. David Kelly has planted the seeds of his dream—a Corporal Punishment Resort. Soon, many people from varied walks of life descend upon this isolated retreat, intent on fulfilling their every desire. Including Marcy Harris, the perfect partner for the lustful Doctor....

## GWYNETH JAMES

### DREAM CRUISE
$4.95/3045-8

Angelia has it all—a brilliant career and a beautiful face to match. But she longs to kick up her high heels and have some fun, so she takes an island vacation and vows to leave her sexual inhibitions behind. From the moment her plane takes off, she finds herself in one hot and steamy encounter after another!

## LIZBETH DUSSEAU

### THE APPLICANT
$6.50/501-8

"Adventuresome young women who enjoys being submissive sought by married couple in early forties. Expect no limits." Hilary answers an ad, hoping to find someone who can meet her special needs. The beautiful Liza turns out to be a flawless mistress, and together with her husband, Oliver, she trains Hilary to be the perfect servant.

### SPANISH HOLIDAY
$4.95/185-3

"She didn't know what to make of Sam Jacobs. He was undoubtedly the most remarkable man she'd ever met...." Lauren didn't mean to fall in love with the enigmatic Sam, but a once-in-a-lifetime European vacation gives her all the evidence she needs that this hot, insatiable man might be the one for her....

# MASQUERADE BOOKS

## ANTHONY BOBARZYNSKI
### STASI SLUT
$4.95/3050-4

Adina lives in East Germany, where she can only dream about the freedoms of the West. She begins to despair of ever living in a more sexually liberated world. But then she meets a group of ruthless and corrupt STASI agents. They use her body for their own perverse gratification, while she opts to use her many sensual talents in a final bid for total freedom!

## JOCELYN JOYCE
### PRIVATE LIVES
$4.95/309-0

The lecherous habits of the illustrious make for a sizzling tale of French erotic life. A widow has a craving for a young busboy; he's sleeping with a rich businessman's wife; her husband is minding his sex business elsewhere! Wild, uninhibited sexual entanglements run through this tale of upper-crust lust!

### SABINE
$4.95/3046-6

There is no one who can refuse her once she casts her spell; no lover can do anything less than give up his whole life for her. Great men and empires fall at her feet; but she is haughty, distracted, impervious. It is the eve of WW II, and Sabine must find a new lover equal to her talents and her tastes.

### THE JAZZ AGE
$4.95/48-3

The time is the Roaring 20s. An attorney becomes suspicious of his mistress while his wife has an interlude with a lesbian lover. *The Jazz Age* is a romp of erotic realism from the heyday of the flapper and the speakeasy—when rules existed to be broken!

### THE WOMEN OF BABYLON
$4.95/171-3

"She adored it. Oh, what an amusement! she thought. Axel Gruning was now one of her conquests...." With the lusty abandon of the harlot Babylon, some very independent women set their sights on ensnaring the hearts—and more—of every man in sight!

## SARAH JACKSON
### SANCTUARY
$5.95/318-X

*Sanctuary* explores both the unspeakable debauchery of court life and the unimaginable privations of monastic solitude, leading the voracious and the virtuous on a collision course that brings history to throbbing life.

### THE WILD HEART
$4.95/3007-5

A luxury hotel is the setting for this artful web of sex, desire, and love. A newlywed sees sex as a duty, while her hungry husband tries to awaken her to its tender joys. A Parisian entertains wealthy guests for the love of money. Each episode provides a perverse new variation.

## SARA H. FRENCH
### MASTER OF TIMBERLAND
$5.95/327-9

A tale of sexual slavery at the ultimate paradise resort—where sizzling submissives serve their masters without question. One of our bestselling titles, this trek to Timberland has ignited passions the world over—and stands poised to become one of modern erotica's legendary tales.

## MARY LOVE
### ANGELA
$6.95/545-X

Angela's game is "look but don't touch," and she drives everyone mad with desire, dancing for their pleasure but never allowing a single caress. Soon her sensual spell is cast, and she's the only one who can break it!

### MASTERING MARY SUE
$5.95/351-1

Mary Sue is a rich nymphomaniac whose husband is determined to declare her mentally incompetent and gain control of her fortune. He brings her to a castle where, to Mary Sue's delight, she is subjected to a veritable sex-fest! Soon it becomes clear that Mary Sue can never get enough—and is intent on everyone getting in on the act....

### THE BEST OF MARY LOVE
$4.95/3099-7

One of modern erotica's most daring writers is here represented by her most scalding passages. Mary Love leaves no coupling untried and no extreme unexplored in these scandalous selections from *Mastering Mary Sue*, *Ecstasy on Fire*, *Vice Park Place*, *Wanda*, and *Naughtier at Night*.

### WANDA
$4.95/002-4

Wanda just can't help it. Ever since she moved to Greenwich Village, she's been overwhelmed by the desire to be totally, utterly naked! By day, she finds herself inspired by a pornographic novel whose main character's insatiable appetites seem to match her own. At night she parades her quivering, nubile flesh in a non-stop sex show for her neighbors. An electrifying exhibitionist gone wild!

**BUY ANY 4 BOOKS & CHOOSE 1 ADDITIONAL BOOK, OF EQUAL OR LESSER VALUE, AS YOUR FREE GIFT**

# MASQUERADE BOOKS

## AMARANTHA KNIGHT

**The Darker Passions: THE PICTURE OF DORIAN GRAY**
$6.50/342-2

Knight's take on the fabulously decadent tale of highly personal changes. One woman finds her most secret desires laid bare by a portrait far more revealing than she could have imagined. Soon she benefits from a skillful masquerade.

**THE DARKER PASSIONS READER**
$6.50/432-1

The best moments from Knight's phenomenally popular Darker Passions series. Here are the most eerily erotic passages from her acclaimed sexual reworkings of *Dracula, Frankenstein, Dr. Jekyll & Mr. Hyde* and *The Fall of the House of Usher.*

**The Darker Passions: THE FALL OF THE HOUSE OF USHER**
$6.50/528-X

Two weary travelers arrive at a dark and foreboding mansion, where they fall victim to the many bizarre appetites of its residents. The Master and Mistress of the house of Usher indulge in every form of decadence, and initiate their guests into the many pleasures to be found in submission.

**The Darker Passions: DR. JEKYLL AND MR. HYDE**
$4.95/227-2

It is a story of incredible transformations. Explore the steamy possibilities of a tale where no one is quite who—or what—they seem. Victorian bedrooms explode with hidden demons!

**The Darker Passions: FRANKENSTEIN**
$5.95/248-5

What if you could create a living human? What shocking acts could it be taught to perform, to desire? Find out what pleasures await those who play God....

**The Darker Passions: DRACULA**
$5.95/326-0

"Well-written and imaginative...taking us through the sexual and sadistic scenes with details that keep us reading.... A classic in itself has been added to the shelves." —*Divinity*

The infamous erotic revisioning of Bram Stoker's classic.

## THE PAUL LITTLE LIBRARY

**ROOMMATE'S SECRET**
$8.95/557-3/Trade paperback

What are the secrets young ladies hide—even from their trusted roommates? Here are the many exploits of one woman forced to make ends meet by the most ancient of methods. From the misery of early impoverishment to the delight of ill-gotten gains, Elda learns to rely on her considerable sensual talents.

**LOVE SLAVE/PECULIAR PASSIONS OF LADY MEG**
$8.95/529-8/Trade paperback

Two classics from erotica's most popular author! What does it take to acquire a willing *Love Slave* of one's own? What are the appetites that lurk beneath *Lady Meg*? The notoriously depraved Paul Little spares no lascivious detail in these two relentless tales!

**CELESTE**
$6.95/544-1

It's definitely all in the family for this female duo of sexual dynamics. While traveling through Europe, these two try everything and everyone on their horny holiday.

**ALL THE WAY**
$6.95/509-5

Two excruciating novels from Paul Little in one hot volume! *Going All the Way* features an unhappy man who tries to purge himself of the memory of his lover with a series of quirky and uninhibited lovers. *Pushover* tells the story of a serial spanker and his celebrated exploits.

**THE DISCIPLINE OF ODETTE**
$5.95/334-1

Odette was sure marriage would rescue her from her family's brutal "corrections." To her horror, she discovers that her beloved Jacques has also been raised on discipline—an upbringing he's intent on sharing with Odette. A shocking erotic coupling!

**THE END OF INNOCENCE**
$6.95/546-8

The early days of Women's Emancipation are the setting for this story of some very independent ladies. These women were willing to go to any lengths to fight for their sexual freedom, and willing to endure any punishment in their desire for total liberation. A shockingly sexy historical romp.

**TUTORED IN LUST**
$6.95/547-6

This tale of the initiation and instruction of a carnal college co-ed and her fellow students unlocks the sex secrets of the classroom.

**THE BEST OF PAUL LITTLE**
$6.50/469-0

Known for his fantastic portrayals of punishment and pleasure, Little never fails to push readers over the edge of sensual excitement. His best scenes are here collected for the enjoyment of all erotic connoisseurs.

**THE PRISONER**
$5.95/330-9

Judge Black has built a secret room below a penitentiary, where he sentences his female prisoners to hours of exhibition and torment while his friends watch. Judge Black's brand of rough justice keeps his lovely captives on the brink of utter pleasure!

# MASQUERADE BOOKS

### TEARS OF THE INQUISITION
$4.95/146-2

A thoroughly staggering account of pleasure and punishment, set in an age of rampant corruption and brutal abuses of power. "There was a tickling inside her as her nervous system reminded her she was ready for sex. But before her was...the Inquisitor!"

### DOUBLE NOVEL
$4.95/86-6

*The Metamorphosis of Lisette Joyaux* tells the story of a young woman initiated into an incredible world world of lesbian lusts. *The Story of Monique* reveals the twisted sexual rituals that beckon the ripe and willing Monique.

### CAPTIVE MAIDENS
$5.95/440-2

Three beautiful young women find themselves powerless against the debauched landowners of 1824 England. They are banished to a sex colony, and corrupted by every imaginable perversion.

### SLAVE ISLAND
$5.95/441-0

A leisure cruise is waylaid by Lord Henry Philbrock, a sadistic genius. The ship's passengers are kidnapped and spirited to his island prison, where the women are trained to accommodate the most bizarre sexual cravings of the rich, the famous, the pampered and the perverted.

## ALIZARIN LAKE

### CLARA
$6.95/548-4

The mysterious death of a beautiful woman leads her old boyfriend on a harrowing journey of discovery. His search uncovers a woman on a quest for deeper and more unusual sensations, each more shocking than the one before!

### SEX ON DOCTOR'S ORDERS
$5.95/402-X

A chronicle of selfless devotion to mankind! Beth, a nubile young nurse, uses her considerable skills to further medical science by offering incomparable and insatiable assistance in the gathering of important specimens. Soon she's involved everyone in her important work—including the horny doctor himself.

### THE EROTIC ADVENTURES OF HARRY TEMPLE
$4.95/127-6

Harry Temple's memoirs chronicle his incredibly amorous adventures—from his initiation at the hands of insatiable sirens, through his stay at a house of hot repute, to his encounters with a chastity-belted nympho, and much more!

### MORE EROTIC ADVENTURES OF HARRY TEMPLE
$4.95/67-X

Harry Temple's lustful adventures continue. this time he begins his amorous pursuits by deflowering the ample and eager Aurora. Harry soon discovers that his little protégée is more than able to match him at every lascivious game and very willing to display her own talents. An education in sensuality that only Harry Temple can provide!

### MISS HIGH HEELS
$4.95/3066-0

It was a delightful punishment few men dared to dream of. Who could have predicted how far it would go? Forced by his wicked sisters to dress and behave like a proper lady, Dennis Beryl finds he enjoys life as Denise much more!

## JOHN NORMAN

### TARNSMAN OF GOR
$6.95/486-0

This controversial series returns! Tarl Cabot is transported to Gor. He must quickly accustom himself to the ways of this world, including the caste system which exalts some as Priest-Kings or Warriors, and debases others as slaves. The beginning of the mammoth epic which made Norman a controversial success—as well as a household name among fans of both science fiction and dominance/submission.

### OUTLAW OF GOR
$6.95/487-9

Tarl Cabot returns to Gor, to reclaim both his woman and his role of Warrior. But upon arriving, he discovers that his name, his city and the names of those he loves have become unspeakable. Cabot has become an outlaw, and must discover his new purpose on this strange planet, where danger stalks the outcast, and even simple answers have their price....

### PRIEST-KINGS OF GOR
$6.95/488-7

Tarl Cabot searches for his lovely wife Talena. Does she live, or was she destroyed by the all-powerful Priest-Kings? Cabot is determined to find out—even while knowing that no one who has approached the mountain stronghold of the Priest-Kings has ever returned alive....

### NOMADS OF GOR
$6.95/527-1

Cabot finds his way across Gor, pledged to serve the Priest-Kings in their quest for survival. Unfortunately for Cabot, his mission leads him to the savage Wagon People—nomads who may very well kill before surrendering any secrets....

**BUY ANY 4 BOOKS & CHOOSE 1 ADDITIONAL BOOK, OF EQUAL OR LESSER VALUE, AS YOUR FREE GIFT**

# MASQUERADE BOOKS

### ASSASSIN OF GOR
$6.95/538-7
*Assassin of Gor* exposes the brutal caste system of Gor at its most unsparing: from the Assassin Kuurus, on a mission of bloody vengeance, to Pleasure Slaves, tirelessly trained in the ways of personal ecstasy. From one social stratum to the next, the inhabitants of Counter-Earth pursue and are pursued by all-too human passions—and the inescapable destinies that await their caste...

### RAIDERS OF GOR
$6.95/558-1
Tarl Cabot descends into the depths of Port Kar—the darkest, most degenerate port city of the Counter-Earth. There, among pirates, cutthroats and brigands, Cabot learns the ways of Kar, whose residents are renowned for the iron grip in which they hold their voluptuous slaves....

## ELAINE PLATERO
### LESSONS AND LOVERS
$4.95/196-9
"Stunned by her spanking, Hettie felt like a sex-doll for the other two, a living breathing female body to demonstrate the responses and vulnerabilities of womankind to a young man who was hungry for knowledge...." When a repressed widow, her all-too-willing manservant, a voluptuous doctor and an anxious neophyte take a country weekend together, crucial lessons are learned by all—through the horny formulas of Sexual Geometry!

## SYDNEY ST. JAMES
### RIVE GAUCHE
$5.95/317-1
The Latin Quarter, Paris, circa 1920. Expatriate bohemians couple with abandon—before eventually abandoning their ambitions amidst the intoxicating temptations waiting to be indulged in every bedroom.

### GARDEN OF DELIGHT
$4.95/3058-X
A vivid account of sexual awakening that follows an innocent but insatiably curious young woman's journey from the furtive, forbidden joys of dormitory life to the unabashed carnality of the wild world.

## DON WINSLOW
### THE FALL OF THE ICE QUEEN
$6.50/520-4
Rahn the Conqueror chose a true beauty as his Consort. But the regal disregard with which she treated Rahn was not to be endured. It was decided that she would submit to his will, and learn to serve her lord in the fashion he had come to expect. And as so many had learned, Rahn's depraved expectations have made his court infamous.

### PRIVATE PLEASURES
$6.50/504-2
Frantic voyeurs, licentious exhibitionists, and everyday lovers are here displayed in all their wanton glory—proving again that fleshly pleasures have no more apt chronicler than Don Winslow.

### THE INSATIABLE MISTRESS OF ROSEDALE
$6.50/494-1
Edward and Lady Penelope reside in mysterious Rosedale manor. While Edward is a true connoisseur of sexual perversion, it is Lady Penelope whose mastery of complete sensual pleasure makes their home infamous. Indulging one another's bizarre whims is a way of life for this wicked couple....

### SECRETS OF CHEATEM MANOR
$6.50/434-8
Edward returns to his late father's estate, to find it being run by the majestic Lady Amanda. Edward can hardly believe his luck—Lady Amanda is assisted by her two beautiful, lonely daughters, Catherine and Prudence. What the randy young man soon comes to realize is the love of discipline that all three beauties share.

### KATERINA IN CHARGE
$5.95/409-7
When invited to a country retreat by a mysterious couple, two randy young ladies can hardly resist! But do they have any idea what they're in for? Whatever the case, the imperious Katerina will make her desires known very soon—and demand that they be fulfilled...

### THE MANY PLEASURES OF IRONWOOD
$5.95/310-3
Seven lovely young women are employed by The Ironwood Sportsmen's Club, where their natural talents in the sensual arts are put to creative use. A small and exclusive club with seven carefully selected sexual connoisseurs.

### CLAIRE'S GIRLS
$5.95/442-9
You knew when she walked by that she was something special. She was one of Claire's girls, a woman carefully dressed and groomed to fill a role, to capture a look, to fit an image crafted by the sophisticated proprietress of an exclusive escort agency.

## MARCUS VAN HELLER
### KIDNAP
$4.95/90-4
P.I. Harding is called in to investigate a mysterious kidnapping case involving the rich and powerful. Along the way he has the pleasure of "interrogating" an exotic dancer named Jeanne and a beautiful English reporter, as he finds himself enmeshed in the sleazy international underworld.

# MASQUERADE BOOKS

### ADAM & EVE
$4.95/93-9

Adam and Eve long to escape their dull lives by achieving stardom—she in the theater, and he in the art world. They throw aside all inhibitions, and Eve soon finds herself spread-eagle on the casting couch, while Adam must join a bizarre sex cult to further his artistic career.

## N. WHALLEN
### TAU'TEVU
$6.50/426-7

In a mysterious and exotic land, the statuesque and beautiful Vivian learns to subject herself to the hand of a domineering man. He systematically helps her prove her own strength, and brings to life in her an unimagined sensual fire.

## ALEXANDER TROCCHI
### YOUNG ADAM
$4.95/52-1

Two British barge operators discover a girl drowned in the river Clyde. Her lover, a plumber, is arrested for her murder. But he is innocent. Joe, the barge assistant, knows that. As the plumber is tried and sentenced to hang, this knowledge lends poignancy to Joe's romances with the women along the river whom he will love then... well, read on.

## ISADORA ALMAN
### ASK ISADORA
$4.95/61-0

An essential volume, collecting six years' worth of Isadora Alman's syndicated columns on sex and relationships. Alman's been called a "hip Dr. Ruth," and a "sexy Dear Abby," based upon the wit of her advice. Today's world is more perplexing than ever—and Alman is just the expert to help untangle the most personal of knots.

## THE CLASSIC COLLECTION
### THE ENGLISH GOVERNESS
$5.95/373-2

When Lord Lovell's son was expelled from his prep school for masturbation, his father hired a very proper governess to tutor the boy—giving her strict instructions not to spare the rod to break him of his bad habits. But governess Harriet Marwood was addicted to domination.

### PROTESTS, PLEASURES, RAPTURES
$5.95/400-3

Invited for an allegedly quiet weekend at a country vicarage, a young woman is stunned to find herself surrounded by shocking acts of sexual sadism. Soon her curiosity is piqued, and she begins to explore her own capacities for delicious sexual cruelty.

### THE YELLOW ROOM
$5.95/378-3

The "yellow room" holds the secrets of lust, lechery, and the lash. There, bare-bottomed, spread-eagled, and open to the world, demure Alice Darvell soon learns to love her lickings.

### SCHOOL DAYS IN PARIS
$5.95/325-2

Few Universities provide the profound and pleasurable lessons one learns in after-hours study—particularly if one is young and available, and lucky enough to have Paris as a playground. Here are all the randy pursuits of young adulthood.

### MAN WITH A MAID
$4.95/307-4

The adventures of Jack and Alice have delighted readers for eight decades! A classic of its genre, *Man with a Maid* tells a tale of desire, revenge, and submission. Over 200,000 copies in print!

## MASQUERADE READERS
### INTIMATE PLEASURES
$4.95/38-6

Indulge your most private penchants with this specially chosen selection. Try a tempting morsel of *The Prodigal Virgin* and *Eveline*, or the bizarre public displays of carnality in *The Gilded Lily* and *The Story of Monique*. Many other selections guaranteed to have you begging for more!

## CLASSIC EROTIC BIOGRAPHIES
### JENNIFER AGAIN
$4.95/220-5

"In her dream she was naked, but there was no one on the streets to see her nakedness. Then she turned a corner, and a tall man was standing before her in the middle of the eerily empty street. She didn't know him, yet he seemed to know her: His lips formed her name: Jennifer...."
Once again, the insatiable Jennifer seizes the day and extracts every last drop of sensual pleasure!

### JENNIFER III
$5.95/292-2

The adventures of erotica's most daring heroine. Jennifer has a photographer's eye for details—particularly of the male variety! One by one, her subjects submit to her demands for pleasure.

### PAULINE
$4.95/129-2

From rural America to the royal court of Austria, Pauline follows her ever-growing sexual desires as she rises to the top of the Opera world. "I would never see them again. Why shouldn't I give myself to them that they might become more and more inspired to deeds of greater lust!"

**BUY ANY 4 BOOKS & CHOOSE 1 ADDITIONAL BOOK, OF EQUAL OR LESSER VALUE, AS YOUR FREE GIFT**

# MASQUERADE BOOKS

## RHINOCEROS

### JOHN NORMAN
**IMAGINATIVE SEX**
$7.95/561-1
In 1974, the author of the controversial and popular Gor novels unleashed his vision for an exciting, fulfilling sex life for all. *Imaginative Sex* outlines John Norman's philosophy on relations between the sexes, and presents fifty-three scenarios designed to reintroduce fantasy and intimacy to the bedroom.

### KATHLEEN K.
**SWEET TALKERS**
$6.95/516-6
"If you enjoy eavesdropping on explicit conversations about sex... this book is for you."    —*Spectator*

Kathleen K. ran a phone-sex company in the late 80s, and she opens up her diary for a very thought provoking peek at the life of a phone-sex operator. Transcripts of actual conversations are included.

Trade /$12.95/192-6

### THOMAS S. ROCHE
**DARK MATTER**
$6.95/484-4
"*Dark Matter* is sure to please gender outlaws, bodymod junkies, goth vampires, boys who wish they were dykes, and anybody who's not to sure where the fine line should be drawn between pleasure and pain. It's a handful."—Pat Califia

"Here is the erotica of the cumming millennium.... You will be deliciously disturbed, but never disappointed."
—Poppy Z. Brite

**NOIROTICA: An Anthology of Erotic Crime Stories (Ed.)**
$6.95/390-2
A collection of darkly sexy tales, taking place at the crossroads of the crime and erotic genres. Here are some of today's finest writers of sexual fiction, all of whom explore the murky terrain where desire runs irrevocably afoul of the law.

### ROMY ROSEN
**SPUNK**
$6.95/492-5
Casey, a lovely model poised upon the verge of super-celebrity, falls for an insatiable young rock singer—not suspecting that his sexual appetite has led him to experiment with a dangerous new aphrodisiac. Soon, Casey becomes addicted to the drug, and her craving plunges her into a strange underworld, where the only chance for redemption lies with a shadowy young man with a secret of his own.

### MOLLY WEATHERFIELD
**CARRIE'S STORY**
$6.95/485-2
"I was stunned by how well it was written and how intensely foreign I found its sexual world.... And, since this is a world I don't frequent... I thoroughly enjoyed the National Geo tour."
—*bOING bOING*

"Hilarious and harrowing... just when you think things can't get any wilder, they do."    —*Black Sheets*

"I had been Jonathan's slave for about a year when he told me he wanted to sell me at an auction. I wasn't in any condition to respond when he told me this…" Desire and depravity run rampant in this story of uncompromising mastery and irrevocable submission. A unique piece of erotica that is both thoughtful and hot!

### CYBERSEX CONSORTIUM
**CYBERSEX: The Perv's Guide to Finding Sex on the Internet**
$6.95/471-2
You've heard the objections: cyberspace is soaked with sex, mired in immorality. Okay—so where is it!? Tracking down the good stuff—the real good stuff—can waste an awful lot of expensive time, and frequently leave you high and dry. The Cybersex Consortium presents an easy-to-use guide for those intrepid adults who know what they want. No horny hacker can afford to pass up this map to the kinkiest rest stops on the Info Superhighway.

### AMELIA G, EDITOR
**BACKSTAGE PASSES**
$6.95/438-0
Amelia G, editor of the goth-sex journal *Blue Blood*, has brought together some of today's most irreverent writers, each of whom has outdone themselves with an edgy, antic tale of modern lust. Punks, metalheads, and grunge-trash roam the pages of *Backstage Passes*, and no one knows their ways better…

### GERI NETTICK WITH BETH ELLIOT
**MIRRORS: Portrait of a Lesbian Transsexual**
$6.95/435-6
The alternately heartbreaking and empowering story of one woman's long road to full selfhood. Born a male, Geri Nettick knew something just didn't fit. And even after coming to terms with her own gender dysphoria—and taking steps to correct it—she still fought to be accepted by the lesbian feminist community to which she felt she belonged. A true tale of struggle and discovery.

# MASQUERADE BOOKS

## DAVID MELTZER

**UNDER**
$6.95/290-6
The story of a 21st century sex professional living at the bottom of the social heap. After surgeries designed to increase his physical allure, corrupt government forces drive the cyber-gigolo underground—where even more bizarre cultures await him.

**ORF**
$6.95/110-1
He is the ultimate musician-hero—the idol of thousands, the fevered dream of many more. And like many musicians before him, he is misunderstood, misused—and totally out of control. Every last drop of feeling is squeezed from a modern-day troubadour and his lady love.

## LAURA ANTONIOU, EDITOR

**NO OTHER TRIBUTE**
$6.95/294-9
A collection sure to challenge Political Correctness in a way few have before, with tales of women kept in bondage to their lovers by their deepest passions. Love pushes these women beyond acceptable limits, rendering them helpless to deny anything to the men and women they adore.

**SOME WOMEN**
$6.95/300-7
Over forty essays written by women actively involved in consensual dominance and submission. Pro doms, lifestyle leatherdykes, titleholders—women from every walk of life lay bare their true feelings about explosive issues.

**BY HER SUBDUED**
$6.95/281-7
These tales all involve women in control—of their lives, their loves, their men. So much in control that they can remorselessly break rules to become powerful goddesses of the men who sacrifice all to worship at their feet.

## TRISTAN TAORMINO & DAVID AARON CLARK, EDS.

**RITUAL SEX**
$6.95/391-0
The many contributors to *Ritual Sex* know—and demonstrate—that body and soul share more common ground than society feels comfortable acknowledging. From memoirs of ecstatic revelation, to quests to reconcile sex and spirit, *Ritual Sex* provides an unprecedented look at private life.

## TAMMY JO ECKHART

**AMAZONS: Erotic Explorations of Ancient Myths**
$7.95/534-4
The Amazon—the fierce, independent woman warrior—appears in the traditions of many cultures, but never before has the full erotic potential of this archetype been explored with such imagination and energy. Powerful pleasures await anyone lucky enough to encounter Eckhart's legendary spitfires.

**PUNISHMENT FOR THE CRIME**
$6.95/427-5
Peopled by characters of rare depth, these stories explore the true meaning of dominance and submission. From an encounter between two of society's most despised individuals, to the explorations of longtime friends, these tales take you where few others have ever dared....

## AMARANTHA KNIGHT, ED.

**SEDUCTIVE SPECTRES**
$6.95/464-X
Breathtaking tours through the erotic supernatural via the imaginations of today's best writers. Never have ghostly encounters been so alluring, thanks to a cast of otherworldly characters well-acquainted with the pleasures of the flesh.

**SEX MACABRE**
$6.95/392-9
Horror tales designed for dark and sexy nights. Amarantha Knight—the woman behind the Darker Passions series—has gathered together erotic stories sure to make your skin crawl, and heart beat faster.

**FLESH FANTASTIC**
$6.95/352-X
Humans have long toyed with the idea of "playing God": creating life from nothingness, bringing life to the inanimate. Now Amarantha Knight collects stories exploring not only the act of Creation, but the lust that follows. Includes work by some of today's edgiest writers.

## GARY BOWEN

**DIARY OF A VAMPIRE**
$6.95/331-7
"Gifted with a darkly sensual vision and a fresh voice, [Bowen] is a writer to watch out for." —Cecilia Tan
Rafael, a red-blooded male with an insatiable hunger for the same, is the perfect antidote to the effete malcontents haunting bookstores today. The emergence of a bold and brilliant vision, rooted in past and present.

**BUY ANY 4 BOOKS & CHOOSE 1 ADDITIONAL BOOK, OF EQUAL OR LESSER VALUE, AS YOUR FREE GIFT**

# MASQUERADE BOOKS

## RENÉ MAIZEROY
### FLESHLY ATTRACTIONS
$6.95/299-X

Lucien was the son of the wantonly beautiful actress, Marie-Rose Hardanges. When she decides to let a "friend" introduce her son to the pleasures of love, Marie-Rose could not have foretold the excesses that would lead to her own ruin and that of her cherished son.

## JEAN STINE
### THRILL CITY
$6.95/411-9

*Thrill City* is the seat of the world's increasing depravity, and this classic novel transports you there with a vivid style you'd be hard pressed to ignore. No writer is better suited to describe the extremes of this modern Babylon.

### SEASON OF THE WITCH
$6.95/268-X

"A future in which it is technically possible to transfer the total mind...of a rapist killer into the brain dead but physically living body of his female victim. Remarkable for intense psychological technique. There is eroticism but it is necessary to mark the differences between the sexes and the subtle altering of a man into a woman." —*The Science Fiction Critic*

## GRANT ANTREWS
### ROGUES GALLERY
$6.95/522-0

A stirring evocation of dominant/submissive love. Two doctors meet and slowly fall in love. Once Beth reveals her hidden desires to Jim, the two explore the forbidden acts that will come to define their distinctly exotic affair.

### MY DARLING DOMINATRIX
$6.95/447-X

When a man and a woman fall in love, it's supposed to be simple, uncomplicated, easy—unless that woman happens to be a dominatrix. This highly praised and unpretentious love story captures the richness and depth of this very special kind of love without leering or smirking.

### SUBMISSIONS
$6.95/207-8

Antrews portrays the very special elements of the dominant/submissive relationship with restraint—this time with the story of a lonely man, a winning lottery ticket, and a demanding dominatrix.

## LAURA ANTONIOU writing as "Sara Adamson"
### THE MARKETPLACE
$6.95/3096-2

The volume that introduced the Marketplace to the world—and established it as one of the most popular realms in contemporary SM fiction. The thrilling overview of this ultimate slave-ring.

### THE SLAVE
$6.95/173-X

One talented submissive longs to join the ranks of those who have proven themselves worthy of entry into the Marketplace. But as all applicants soon discover, the price is staggeringly high....

### THE TRAINER
$6.95/249-3

The Marketplace Trilogy concludes with the story of the trainers, and the desires and paths that led them to become the ultimate figures of authority.

## JOHN WARREN
### THE TORQUEMADA KILLER
$6.95/367-8

Detective Eva Hernandez gets her first "big case": a string of vicious murders taking place within New York's SM community. Eva assembles the evidence, revealing a picture of a world misunderstood and under attack—and gradually comes to understand her own place within it.

### THE LOVING DOMINANT
$6.95/218-3

Everything you need to know about an infamous sexual variation—and an unspoken type of love. Warren guides readers through this world and reveals the too-often hidden basis of the D/S relationship: care, trust and love.

## DAVID AARON CLARK
### SISTER RADIANCE
$6.95/215-9

A meditation on love, sex, and death. The vicissitudes of lust and romance are examined against a backdrop of urban decay in this testament to the allure—and inevitability—of the forbidden.

### THE WET FOREVER
$6.95/117-9

The story of Janus and Madchen—a small-time hood and a beautiful sex worker on the run—examines themes of loyalty, sacrifice, redemption and obsession amidst Manhattan's sex parlors and underground S/M clubs.

## MICHAEL PERKINS
### EVIL COMPANIONS
$6.95/3067-9

*Evil Companions* has been hailed as "a frightening classic." A young couple explores the nether reaches of the erotic unconscious in a shocking confrontation with the extremes of passion.

### THE SECRET RECORD:
### Modern Erotic Literature
$6.95/3039-3

Michael Perkins surveys the field with authority and unique insight. Updated and revised to include the latest trends, tastes, and developments in this misunderstood and maligned genre.

# MASQUERADE BOOKS

### AN ANTHOLOGY OF CLASSIC ANONYMOUS EROTIC WRITING
$6.95/140-3

Michael Perkins has collected the very best passages from the world's most enduring erotic writing. "Anonymous" is one of the most infamous bylines in publishing history—and these steamy excerpts show why!

## LIESEL KULIG
### LOVE IN WARTIME
$6.95/3044-X

Madeleine knew that the handsome SS officer was a dangerous man, but she was just a cabaret singer in Nazi-occupied Paris, trying to survive in a perilous time. When Josef fell in love with her, he discovered that a beautiful woman can sometimes be as dangerous as any warrior.

## HELEN HENLEY
### ENTER WITH TRUMPETS
$6.95/197-7

Helen Henley was told that women just don't write about sex—much less the taboos she was so interested in exploring. So Henley did it alone, flying in the face of "tradition" by writing this touching tale of arousal and devotion in one couple's kinky relationship.

## ALICE JOANOU
### BLACK TONGUE
$6.95/258-2

"Joanou has created a series of sumptuous, brooding, dark visions of sexual obsession, and is undoubtedly a name to look out for in the future."
—*Redeemer*

Exploring lust at its most florid and unsparing, *Black Tongue* is a trove of baroque fantasies—each redolent of forbidden passions.

### TOURNIQUET
$6.95/3060-1

A heady collection of stories and effusions from the pen of one our most dazzling young writers. Strange tales abound in this complex and riveting series of meditations on desire.

### CANNIBAL FLOWER
$4.95/72-6

"She is waiting in her darkened bedroom, as she has waited throughout history, to seduce the men who are foolish enough to be blinded by her irresistible charms.... She is the goddess of sexuality, and *Cannibal Flower* is her haunting siren song."
—Michael Perkins

## PHILIP JOSÉ FARMER
### A FEAST UNKNOWN
$6.95/276-0

"Sprawling, brawling, shocking, suspenseful, hilarious..."
—Theodore Sturgeon

Farmer's supreme anti-hero returns. "I was conceived and born in 1888." Slowly, Lord Grandrith—armed with the belief that he is the son of Jack the Ripper—tells the story of his remarkable and unbridled life. His story begins with his discovery of the secret of immortality—and progresses to encompass the furthest extremes of human behavior.

### FLESH
$6.95/303-1

The author of the mind-blowing classic *The Image of the Beast* returns with one of his most infamous science fiction yarns. Space Commander Stagg explored the galaxies for 800 years, and could only hope that he would be welcomed home by an adoring—or at least appreciative—public. Upon his return, the hero Stagg is made the centerpiece of an incredible public ritual—one that will repeatedly take him to the heights of ecstasy, and inexorably drag him toward the depths of hell.

## SAMUEL R. DELANY
### THE MAD MAN
$8.99/408-9

"Reads like a pornographic reflection of Peter Ackroyd's *Chatterton* or A. S. Byatt's *Possession*.... Delany develops an insightful dichotomy between [his protagonist]'s two worlds: the one of cerebral philosophy and dry academia, the other of heedless, 'impersonal' obsessive sexual extremism. When these worlds finally collide...the novel achieves a surprisingly satisfying resolution...."
—*Publishers Weekly*

Graduate student John Marr researches the life of Timothy Hasler: a philosopher whose career was cut tragically short over a decade earlier. On another front, Marr finds himself increasingly drawn toward shocking, depraved sexual entanglements with the homeless men of his neighborhood, until it begins to seem that Hasler's death might hold some key to his own life as a gay man in the age of AIDS. Unquestionably one of Samuel R. Delany's most challenging novels, and a must for any reader concerned with the state of the erotic in modern literature.

---

**BUY ANY 4 BOOKS & CHOOSE 1 ADDITIONAL BOOK, OF EQUAL OR LESSER VALUE, AS YOUR FREE GIFT**

# MASQUERADE BOOKS

## DANIEL VIAN

**ILLUSIONS**
$6.95/3074-1
International lust. Two tales of danger and desire in Berlin on the eve of WWII. From private homes to lurid cafés, passion is exposed in stark contrast to the brutal violence of the time, as desperate people explore their darkest sexual desires. A hallucinatory volume of unquenchable desires.

**PERSUASIONS**
$4.95/183-7
"The stockings are drawn tight by the suspender belt, tight enough to be stretched to the limit just above the middle part of her thighs, tight enough so that her calves glow through the sheer silk..." A double novel, including the classics *Adagio* and *Gabriela and the General*, this volume traces lust around the globe.

## ANDREI CODRESCU

**THE REPENTANCE OF LORRAINE**
$6.95/329-5
"One of our most prodigiously talented and magical writers."
—*NYT Book Review*

By the acclaimed author of *The Hole in the Flag* and *The Blood Countess*. An aspiring writer, a professor's wife, a secretary, gold anklets, Maoists, Roman harlots—and more—swirl through this spicy tale of a harried quest for a mythic artifact. Written when the author was a young man, this lusty yarn was inspired by the heady days of the Sixties. Includes a new introduction by the author, detailing the events that inspired *Lorraine's* creation.

## TUPPY OWENS

**SENSATIONS**
$6.95/3081-4
Tuppy Owens tells the unexpurgated story of the making of *Sensations*—the first big-budget sex flick. Originally commissioned to appear in book form after the release of the film in 1975, *Sensations* is finally released under Masquerade's stylish Rhinoceros imprint. A rare peek behind the scenes of a porn-flick, from the genre's early, ground-breaking days.

## SOPHIE GALLEYMORE BIRD

**MANEATER**
$6.95/103-9
Through a bizarre act of creation, a man attains the "perfect" lover—by all appearances a beautiful, sensuous woman, but in reality something far darker. Once brought to life she will accept no mate, seeking instead the prey that will sate her hunger for vengeance. A biting take on the war of the sexes.

## LEOPOLD VON SACHER-MASOCH

**VENUS IN FURS**
$6.95/3089-X
The first uncompromising exploration of the dominant/submissive relationship in literature. The alliance of Severin and Wanda epitomizes Sacher-Masoch's dark obsession with a cruel, controlling goddess and the urges that drive the man held in her thrall.

# BADBOY

## KITTY TSUI WRITING AS "ERIC NORTON"

**SPARKS FLY**
$6.95/551-4
The acclaimed author of *Breathless* explores the highest highs—and most wretched depths—of life as Eric Norton, a beautiful wanton living San Francisco's high life. *Sparks Fly* traces Norton's rise, fall, and resurrection, vividly marking the way with the personal affairs that give life meaning. Scaldingly hot and totally revealing.

## BARRY ALEXANDER

**ALL THE RIGHT PLACES**
$6.95/482-8
Stories filled with hot studs in lust and love. From modern masters and slaves to medieval royals and their subjects, Alexander explores the mating rituals men have engaged in for centuries—all in the name of sometimes hidden desires...

## MICHAEL FORD, EDITOR

**BUTCHBOYS:**
**Stories For Men Who Need It Bad**
$6.50/523-9
A big volume of tales dedicated to the rough-and-tumble type who can make a man weak at the knees. Some of today's best erotic writers explore the many possible variations on the age-old fantasy of the dominant man.

## WILLIAM J. MANN, EDITOR

**GRAVE PASSIONS:**
**Gay Tales of the Supernatural**
$6.50/405-4
A collection of the most chilling tales of passion currently being penned by today's most provocative gay writers. Unnatural transformations, otherworldly encounters, and deathless desires make for a collection sure to keep readers up late at night—for a variety of reasons!

# MASQUERADE BOOKS

## J.A. GUERRA, EDITOR

**COME QUICKLY:**
**For Boys on the Go**
$6.50/413-5

Here are over sixty of the hottest fantasies around—all designed to get you going in less time than it takes to dial 976. Julian Anthony Guerra, the editor behind the popular *Men at Work* and *Badboy Fantasies*, has put together this volume especially for you—a busy man on a modern schedule, who still appreciates a little old-fashioned action.

## JOHN PRESTON

**HUSTLING: A Gentleman's Guide to the Fine Art of Homosexual Prostitution**
$6.50/517-4

"...Unrivaled. For any man even vaguely contemplating going into business this tome has got to be the first port of call."
—*Divinity*

"Fun and highly literary. What more could you expect form such an accomplished activist, author and editor?" —*Drummer*

John Preston solicited the advice and opinions of "working boys" from across the country in his effort to produce the ultimate guide to the hustler's world. *Hustling* covers every practical aspect of the business, from clientele and payment options to "specialties," sidelines and drawbacks. Trade $12.95/137-3

**MR. BENSON**
$4.95/3041-5

Jamie is an aimless young man lucky enough to encounter Mr. Benson. He is soon led down the path of erotic enlightenment, learning to accept this man as his master. Jamie's incredible adventures never fail to excite—especially when the going gets rough!

**TALES FROM THE DARK LORD**
$5.95/323-6

Twelve stunning works from the man *Lambda Book Report* called "the Dark Lord of gay erotica." The relentless ritual of lust and surrender is explored in all its manifestations in this heart-stopping triumph of authority and vision from the Dark Lord!

**TALES FROM THE DARK LORD II**
$4.95/176-4

**THE ARENA**
$4.95/3083-0

Preston's take on the ultimate sex club. Men go there to unleash beasts, to let demons roam free, to abolish all limits. Only the author of Mr. Benson could have imagined so perfect an institution for the satisfaction of masculine desires.

**THE HEIR•THE KING**
$4.95/3048-2

Two complete novels in one special volume. The ground-breaking and controversial *The Heir*, written in the lyric voice of the ancient myths, tells the story of a world where slaves and masters create a new sexual society. *The King* tells the story of a soldier who discovers his monarch's most secret desires.

**THE MISSION OF ALEX KANE**
**SWEET DREAMS**
$4.95/3062-8

It's the triumphant return of gay action hero Alex Kane! In *Sweet Dreams*, Alex travels to Boston where he takes on a street gang that stalks gay teenagers.

**GOLDEN YEARS**
$4.95/3069-5

When evil threatens the plans of a group of older gay men, Kane's got the muscle to take it head on. Along the way, he wins the support—and very specialized attentions—of a cowboy plucked right out of the Old West.

**DEADLY LIES**
$4.95/3076-8

Politics is a dirty business and the dirt becomes deadly when a political smear campaign targets gay men. Who better to clean things up than Alex Kane! Alex comes to protect the lives of gay men imperiled by lies and deceit.

**STOLEN MOMENTS**
$4.95/3098-9

Houston's evolving gay community is victimized by a malicious newspaper editor who is more than willing to sacrifice gays on the altar of circulation. He never counted on Alex Kane, fearless defender of gay dreams and desires.

**SECRET DANGER**
$4.95/111-X

Homophobia: a pernicious social ill not confined by America's borders. Alex Kane and the faithful Danny are called to a small European country, where a group of gay tourists is being held hostage by ruthless terrorists. Luckily, the Mission of Alex Kane stands as firm foreign policy.

**LETHAL SILENCE**
$4.95/125-X

The Mission of Alex Kane thunders to a conclusion. Chicago becomes the scene of the right-wing's most noxious plan—facilitated by unholy political alliances. Alex and Danny head to the Windy City to take up battle with the mercenaries who would squash gay men underfoot.

**BUY ANY 4 BOOKS & CHOOSE 1 ADDITIONAL BOOK, OF EQUAL OR LESSER VALUE, AS YOUR FREE GIFT**

# MASQUERADE BOOKS

## MATT TOWNSEND
**SOLIDLY BUILT**
$6.50/416-X
It's Tool Time! Matt Townsend—one of today's most promising eroticists—debuts with the tale of the tumultuous relationship between Jeff, a young photographer, and Mark, the butch electrician hired to wire Jeff's new home. For Jeff, it's love at first sight; Mark, however, has more than a few hang-ups. Soon, both are forced to reevaluate their outlooks, and are assisted by a variety of hot men....

## JAY SHAFFER
**SHOOTERS**
$5.95/284-1
Hot sex for no-nonsense guys. No mere catalog of random acts, *Shooters* tells the stories of a variety of stunning men and the ways they connect in sexual and non-sexual ways. A virtuoso storyteller, Shaffer always gets his man.

**ANIMAL HANDLERS**
$4.95/264-7
In Shaffer's world, each and every man finally succumbs to the animal urges deep inside. And if there's any creature that promises a wild time, it's a beast who's been caged for far too long. Shaffer has one of the keenest eyes for the nuances of male passion.

**FULL SERVICE**
$4.95/150-0
Wild men build up steam until they finally let loose. No-nonsense guys bear down hard on each other as they work their way toward release in this finely detailed assortment of masculine fantasies. One of gay erotica's most insightful chroniclers of male passion.

## D. V. SADERO
**IN THE ALLEY**
$4.95/144-6
Hardworking men—from cops to carpenters—bring their own special skills and impressive tools to the most satisfying job of all: capturing and breaking the male sexual beast. Hot, incisive and way over the top.

## SCOTT O'HARA
**DO-IT-YOURSELF PISTON POLISHING**
$6.50/489-5
Longtime sex-pro Scott O'Hara draws upon his acute powers of seduction to lure you into a world of hard, horny men long overdue for a tune-up. Pretty soon, you'll pop your own hood for the servicing you know you need....

## SUTTER POWELL
**EXECUTIVE PRIVILEGES**
$6.50/383-X
No matter how serious or sexy a predicament his characters find themselves in, Powell conveys the sheer exuberance of their encounters with a warm humor rarely seen in contemporary gay erotica.

## GARY BOWEN
**WESTERN TRAILS**
$6.50/477-1
A wild roundup of tales devoted to life on the lone prairie. Gary Bowen has collected the very best contemporary cowboy stories. Some of gay literature's brightest stars tell the sexy truth about the many ways a rugged stud found to satisfy himself—and his buddy—in the Very Wild West.

**MAN HUNGRY**
$5.95/374-0
By the author of *Diary of a Vampire*. A riveting collection of stories from one of gay erotica's new stars. Dipping into a variety of genres, Bowen crafts tales of lust unlike anything being published today.

## KYLE STONE
**HOT BAUDS 2**
$6.50/479-8
Stone conducted another heated search through the world's randiest gay bulletin boards, resulting in one of the most scalding follow-ups ever published. Sexy, shameless, and user-friendly.

**HOT BAUDS**
$5.95/285-X
Stone combed cyberspace for the hottest fantasies of the world's horniest hackers. Stone has assembled the first collection of the raunchy erotica so many gay men surf the Net for.

**FIRE & ICE**
$5.95/297-3
A collection of stories from the author of the infamous adventures of PB 500. Randy, powerful, and just plain bad, Stone's characters always promise one thing: enough hot action to burn away your desire for anyone else....

**FANTASY BOARD**
$4.95/212-4
Explore the foreseeable future—through the intertwined lives of a collection of randy computer hackers. On the Lambda Gate BBS, every horny male is in search of virtual satisfaction!

**THE CITADEL**
$4.95/198-5
The sequel to *The Initiation of PB 500*. Micah—now known only as '500'—will face new challenges and hardships after his entry into the forbidding Citadel. Only his master knows what awaits—and whether Micah will again distinguish himself as the perfect instrument of pleasure....

# MASQUERADE BOOKS

### THE INITIATION OF PB 500
$4.95/141-1

He is a stranger on their planet, unschooled in their language, and ignorant of their customs. But this man, Micah—now known only by his number—will soon be trained in every detail of erotic service. He must begin proving himself worthy of the master who has chosen him....

### RITUALS
$4.95/168-3

Via a computer bulletin board, a young man finds himself drawn into a series of sexual rites that transform him into the willing slave of a mysterious stranger. All vestiges of his former life are thrown off, and he learns to live for his Master's touch....

## ROBERT BAHR
### SEX SHOW
$4.95/225-6

Luscious dancing boys. Brazen, explicit acts. Take a seat, and get very comfortable, because the curtain's going up on a show no discriminating appetite can afford to miss.

## JASON FURY
### THE ROPE ABOVE, THE BED BELOW
$4.95/269-8

A vicious murderer is preying upon New York's go-go boys. In order to solve this mystery and save lives, each studly suspect must lay bare his soul—and more!

### ERIC'S BODY
$4.95/151-9

Fury's sexiest tales are collected in book form for the first time. Follow the irresistible Jason through sexual adventures unlike any you have ever read....

### 1 900 745-HUNG

THE connection for hot handfuls of eager guys! No credit card needed—so call now for access to the hottest party line available. Spill it all to bad boys from across the country! (Must be over 18.) Pick one up now.... $3.98 per min.

## LARS EIGHNER
### WHISPERED IN THE DARK
$5.95/286-9

A volume demonstrating Eighner's unique combination of strengths: poetic descriptive power, an unfailing ear for dialogue, and a finely tuned feeling for the nuances of male passion.

### AMERICAN PRELUDE
$4.95/170-5

Eighner is widely recognized as one of our best, most exciting gay writers. He is also one of gay erotica's true masters—and *American Prelude* shows why. Wonderfully written, blisteringly hot tales of all-American lust between oversexed studs.

### B.M.O.C.
$4.95/3077-6

In a college town known as "the Athens of the Southwest," studs of every stripe are up all night—studying, naturally. Relive university life the way it was supposed to be, with a cast of handsome honor students majoring in Human Homosexuality.

## DAVID LAURENTS, EDITOR
### SOUTHERN COMFORT
$6.50/466-6

Editor David Laurents now unleashes a collection of tales focusing on the American South—stories reflecting not only Southern literary tradition, but the many sexy contributions the region has made to the iconography of the American Male.

### WANDERLUST:
### Homoerotic Tales of Travel
$5.95/395-3

A volume dedicated to the special pleasures of faraway places. Celebrate the freedom of the open road, and the allure of men who stray from the beaten path....

### THE BADBOY BOOK OF EROTIC POETRY
$5.95/382-1

Erotic poetry has long been the problem child of the literary world—highly creative and provocative, but somehow too frank to be "art." *The Badboy Book of Erotic Poetry* restores eros to its place of honor in contemporary gay writing.

## AARON TRAVIS
### BIG SHOTS
$5.95/448-8

Two fierce tales in one electrifying volume. In *Beirut*, Travis tells the story of ultimate military power and erotic subjugation; *Kip*, Travis's hyper-sexed and sinister take on film noir, appears in unexpurgated form for the first time.

### EXPOSED
$4.95/126-8

A volume of shorter Travis tales, each providing a unique glimpse of the horny gay male in his natural environment! Cops, college jocks, ancient Romans—even Sherlock Holmes and his loyal Watson—cruise these pages, fresh from the throbbing pen of one of our hottest authors.

**BUY ANY 4 BOOKS & CHOOSE 1 ADDITIONAL BOOK, OF EQUAL OR LESSER VALUE, AS YOUR FREE GIFT**

# MASQUERADE BOOKS

## BEAST OF BURDEN
$4.95/105-5

Innocents surrender to the brutal sexual mastery of their superiors, as taboos are shattered and replaced with the unwritten rules of masculine conquest. Intense, extreme—and totally Travis.

## IN THE BLOOD
$5.95/283-3

Written when Travis had just begun to explore the true power of the erotic imagination, these stories laid the groundwork for later masterpieces. Among the many rewarding rarities included in this special volume: "In the Blood"—a heart-pounding descent into sexual vampirism.

## THE FLESH FABLES
$4.95/243-4

One of Travis' best collections. *The Flesh Fables* includes "Blue Light," his most famous story, as well as other masterpieces that established him as the erotic writer to watch.

## SLAVES OF THE EMPIRE
$4.95/3054-7

"A wonderful mythic tale. Set against the backdrop of the exotic and powerful Roman Empire, this wonderfully written novel explores the timeless questions of light and dark in male sexuality. The locale may be the ancient world, but these are the slaves and masters of our time...."    —John Preston

### BOB VICKERY
## SKIN DEEP
$4.95/265-5

So many varied beauties no one will go away unsatisfied. No tantalizing morsel of manflesh is overlooked—or left unexplored! Beauty may be only skin deep, but a handful of beautiful skin is a tempting proposition.

### JR
## FRENCH QUARTER NIGHTS
$5.95/337-6

Sensual snapshots of the many places where men get down and dirty—from the steamy French Quarter to the steam room at the old Everard baths. These are nights you'll wish would go on forever....

### TOM BACCHUS
## RAHM
$5.95/315-5

The imagination of Tom Bacchus brings to life an extraordinary assortment of characters, from the Father of Us All to the cowpoke next door, the early gay literati to rude, queercore mosh rats.

## BONE
$4.95/177-2

Queer musings from the pen of one of today's hottest young talents. A fresh outlook on fleshly indulgence yields more than a few pleasant surprises. Horny Tom Bacchus maps out the tricking ground of a new generation.

### KEY LINCOLN
## SUBMISSION HOLDS
$4.95/266-3

A bright young talent unleashes his first collection of gay erotica. From tough to tender, the men between these covers stop at nothing to get what they want. These sweat-soaked tales show just how bad boys can really get.

### CALDWELL/EIGHNER
## QSFX2
$5.95/278-7

The wickedest, wildest, other-worldliest yarns from two master storytellers—Clay Caldwell and Lars Eighner. Both eroticists take a trip to the furthest reaches of the sexual imagination, sending back ten stories proving that as much as things change, one thing will always remain the same....

### CLAY CALDWELL
## JOCK STUDS
$6.50/472-0

Scalding tales of pumped bodies and raging libidos. Swimmers, runners, football players... whatever your sport might be, there's a man waiting for you in these pages. Waiting to peel off that uniform and claim his reward for a game well-played....

## ASK OL' BUDDY
$5.95/346-5

Set in the underground SM world, Caldwell takes you on a journey of discovery—where men initiate one another into the secrets of the rawest sexual realm of all. And when each stud's initiation is complete, he takes part in the training of another hungry soul...

## STUD SHORTS
$5.95/320-1

"If anything, Caldwell's charm is more powerful, his nostalgia more poignant, the horniness he captures more sweetly, achingly acute than ever."    —Aaron Travis

A new collection of this legend's latest sex-fiction. Caldwell tells all about cops, cadets, truckers, farmboys (and many more) in these dirty jewels.

## TAILPIPE TRUCKER
$5.95/296-5

Trucker porn! In prose as free and unvarnished as a cross-country highway, Caldwell tells the truth about Trag and Curly—two men hot for the feeling of sweaty manflesh. Together, they pick up—and turn out—a couple of thrill-seeking punks.

## SERVICE, STUD
$5.95/336-8

Another look at the gay future. The setting is the Los Angeles of a distant future. Here the all-male populace is divided between the served and the servants—guaranteeing the erotic satisfaction of all involved.

# MASQUERADE BOOKS

## QUEERS LIKE US
$4.95/262-0

"Caldwell at his most charming." —Aaron Travis

For years the name Clay Caldwell has been synonymous with the hottest, most finely crafted gay tales available. *Queers Like Us* is one of his best: the story of a randy mailman's trek through a landscape of willing, available studs.

## ALL-STUD
$4.95/104-7

This classic, sex-soaked tale takes place under the watchful eye of Number Ten: an omniscient figure who has decreed unabashed promiscuity as the law of his all-male land.

## CLAY CALDWELL AND AARON TRAVIS

### TAG TEAM STUDS
$6.50/465-8

Thrilling tales from these two legendary eroticists. The wrestling world will never seem the same, once you've made your way through this assortment of sweaty, virile studs. But you'd better be wary—should one catch you off guard, you just might spend the rest of the night pinned to the mat....

## LARRY TOWNSEND

### LEATHER AD: M
$5.95/380-5

The first of this two-part classic. John's curious about what goes on between the leatherclad men he's fantasized about. He takes out a personal ad, and starts a journey of self-discovery that will leave no part of his life unchanged.

### LEATHER AD: S
$5.95/407-0

The tale continues—this time told from a Top's perspective. A simple ad generates many responses, and one man finds himself in the enviable position of putting these studs through their paces....

## 1 800 906-HUNK

Hardcore phone action for real men. A scorching assembly of studs is waiting for your call—and eager to give you the headtrip of your life! Totally live, guaranteed one-on-one encounters. (Must be over 18.) No credit card needed. $3.98 per minute.

## BEWARE THE GOD WHO SMILES
$5.95/321-X

Two lusty young Americans are transported to ancient Egypt—where they are embroiled in regional warfare and taken as slaves by barbarians. The key to escape lies in their rampant libidos.

## 2069 TRILOGY
(This one-volume collection only $6.95)244-2

The early science-fiction trilogy in one volume! Set in the future, the *2069 Trilogy* includes the tight plotting and shameless all-male sex action that established Townsend as one of erotica's masters.

## MIND MASTER
$4.95/209-4

Who better to explore the territory of erotic dominance than an author who helped define the genre—and knows that ultimate mastery always transcends the physical.

## THE LONG LEATHER CORD
$4.95/201-9

Chuck's stepfather never lacks money or clandestine male visitors with whom he enacts intense sexual rituals. As Chuck comes to terms with his own desires, he begins to unravel the mystery behind his stepfather's secret life.

## THE SCORPIUS EQUATION
$4.95/119-5

The story of a man caught between the demands of two galactic empires. Our randy hero must match wits—and more—with the incredible forces that rule his world.

## MAN SWORD
$4.95/188-8

The *très gai* tale of France's King Henri III, who encounters enough sexual schemers and politicos to alter one's picture of history forever!

## THE FAUSTUS CONTRACT
$4.95/167-5

*Two attractive young men desperately need $1000. Will do anything. Travel OK. Danger OK. Call anytime...* Two cocky young hustlers get more than they bargained for in this story of lust and its discontents.

## CHAINS
$4.95/158-6

Picking up street punks has always been risky, but here it sets off a string of events that must be read to be believed. Townsend at his grittiest.

## KISS OF LEATHER
$4.95/161-6

A look at the acts and attitudes of an earlier generation of gay leathermen, *Kiss of Leather* is full to bursting with gritty, raw action. Sensual pain and pleasure mix in this tightly plotted tale.

## RUN, LITTLE LEATHER BOY
$4.95/143-8

A chronic underachiever, Wayne seems to be going nowhere fast. He finds himself drawn to the masculine intensity of a dark and mysterious sexual underground, where he soon finds many goals worth pursuing....

**BUY ANY 4 BOOKS & CHOOSE 1 ADDITIONAL BOOK, OF EQUAL OR LESSER VALUE, AS YOUR FREE GIFT**

# MASQUERADE BOOKS

**RUN NO MORE**
$4.95/152-7
The continuation of Larry Townsend's legendary *Run, Little Leather Boy*. This volume follows the further adventures of Townsend's leatherclad narrator as he travels every sexual byway available to the S/M male. A novel of self-discovery by the author who almost single-handedly created the genre of gay SM erotica.

**THE SEXUAL ADVENTURES OF SHERLOCK HOLMES**
$4.95/3097-0
A scandalously sexy take on this legendary sleuth. "A Study in Scarlet" is transformed to expose Mrs. Hudson as a man in drag, the Diogenes Club as an S/M arena, and clues only the redoubtable—and very horny—Sherlock Holmes could piece together. A baffling tale of sex and mystery.

**THE GAY ADVENTURES OF CAPTAIN GOOSE**
$4.95/169-1
Hot young Jerome Gander is sentenced to serve aboard the H.M.S. Faerigold—a ship manned by the most hardened, unrepentant criminals. In no time, Gander becomes well-versed in the ways of horny men at sea, and the Faerigold becomes the most notorious vessel to ever set sail.

## DONALD VINING
**CABIN FEVER AND OTHER STORIES**
$5.95/338-4
"Demonstrates the wisdom experience combined with insight and optimism can create."  —*Bay Area Reporter*

Eighteen blistering stories in celebration of the most intimate of male bonding. Time after time, Donald Vining's men succumb to nature, and reaffirm both love and lust in modern gay life.

## DEREK ADAMS
**PRISONER OF DESIRE**
$6.50/439-9
Scalding fiction from one of Badboy's most popular authors. The creator of horny P.I. Miles Diamond returns with this volume bursting with red-blooded, sweat-soaked excursions through the modern gay libido.

**THE MARK OF THE WOLF**
$5.95/361-9
The past comes back to haunt one well-off stud, whose unslakeable thirsts lead him into the arms of many men—and the midst of a mystery.

**MY DOUBLE LIFE**
$5.95/314-7
Every man leads a double life, dividing his hours between the mundanities of the day and the pursuits of the night. Adams shines a little light on the wicked things men do when no one's looking.

**HEAT WAVE**
$4.95/159-4
"His body was draped in baggy clothes, but there was hardly any doubt that they covered anything less than perfection.... His slacks were cinched tight around a narrow waist, and the rise of flesh pushing against the thin fabric promised a firm, melon-shaped ass...."

**MILES DIAMOND AND THE DEMON OF DEATH**
$4.95/251-5
Miles always find himself in the stickiest situations—with any stud whose path he crosses! His adventures with "The Demon of Death" promise another carnal carnival.

**THE ADVENTURES OF MILES DIAMOND**
$4.95/118-7
Derek Adams' take on the classic American archetype of the hardboiled private eye. "The Case of the Missing Twin" promises to be a most rewarding case, packed as it is with randy studs. Miles sets about uncovering all as he tracks down the elusive and delectable Daniel Travis.

## KELVIN BELIELE
**IF THE SHOE FITS**
$4.95/223-X
An essential and winning volume of tales exploring a world where randy boys can't help but do what comes naturally—as often as possible! Sweaty male bodies grapple in pleasure, proving the old adage: if the shoe fits, one might as well slip right in....

## JAMES MEDLEY
**THE REVOLUTIONARY & OTHER STORIES**
$6.50/417-8
Billy, the son of the station chief of the American Embassy in Guatemala, is kidnapped and held for ransom. Frightened at first, Billy gradually develops an unimaginably close relationship with Juan, the revolutionary assigned to guard him.

**HUCK AND BILLY**
$4.95/245-0
Young love is always the sweetest. Young lust, on the other hand, knows no bounds—and is often the hottest of one's life! Huck and Billy explore the desires that course through their bodies, determined to plumb the depths of passion.

## FLEDERMAUS
**FLEDERFICTION: STORIES OF MEN AND TORTURE**
$5.95/355-4
Fifteen blistering paeans to men and their suffering. Unafraid of exploring the nether reaches of pain and pleasure, Fledermaus here unleashes his most thrilling tales in this special volume.

# MASQUERADE BOOKS

## VICTOR TERRY

**MASTERS**
$6.50/418-6
A powerhouse volume of boot-wearing, whip-wielding, bone-crunching bruisers who've got what it takes to make a grown man grovel.

**SM/SD**
$6.50/406-2
Set around a South Dakota town called Prairie, these tales offer compelling evidence that the real rough stuff can still be found where men take what they want despite all rules.

**WHiPs**
$4.95/254-X
Cruising for a hot man? You'd better be, because one way or another, these WHiPs—officers of the Wyoming Highway Patrol—are gonna pull you over for a little impromptu interrogation....

## MAX EXANDER

**DEEDS OF THE NIGHT:**
**Tales of Eros and Passion**
$5.95/348-1
MAXimum porn! Exander's a writer who's seen it all—and is more than happy to describe every inch of it in pulsating detail. A whirlwind tour of the hypermasculine libido.

**LEATHERSEX**
$4.95/210-8
Hard-hitting tales from merciless Max Exander. This time he focuses on the leatherclad lust that draws together only the most willing and talented of tops and bottoms—for an all-out orgy of limitless surrender and control....

**MANSEX**
$4.95/160-8
"Mark was the classic leatherman: a huge, dark stud in chaps, with a big black moustache, hairy chest and enormous muscles. Exactly the kind of men Todd liked—strong, hunky, masculine, ready to take control..."

## TOM CAFFREY

**TALES FROM THE MEN'S ROOM**
$5.95/364-3
Male lust at its most elemental and arousing. If there's a lesson to be learned, it's that the Men's Room is less a place than a state of mind—one that every man finds himself in, day after day....

**HITTING HOME**
$4.95/222-1
Titillating and compelling, the stories in *Hitting Home* make a strong case for there being only one thing on a man's mind.

## "BIG" BILL JACKSON

**EIGHTH WONDER**
200-0/$4.95
"Big" Bill Jackson's always the randiest guy in town—no matter what town he's in. From the bright lights and back rooms of New York to the open fields and sweaty bods of a small Southern town, "Big" Bill always manages to cause a scene, and the more actors he can involve, the better!

## TORSTEN BARRING

**GUY TRAYNOR**
$6.50/414-3
Some call Guy Traynor a theatrical genius; others say he was a madman. All anyone knows for certain is that his productions were the result of blood, sweat and outrageous erotic torture!

**PRISONERS OF TORQUEMADA**
$5.95/252-3
Another volume sure to push you over the edge. How cruel is the "therapy" practiced at Casa Torquemada? Barring is just the writer to evoke such steamy sexual malevolence.

**SHADOWMAN**
$4.95/178-0
From spoiled aristocrats to randy youths sowing wild oats at the local picture show, Barring's imagination works overtime in these steamy vignettes of homolust—past, present and future.

**PETER THORNWELL**
$4.95/149-7
Follow the exploits of Peter Thornwell as he goes from misspent youth to scandalous stardom, all thanks to an insatiable libido and love for the lash.

**THE SWITCH**
$4.95/3061-X
Sometimes a man needs a good whipping, and *The Switch* certainly makes a case! Packed with hot studs and unrelenting passions, these stories established Barring as a writer to be watched.

## BERT McKENZIE

**FRINGE BENEFITS**
$5.95/354-6
From the pen of a widely published short story writer comes a volume of highly immodest tales. Not afraid of getting down and dirty, McKenzie produces some of today's most visceral sextales.

## CHRISTOPHER MORGAN

**STEAM GAUGE**
$6.50/473-9
This volume abounds in manly men doing what they do best—to, with, or for any hot stud who crosses their paths.

---

**BUY ANY 4 BOOKS & CHOOSE 1 ADDITIONAL BOOK, OF EQUAL OR LESSER VALUE, AS YOUR FREE GIFT**

# MASQUERADE BOOKS

**THE SPORTSMEN**
$5.95/385-6
A collection of super-hot stories dedicated to the all-American athlete. Here are enough tales of carnal grand slams, sexy interceptions and highly personal bests to satisfy any hunger. These writers know just the type of guys that make up every red-blooded male's starting line-up....

**MUSCLE BOUND**
$4.95/3028-8
In the NYC bodybuilding scene, Tommy joins forces with sexy Will Rodriguez in a battle of wits and biceps at the hottest gym in town, where the weak are bound and crushed by iron-pumping gods.

## SONNY FORD
**REUNION IN FLORENCE**
$4.95/3070-9
Follow Adrian and Tristan an a sexual odyssey that takes in all ports known to ancient man. From lustful turks to insatiable Mamluks, these two have much more than their hands full, as they spread pleasure throughout the classical world!

## ROGER HARMAN
**FIRST PERSON**
$4.95/179-9
A highly personal collection. Each story takes the form of a confessional—told by men who've got plenty to confess! From the "first time ever" to firsts of different kinds, *First Person* tells truths too hot to be purely fiction.

## J. A. GUERRA, ED.
**SLOW BURN**
$4.95/3042-3
Welcome to the Body Shoppe! Torsos get lean and hard, pecs widen, and stomachs ripple in these sexy stories of the power and perils of physical perfection.

## DAVE KINNICK
**SORRY I ASKED**
$4.95/3090-3
Unexpurgated interviews with gay porn's rank and file. Get personal with the men behind (and under) the "stars," and discover the hot truth about the porn business.

## SEAN MARTIN
**SCRAPBOOK**
$4.95/224-8
From the creator of Doc and Raider comes this hot collection of life's horniest moments—all involving studs sure to set your pulse racing! A brilliantly sexy volume.

## CARO SOLES & STAN TAL, EDS.
**BIZARRE DREAMS**
$4.95/187-X
An anthology of stirring voices dedicated to exploring the dark side of human fantasy. Here are the most talented practitioners of "dark fantasy," the most forbidden sexual realm of all.

## MICHAEL LOWENTHAL, ED.
**THE BADBOY EROTIC LIBRARY Volume I**
$4.95/190-X
Excerpts from *A Secret Life, Imre, Sins of the Cities of the Plain, Teleny* and others demonstrate the uncanny gift for portraying sex between men that led to many of these titles being banned.

**THE BADBOY EROTIC LIBRARY Volume I**
$4.95/211-8
This time, selections are taken from *Mike and Me, Muscle Bound, Men at Work, Badboy Fantasies,* and *Slowburn.*

## ERIC BOYD
**MIKE AND ME**
$5.95/419-4
Mike joined the gym squad to bulk up on muscle. Little did he know he'd be turning on every sexy muscle jock in Minnesota! Hard bodies collide in a series of workouts designed to generate a whole lot more than rips and cuts.

**MIKE AND THE MARINES**
$6.50/497-6
Mike takes on America's most elite corps of studs—running into more than a few good men! Join in on the never-ending sexual escapades of this singularly lustful platoon!

## ANONYMOUS
**A SECRET LIFE**
$4.95/3017-2
Meet Master Charles: only eighteen, and quite innocent, until his arrival at the Sir Percival's Royal Academy, where the daily lessons are supplemented with a crash course in pure sexual heat!

**SINS OF THE CITIES OF THE PLAIN**
$5.95/322-8
indulge yourself in the scorching memoirs of young man-about-town Jack Saul. Jack's positively sinful escapades grow wilder with every chapter!

**IMRE**
$4.95/3019-9
What fiery passions lay hidden behind Lieutenant Imre's emerald eyes? An extraordinary lost classic of obsession, gay erotic desire, and romance in a small European town on the eve of WWI.

# MASQUERADE BOOKS

### TELENY
$4.95/3020-2
Often attributed to Oscar Wilde. A young man dedicates himself to a succession of forbidden pleasures.

### THE SCARLET PANSY
$4.95/189-6
A white-hot gay camp classic. The story of Randall Etrange, travelling the world in search of true love. Along the way, he engages one and all as his journey becomes a sexual odyssey of truly epic proportions. The randiest road novel ever published!

## PAT CALIFIA, ED.
### THE SEXPERT
3034-2/$4.95
Straight from the pages of Advocate Men comes The Sexpert! From penis size to toy care, bar behavior to AIDS awareness, The Sexpert responds to real concerns with uncanny wisdom and a razor wit. The best of this popular columnist's writing, collected for the first time.

# HARD CANDY

## MICHAEL ROWE
### WRITING BELOW THE BELT: Conversation with Erotic Authors
$7.95/540-9
"This is a thoughtful and engaging book, in turns serious and witty." —*Harvard Gay & Lesbian Review*

"Rowe takes this project far beyond its premise and delivers an in-depth and enlightening tour of society's love/hate relationship with sex, morality, and censorship." —*James White Review*

Award-winning journalist Michael Rowe interviewed the best and brightest erotic writers and presents the collected wisdom in *Writing Below the Belt*. In each of these revealing conversations, the personal, the political and the just plain prurient collide and complement one another in fascinating ways.

## BRAD GOOCH
### THE GOLDEN AGE OF PROMISCUITY
$7.95/550-6
"The next best thing to taking a time-machine trip to grovel in the glorious '70s gutter." —*San Francisco Chronicle*

"A solid, unblinking, unsentimental look at a vanished era. Gooch tells us everything we ever wanted to know about the dark and decadent gay subculture in Manhattan before AIDS altered the landscape." —*Kirkus Reviews*

## KEVIN KILLIAN
### ARCTIC SUMMER
$6.95/514-X
An examination of the many secrets lying beneath the placid exterior of America in the 50s. With the story of Liam Reilly—a young gay man of considerable means and numerous secrets—Killian exposes the contradictions of the American Dream.

## STAN LEVENTHAL
### BARBIE IN BONDAGE
$6.95/415-1
Widely regarded as one of the most clear-eyed interpreters of big city gay male life, Leventhal here provides a series of explorations of love and desire between men.

### SKYDIVING ON CHRISTOPHER STREET
$6.95/287-6
"Positively addictive." —Dennis Cooper

Aside from a hateful job, a hateful apartment, a hateful world and an increasingly hateful lover, life seems, well, all right for the protagonist of Stan Leventhal's latest novel. Having already lost most of his friends to AIDS, how could things get any worse? An insightful tale of contemporary urban gay life.

## PATRICK MOORE
### IOWA
$6.95/423-2
Lambda Literary Award Nominee.

"Full of terrific characters etched in acid-sharp prose, soaked through with just enough ambivalence to make it thoroughly romantic." —Felice Picano

One gay man's journey into adulthood, and the roads that bring him home again.

## PAUL T. ROGERS
### SAUL'S BOOK
$7.95/462-3
Winner of the Editors' Book Award
"A masterpiece." —*Village Voice Literary Supplement*

"A first novel of considerable power... Sinbad the Sailor, thanks to the sympathetic imagination of Paul T. Rogers, speaks to us all." —*New York Times Book Review*

The story of a Times Square hustler, Sinbad the Sailor, and Saul, a brilliant, self-destructive, alcoholic, dominating character who may be the only love Sinbad will ever know.

**BUY ANY 4 BOOKS & CHOOSE 1 ADDITIONAL BOOK, OF EQUAL OR LESSER VALUE, AS YOUR FREE GIFT**

# MASQUERADE BOOKS

## WALTER R. HOLLAND
### THE MARCH
$6.95/429-1

Beginning on a hot summer night in 1980, *The March* revolves around a circle of young gay men, and the many others their lives touch. Over time, each character changes in unexpected ways; lives and loves come together and fall apart, as society itself is horribly altered by the onslaught of AIDS.

## RED JORDAN AROBATEAU
### LUCY AND MICKEY
$6.95/311-2

"A necessary reminder to all who blissfully—some may say ignorantly—ride the wave of lesbian chic into the main-stream." —Heather Findlay

The story of Mickey—an uncompromising butch—and her long affair with Lucy, the femme she loves.

### DIRTY PICTURES
$5.95/345-7

"Red Jordan Arobateau is the Thomas Wolfe of lesbian literature... She's a natural—raw talent that is seething, passionate, hard, remarkable."
—Lillian Faderman, editor of *Chloe Plus Olivia*

*Dirty Pictures* is the story of a lonely butch tending bar—and the femme she finally calls her own.

## LARS EIGHNER
### GAY COSMOS
$6.95/236-1

A title sure to appeal not only to Eighner's gay fans, but the many converts who first encountered his moving nonfiction work. Praised by the press, *Gay Cosmos* is an important contribution to the area of Gay and Lesbian Studies.

## DONALD VINING
### A GAY DIARY
$8.95/451-8

"*A Gay Diary* is, unquestionably, the richest historical document of gay male life in the United States that I have ever encountered...." —*Body Politic*

Vining's *Diary* portrays a vanished age and the lifestyle of a gay generation too frequently forgotten.

## FELICE PICANO
### AMBIDEXTROUS
$6.95/275-2

"Makes us remember what it feels like to be a child..."
—*The Advocate*

Picano's first "memoir in the form of a novel" tells all: home life, school face-offs, the ingenuous sophistications of his first sexual steps. In three years' time, he's had his first gay fling—and is on his way to becoming the writer he is today.

### MEN WHO LOVED ME
$6.95/274-4

"Zesty...spiked with adventure and romance...a distinguished and humorous portrait of a vanished age." —*Publishers Weekly*

In 1966, Picano abandoned New York, determined to find true love in Europe. Upon returning, he plunges into the city's thriving gay community of the 1970s.

### THE LURE
$6.95/398-8

A Book-of-the-Month-Club Selection

"The subject matter, plus the authenticity of Picano's research are, combined, explosive. Felice Picano is one hell of a writer."
—Stephen King

After witnessing a brutal murder, Noel is recruited by the police, to assist as a lure for the killer. Undercover, he moves deep into the freneticism of Manhattan's gay highlife—where he gradually becomes aware of the darker forces at work in his life. In addition to the mystery behind his mission, he begins to recognize changes: in his relationships with the men around him, in himself...

## WILLIAM TALSMAN
### THE GAUDY IMAGE
$6.95/263-9

"To read *The Gaudy Image* now...it is to see first-hand the very issues of identity and positionality with which gay men were struggling in the decades before Stonewall. For what Talsman is dealing with...is the very question of how we conceive ourselves gay." —from the introduction by Michael Bronski

## ROSEBUD
### THE ROSEBUD READER
$5.95/319-8

Rosebud has contributed greatly to the burgeoning genre of lesbian erotica. Here are the finest moments from Rosebud's contemporary classics.

## LESLIE CAMERON
### WHISPER OF FANS
$6.50/542-5

"Just looking into her eyes, she felt that she knew a lot about this woman. She could see strength, boldness, a fresh sense of aliveness that rocked her to the core. In turn she felt open, revealed under the woman's gaze—all her secrets already told...." A fresh look at love between women.

## RACHEL PEREZ
### ODD WOMEN
$6.50/526-3

These women are sexy, smart, tough—some even say odd. But who cares! An assortment of Sapphic sirens proves once and for all that comely ladies come best in pairs.

# MASQUERADE BOOKS

## RANDY TUROFF
### LUST NEVER SLEEPS
$6.50/475-5
A rich volume of highly erotic, powerfully real fiction. Turoff depicts a circle of modern women connected through the bonds of love, friendship, ambition, and lust with accuracy and compassion.

## RED JORDAN AROBATEAU
### ROUGH TRADE
$6.50/470-4
Famous for her unflinching portrayal of lower-class dyke life and love, Arobateau outdoes herself with these tales of butch/femme affairs and unrelenting passions.

### BOYS NIGHT OUT
$6.50/463-1
Short fiction from this lesbian literary sensation. As always, Arobateau takes a good hard look at the lives of everyday women, noting well the struggles and triumphs each woman experiences.

## ALISON TYLER
### COME QUICKLY: For Girls on the Go
$6.95/428-3
Here are over sixty of the hottest fantasies around—all designed to get you going in less time than it takes to dial 976. A volume especially for you—a modern girl on a modern schedule, who still appreciates a little old-fashioned action.

### VENUS ONLINE
$6.50/521-2
Lovely Alexa spends her days in a boring bank job, saving her energies for the night. Then Alexa goes online, living out virtual adventures that become more real with each session. Soon Alexa—aka Venus—feels her erotic imagination growing beyond anything she could have imagined.

### DARK ROOM: An Online Adventure
$6.50/455-0
Dani, a successful photographer, can't bring herself to face the death of her lover, Kate. Determined to keep the memory of her lover alive, Dani goes online under Kate's screen alias—and begins to uncover the truth behind the crime.

### BLUE SKY SIDEWAYS & OTHER STORIES
$6.50/394-5
A variety of women, and their many breathtaking experiences with lovers, friends—and even the occasional sexy stranger. From blossoming young beauties to fearless vixens, Tyler finds the sexy pleasures of everyday life.

### DIAL "L" FOR LOVELESS
$5.95/386-4
Katrina Loveless—a private eye talented enough to give Sam Spade a run for his money. In her first case, Katrina investigates a murder implicating a host of society's darlings—while working herself into a variety of highly compromising knots!

### THE VIRGIN
$5.95/379-1
Veronica answers a personal ad in the "Women Seeking Women" category—and discovers a whole sensual world she never knew existed! And she never dreamed she'd be prized as a virgin all over again, by someone who would deflower her with a passion no man could ever show....

## K. T. BUTLER
### TOOLS OF THE TRADE
$5.95/420-8
A sparkling mix of lesbian erotica and humor. An encounter with ice cream, cappuccino and chocolate cake; an affair with a complete stranger; a pair of faulty handcuffs; and love on a drafting table.

## LOVECHILD
### GAG
$5.95/369-4
One of the bravest, most cutting young writers you'll ever encounter. The poems in *Gag* take on American hypocrisy with uncommon energy, and announce Lovechild as a writer of unforgettable rage.

## ELIZABETH OLIVER
### PAGAN DREAMS
$5.95/295-7
Cassidy and Samantha plan a vacation at a secluded bed-and-breakfast, hoping for a little personal time alone. But the lovers are plunged into a world of dungeons and pagan rites, as evil Anastasia steals Samantha for her own.

### THE SM MURDER: Murder at Roman Hill
$5.95/353-8
Intrepid lesbian P.I.s Leslie Patrick and Robin Penny take on a really hot case: the murder of the notorious Felicia Roman. The circumstances of the crime lead them through the leatherdyke underground, where motives—and desires—run deep.

## SUSAN ANDERS
### CITY OF WOMEN
$5.95/375-9
Stories dedicated to women and the passions that draw them together. Designed strictly for the sensual pleasure of women, these tales are set to ignite flames of passion from coast to coast.

**BUY ANY 4 BOOKS & CHOOSE 1 ADDITIONAL BOOK, OF EQUAL OR LESSER VALUE, AS YOUR FREE GIFT**

# MASQUERADE BOOKS

**PINK CHAMPAGNE**
$5.95/282-5
Tasty, torrid tales of butch/femme couplings. Tough as nails or soft as silk, these women seek out their antitheses, intent on working out the details of their own personal theory of difference.

## LAURA ANTONIOU, EDITOR
**LEATHERWOMEN**
$4.95/3095-4
These fantasies break every rule imposed on women's fantasies. The hottest stories from some of today's most outrageous writers make this an unforgettable volume.

**LEATHERWOMEN II**
$4.95/229-9
Another groundbreaking volume of writing from women on the edge, sure to ignite libidinal flames in any reader. Leave taboos behind, because these Leatherwomen know no limits....

## AARONA GRIFFIN
**PASSAGE AND OTHER STORIES**
$4.95/3057-1
An S/M romance. Lovely Nina is frightened by her lesbian passions, until she finds herself infatuated with a woman she spots at a local café.

## VALENTINA CILESCU
**MY LADY'S PLEASURE:**
**Mistress with a Maid, Volume 1**
$5.95/412-7
Claudia Dungarrow, a lovely, powerful, but mysterious professor, attempts to seduce virginal Elizabeth Stanbridge, setting off a chain of events that eventually ruins her career. Claudia vows revenge—and makes her foes pay deliciously....

**DARK VENUS:**
**Mistress with a Maid, Volume 2**
$6.50/481-X
Claudia Dungarrow's quest for ultimate erotic dominance continues in this scalding second volume! How many maidens will fall prey to her insatiable appetite?

**BODY AND SOUL:**
**Mistress With a Maid, volume 3**
$6.50/515-8
Dr. Claudia Dungarrow returns for yet another tour of depravity, subjugating every maiden in sight to her ruthless sexual whims. But she has yet to hold Elizabeth in submission. Will she ever?

**THE ROSEBUD SUTRA**
$4.95/242-6
"Women are hardly ever known in their true light, though they may love others, or become indifferent towards them, may give them delight, or abandon them, or may extract from them all the wealth that they possess." So says *The Rosebud Sutra*—a volume promising women's secrets.

**MISTRESS MINE**
$6.50/502-6
Sophia Cranleigh sits in prison, accused of authoring the "obscene" *Mistress Mine*. What she has done, however, is merely chronicle the events of her life. For Sophia has led no ordinary life, but has slaved and suffered—deliciously—under the hand of the notorious Mistress Malin.

**THE HAVEN**
165-9/$4.95
$4.95/165-9
The shocking story of a dangerous woman on the run—and the innocents she takes with her on a trip to Hell. J craves domination, and her perverse appetites lead her to the Haven: the isolated sanctuary Ros and Annie call home. Soon J forces her way into their world, bringing unspeakable lust and cruelty into their staid lives.

## LINDSAY WELSH
**SECOND SIGHT**
$6.50/507-7
During an attack by a gang of homophobic youths, Dana is thrown onto subway tracks—touching the deadly third rail. Miraculously, she survives, and finds herself endowed with superhuman powers. Dana decides to devote her powers to the protection of her lesbian sisters, no matter how daunting the danger they face.

**NASTY PERSUASIONS**
$6.50/436-4
A hot peek into the behind-the-scenes operations of Rough Trade—one of the world's most famous lesbian clubs. Join Slash, Ramone, Cherry and many others as they bring one another to the height of torturous ecstasy—all in the name of keeping Rough Trade the premier name in sexy entertainment for women.

**MILITARY SECRETS**
$5.95/397-X
Colonel Candice Sproule heads a highly specialized boot camp. Assisted by three dominatrix sergeants, Candice takes on the talented submissives sent to her by secret military contacts. Then along comes Jesse—whose pleasure in being served matches the Colonel's own.

**ROMANTIC ENCOUNTERS**
$5.95/359-7
Julie, the most powerful editor of romance novels in the industry, spends her days igniting women's passions through books—and her nights fulfilling those needs with a variety of licentious lovers. Finally, Julie's worlds come together explosively!

**THE BEST OF LINDSAY WELSH**
$5.95/368-6
Lindsay Welsh was one of Rosebud's early bestsellers, and remains one of our most popular writers. This sampler is set to introduce some of the hottest lesbian erotica to a wider audience.

# MASQUERADE BOOKS

**NECESSARY EVIL**
$5.95/277-9
When her Mistress proves too systematic, too by-the-book, one lovely submissive takes the ultimate chance—choosing and creating a Mistress who'll fulfill her heart's desire. Little did she know how difficult it would be—and, in the end, rewarding....

**A VICTORIAN ROMANCE**
$5.95/365-1
A young Englishwoman realizes her dream—a trip abroad under the guidance of her eccentric maiden aunt. Soon, blossoming Elaine comes to discover her own sexual talents, as a hot-blooded Parisian named Madelaine takes her Sapphic education in hand.

**A CIRCLE OF FRIENDS**
$4.95/250-7
The story of a remarkable group of women. The women pair off to explore all the possibilities of lesbian passion, until finally it seems that there is nothing—and no one—they have not dabbled in.

**BAD HABITS**
$5.95/446-1
"Talk about passing the wet test!... If you like hot, lesbian erotica, run—don't walk—and pick up a copy of *Bad Habits*."
—Lambda Book Report

What does one do with a poorly trained slave? Break her of her bad habits, of course! An immediate favorite with women nationwide, and an incredible bestseller.

## ANNABELLE BARKER
**MOROCCO**
$6.50/541-7
A luscious young woman stands to inherit a fortune—if she can only withstand the ministrations of her cruel guardian until her twentieth birthday. With two months left, Lila makes a bold bid for freedom, only to find that liberty has its own excruciating and delicious price....

## A.L. REINE
**DISTANT LOVE & OTHER STORIES**
$4.95/3056-3
In the title story, Leah Michaels and her lover, Ranelle, have had four years of blissful, smoldering passion together. When Ranelle is out of town, Leah records an audio "Valentine:" a cassette filled with erotic reminiscences....

# A RICHARD KASAK BOOK

## PAT CALIFIA
**DIESEL FUEL: Passionate Poetry**
$12.95/535-2
"Dead-on direct, these poems burn, pierce, penetrate, soak, and sting.... Califia leaves no sexual stone unturned, clearing new ground for us all." —Gerry Gomez Pearlberg

An extraordinary volume from this renowned sexual pioneer. The author of such best-selling—and infamous—volumes as *Sensuous Magic* and *Macho Sluts*, reveals herself to be a poet of unusual power and frankness, in this first collection of verse. One of this year's must-read explorations of underground culture.

**SENSUOUS MAGIC**
$12.95/458-5
"*Sensuous Magic* is clear, succinct and engaging even for the reader for whom S/M isn't the sexual behavior of choice.... When she is writing about the dynamics of sex and the technical aspects of it, Califia is the Dr. Ruth of the alternative sexuality set...." —Lambda Book Report

"Captures the power of what it means to enter forbidden terrain, and to do so safely with someone else, and to explore the healing potential, spiritual aspects and the depth of S/M." —Bay Area Reporter

"Don't take a dangerous trip into the unknown—buy this book and know where you're going!" —SKIN TWO

## SIMON LEVAY
**ALBRICK'S GOLD**
$20.95/518-2/Hardcover
From the man behind the controversial "gay brain" studies comes a chilling tale of medical experimentation run amok. LeVay—a lightning rod for controversy since the publication of The Sexual Brain—has fashioned a classic medical thriller from today's cutting-edge science.
"Well-plotted and imaginative... [Levay's] premise and execution are original and engaging." —Publishers Weekly

## SHAR REDNOUR, EDITOR
**VIRGIN TERRITORY 2**
$12.95/506-9
Focusing on the many "firsts" of a woman's erotic life, *Virgin Territory 2* provides one of the sole outlets for serious discussion of the myriad possibilities available to and chosen by many contemporary lesbians.

---

**BUY ANY 4 BOOKS & CHOOSE 1 ADDITIONAL BOOK, OF EQUAL OR LESSER VALUE, AS YOUR FREE GIFT**

# MASQUERADE BOOKS

**VIRGIN TERRITORY**
$12.95/457-7
An anthology of writing by women about their first-time erotic experiences with other women. Each of these true stories reveals a different, radical perspective on one of the most traditional subjects around: virginity.

## MICHAEL FORD, EDITOR
**ONCE UPON A TIME:**
**Erotic Fairy Tales for Women**
$12.95/449-6
How relevant to contemporary lesbians are the lessons of these age-old tales? Some of the biggest names in contemporary lesbian literature retell their favorite fairy tales, adding their own surprising—and sexy—twists.

**HAPPILY EVER AFTER:**
**Erotic Fairy Tales for Men**
$12.95/450-X
Adapting some of childhood's beloved tales for the adult gay reader, the contributors dig up the subtext of these hitherto "innocent" diversions—adding some surprises of their own along the way.

## MICHAEL BRONSKI, ED.
**TAKING LIBERTIES: Gay Men's Essays on Politics, Culture and Sex**
$12.95/456-9
Lambda Literary Award Nominee

"Offers undeniable proof of a heady, sophisticated, diverse new culture of gay intellectual debate. I cannot recommend it too highly." —Christopher Bram

A collection of some of the most divergent views on the state of gay male culture published in recent years. Some of the community's foremost essayists weigh in on such slippery topics as outing, identity, pornography and much more.

**FLASHPOINT: Gay Male**
**Sexual Writing**
$12.95/424-0
Over twenty of the genre's best writers. Accompanied by Bronski's insightful analysis, each story illustrates the many approaches to sexuality used by today's gay writers. Flashpoint is sure to be one of the most influential volumes ever dedicated to the exploration of gay sexuality.

## HEATHER FINDLAY, ED.
**A MOVEMENT OF EROS:**
**25 Years of Lesbian Erotica**
$12.95/421-6
A roster of stellar talents, each represented by their best work. Tracing the course of the genre from its pre-Stonewall roots to its current renaissance, Findlay examines each piece, placing it within the context of lesbian community and politics.

## CHARLES HENRI FORD & PARKER TYLER
**THE YOUNG AND EVIL**
$12.95/431-3
"*The Young and Evil* creates [its] generation as *This Side of Paradise* by Fitzgerald created his generation."—Gertrude Stein

Originally published in 1933, *The Young and Evil* was an immediate sensation due to its unprecedented portrayal of young gay artists living in New York's notorious Greenwich Village. From drag balls to bohemian flats, these characters followed love and art wherever it led them.

## BARRY HOFFMAN, EDITOR
**THE BEST OF GAUNTLET**
$12.95/202-7
*Gauntlet* has always published the widest possible range of opinions. The most provocative articles have been gathered by editor-in-chief Barry Hoffman, to make *The Best of Gauntlet* a riveting exploration of American society's limits.

## AMARANTHA KNIGHT, ED.
**LOVE BITES**
$12.95/234-5
A volume of tales dedicated to legend's sexiest demon—the Vampire. Not only the finest collection of erotic horror available—but a virtual who's who of promising new talent. A must-read for fans of both the horror and erotic genres.

## MICHAEL ROWE
**WRITING BELOW THE BELT:**
**Conversations with Erotic Authors**
$19.95/363-5
"An in-depth and enlightening tour of society's love/hate relationship with sex, morality, and censorship."
—*James White Review*

Michael Rowe interviewed the best erotic writers and presents the collected wisdom in *Writing Below the Belt*. Rowe speaks frankly with cult favorites such as Pat Califia, crossover success stories like John Preston, and up-and-comers Michael Lowenthal and Will Leber. A chronicle of the insights of this genre's best practitioners.

## LARRY TOWNSEND
**ASK LARRY**
$12.95/289-2
Starting just before the onslaught of AIDS, Townsend wrote the "Leather Notebook" column for *Drummer* magazine. Now, readers can avail themselves of Townsend's collected wisdom, as well as the author's contemporary commentary—a careful consideration of the way life has changed in the AIDS era.

# MASQUERADE BOOKS

## MICHAEL LASSELL
### THE HARD WAY
$12.95/231-0

"Lassell is a master of the necessary word. In an age of tepid and whining verse, his bawdy and bittersweet songs are like a plunge in cold champagne." —Paul Monette

The first collection of renowned gay writer Michael Lassell's poetry, fiction and essays. As much a chronicle of post-Stonewall gay life as a compendium of a remarkable writer's work.

## WILLIAM CARNEY
### THE REAL THING
$10.95/280-9

"Carney gives us a good look at the mores and lifestyle of the first generation of gay leathermen. A chilling mystery/romance novel as well." —Pat Califia

With a new introduction by Michael Bronski. First published in 1968, this uncompromising story of American leathermen received instant acclaim. Out of print even while its legend grew, The Real Thing returns from exile more than twenty-five years after its initial release, detailing the attitudes and practices of an earlier generation of leathermen.

## LAURA ANTONIOU, EDITOR
### LOOKING FOR MR. PRESTON
$23.95/288-4

Interviews, essays and personal reminiscences of John Preston—a man whose career spanned the gay publishing industry. Preston was the author of over twenty books, and edited many more. Ten percent of the proceeds from sale of this book will go to the AIDS Project of Southern Maine, for which Preston served as President of the Board.

## RANDY TUROFF, EDITOR
### LESBIAN WORDS: State of the Art
$10.95/340-6

"This is a terrific book that should be on every thinking lesbian's bookshelf." —Nisa Donnelly

Dorothy Allison, Jewelle Gomez, Judy Grahn, Eileen Myles, Robin Podolsky and many others are represented by some of their best work, looking at not only the current fashionability the media has brought to the lesbian "image," but considerations of the lesbian past via historical inquiry and personal recollections. A must for all interested in the state of the lesbian community.

## ASSOTTO SAINT
### SPELLS OF A VOODOO DOLL
$12.95/393-7

Lambda Literary Award Nominee.

"Angelic and brazen." —Jewelle Gomez

A spellbinding collection of the poetry, lyrics, essays and performance texts of Assotto Saint—one of the most important voices in the renaissance of black gay writing. Saint was the editor of two seminal anthologies: 1991 Lambda Literary Book Award winner, The Road Before Us: 100 Gay Black Poets and Here to Dare: 10 Gay Black Poets.

## EURYDICE
### F/32
$10.95/350-3

"It's wonderful to see a woman...celebrating her body and her sexuality by creating a fabulous and funny tale." —Kathy Acker

With the story of Ela, Eurydice won the National Fiction competition sponsored by Fiction Collective Two and Illinois State University. A funny, disturbing quest for unity, f/32 prompted Frederic Tuten to proclaim "almost any page... redeems us from the anemic writing and banalities we have endured in the past decade..."

## ROBERT PATRICK
### TEMPLE SLAVE
$12.95/191-8

"You must read this book." —Quentin Crisp

"One of the best ways to learn what it was like to be fabulous, gay, theatrical and loved in a time at once more and less dangerous to gay life than our own." —Genre

The story of Greenwich Village and the beginnings of gay theater—told with the wit and stylistic invention for which Patrick is justly famous.

## FELICE PICANO
### DRYLAND'S END
$12.95/279-5

Set five thousand years in the future, Dryland's End takes place in a fabulous techno-empire ruled by intelligent, powerful women. While the Matriarchy has ruled for over two thousand years and altered human society—But is now unraveling. Military rivalries, religious fanaticism and economic competition threaten to destroy the mighty empire.

**BUY ANY 4 BOOKS & CHOOSE 1 ADDITIONAL BOOK, OF EQUAL OR LESSER VALUE, AS YOUR FREE GIFT**

# MASQUERADE BOOKS

## TIM WOODWARD, EDITOR
### THE BEST OF SKIN TWO
$12.95/130-6

*Skin Two* specializes in provocative essays by the finest writers working in the "radical sex" scene. Collected here are the articles and interviews that established the magazine's reputation. Including interviews with cult figures Tim Burton, Clive Barker and Jean Paul Gaultier.

## LUCY TAYLOR
### UNNATURAL ACTS
$12.95/181-0

"A topnotch collection..." —*Science Fiction Chronicle*

A disturbing vision of erotic horror. Unrelenting angels and hungry gods play with souls and bodies in Taylor's murky cosmos: where heaven and hell are merely differences of perspective; where redemption and damnation lie behind the same shocking acts.

## SAMUEL R. DELANY
### THE MOTION OF LIGHT IN WATER
$12.95/133-0

"A very moving, intensely fascinating literary biography from an extraordinary writer....The artist as a young man and a memorable picture of an age." —William Gibson

Award-winning author Samuel R. Delany's autobiography covers the early years of one of science fiction's most important voices. A self-portrait of one of today's most challenging writers.

### THE MAD MAN
$23.95/193-4/hardcover

"What Delany has done here is take the ideas of the Marquis de Sade one step further, by filtering extreme and obsessive sexual behavior through the sieve of post-modern experience...." —*Lambda Book Report*

"Delany develops an insightful dichotomy between [his protagonist]'s two worlds: the one of cerebral philosophy and dry academia, the other of heedless, 'impersonal' obsessive sexual extremism. When these worlds finally collide ... the novel achieves a surprisingly satisfying resolution...." —*Publishers Weekly*

Delany's fascinating examination of human desire. For his thesis, graduate student John Marr researches the life and work of the brilliant Timothy Hasler: a philosopher whose career was cut tragically short over a decade earlier. Marr soon begins to believe that Hasler's death might hold some key to his own life as a gay man in the age of AIDS.

## CARO SOLES, EDITOR
### MELTDOWN!
### An Anthology of Erotic Science Fiction and Dark Fantasy for Gay Men
$12.95/203-5

*Meltdown!* contains the very best examples of the increasingly popular sub-genre of erotic sci-fi/dark fantasy: stories meant to shock and delight, to send a shiver down the spine and start a fire down below.

## GUILLERMO BOSCH
### RAIN
$12.95/232-9

"*Rain* is a trip..." —Timothy Leary

The tale begins on the 1,537th day of drought—when one man comes to know the true depths of thirst. In a quest to sate his hunger for some knowledge of the wide world, he is taken through a series of extraordinary, encounters that promise to change the course of civilization around him.

## RUSS KICK
### OUTPOSTS:
### A Catalog of Rare and Disturbing Alternative Information
$18.95/0202-8

A huge, authoritative guide to some of the most bizarre publications available today! Kick has tracked down and compiled reviews of work penned by political extremists, conspiracy theorists, hallucinogenic pathfinders, sexual explorers, and others.

## CECILIA TAN, EDITOR
### SM VISIONS: The Best of Circlet Press
$10.95/339-2

"Fabulous books! There's nothing else like them." —Susie Bright,

Circlet Press, devoted exclusively to the erotic science fiction and fantasy genre, is now represented by the best of its very best: *SM Visions*—one of the most thrilling and eye-opening rides through the erotic imagination ever published.

## DAVID MELTZER
### THE AGENCY TRILOGY
$12.95/216-7

"...'The Agency' is clearly Meltzer's paradigm of society; a mindless machine of which we are all 'agents,' including those whom the machine supposedly serves...." —Norman Spinrad

A vision of an America consumed and dehumanized by a lust for power.

# MASQUERADE BOOKS

## MICHAEL PERKINS
**THE GOOD PARTS: An Uncensored Guide to Literary Sexuality**
$12.95/186-1
Michael Perkins presents this unprecedented survey of sex as seen/written about in the pages of over 100 major fiction and nonfiction volumes from the past twenty years.

**COMING UP: The World's Best Erotic Writing**
$12.95/370-8
Author and critic Michael Perkins has scoured the field of erotic writing to produce this anthology sure to challenge the limits of even the most seasoned reader. Perkins presents the cream of the current crop.

## MICHAEL LOWENTHAL, ED.
**THE BEST OF THE BADBOYS**
$12.95/233-7
The very best of the leading Badboys is collected here, in this testament to the artistry that has catapulted these "outlaw" authors to bestselling status. John Preston, Aaron Travis, Larry Townsend, and others are here represented by their most provocative work.

## JOHN PRESTON
**MY LIFE AS A PORNOGRAPHER AND OTHER INDECENT ACTS**
$12.95/137-7
"...essential and enlightening... My Life as a Pornographer] is a bridge from the sexually liberated 1970s to the more cautious 1990s, and Preston has walked much of that way as a standard-bearer to the cause for equal rights...." —*Library Journal*

"Not pornography, but rather reflections upon the writing and production of it. In a deeply sex-phobic world, Preston has never shied away from a vision of the redemptive potential of the erotic drive. Better than perhaps anyone in our community, Preston knows how physical joy can bridge differences and make us well."
—*Lambda Book Report*

A collection of renowned author and social critic John Preston's essays, focusing on his work as an erotic writer and proponent of gay rights.

## LARS EIGHNER
**ELEMENTS OF AROUSAL**
$12.95/230-2
A guideline for success with one of publishing's best kept secrets: the novice-friendly field of gay erotic writing. Eighner details his craft, providing the reader with sure advice.

## MARCO VASSI
**A DRIVING PASSION**
$12.95/134-9
Marco Vassi was famous for the lectures he gave regarding sexuality. A Driving Passion collects the insight Vassi brought to these lectures, and distills the philosophy that made him a sensation.

**THE EROTIC COMEDIES**
$12.95/136-5
"The comparison to [Henry] Miller is high praise indeed.... But reading Vassi's work, the analogy holds—for he shares with Miller an unabashed joy in sensuality, and a questing after experience that is the root of all great literature, erotic or otherwise...."   —David L. Ulin, *The Los Angeles Reader*

"...Marco Vassi is our champion sexual energist."   —VLS

Scathing and humorous, these stories reflect Vassi's belief in the power and primacy of Eros in American life. A wry collection for the sexually adventurous.

**THE SALINE SOLUTION**
$12.95/180-2
"I've always read Marco's work with interest and I have the highest opinion not only of his talent but his intellectual boldness."
—Norman Mailer

With the story of one couple's brief affair and the events that lead them to desperately reassess their lives,

**THE STONED APOCALYPSE**
$12.95/132-2
The *Stoned Apocalypse* is Vassi's autobiography, financed by the other groundbreaking erotic writing that made him a cult sensation.

## CHEA VILLANUEVA
**JESSIE'S SONG**
$9.95/235-3
"It conjures up the strobe-light confusion and excitement of urban dyke life.... Read about these dykes and you'll love them."   —Rebecca Ripley

Based largely upon her own experience, Villanueva's work is remarkable for its frankness, and delightful in its iconoclasm.

## STAN TAL, EDITOR
**BIZARRE SEX AND OTHER CRIMES OF PASSION**
$12.95/213-2
Over twenty masterpieces of erotic shock. This incredible volume includes such masters of erotic horror and fantasy as Edward Lee, Lucy Taylor and Nancy Kilpatrick.

**BUY ANY 4 BOOKS & CHOOSE 1 ADDITIONAL BOOK, OF EQUAL OR LESSER VALUE, AS YOUR FREE GIFT**

# ORDERING IS EASY

MC/VISA orders can be placed by calling our toll-free number
PHONE 800-375-2356/FAX 212-986-7355/E-MAIL masqbks@aol.com
or mail this coupon to:
**MASQUERADE DIRECT**
DEPT. BMMQ97 801 2ND AVE., NY, NY 10017

*BUY ANY FOUR BOOKS AND CHOOSE ONE ADDITIONAL BOOK, OF EQUAL OR LESSER VALUE, AS YOUR FREE GIFT.*

| QTY. | TITLE | NO. | PRICE |
|------|-------|-----|-------|
|  |  |  |  |
|  |  |  |  |
|  |  |  |  |
|  |  |  | FREE |
|  |  |  |  |
|  |  |  |  |

We never sell, give or trade any customer's name.

SUBTOTAL

POSTAGE AND HANDLING

TOTAL

In the U.S., please add $1.50 for the first book and 75¢ for each additional book; in Canada, add $2.00 for the first book and $1.25 for each additional book. Foreign countries: add $4.00 for the first book and $2.00 for each additional book. No C.O.D. orders. Please make all checks payable to Masquerade/Direct. Payable in U.S. currency only. NY state residents add 8.25% sales tax. Please allow 4–6 weeks for delivery. Payable in U.S. currency only.

NAME _____

ADDRESS _____

CITY _____ STATE _____ ZIP _____

TEL( ) _____

E-MAIL _____

PAYMENT:  ☐ CHECK   ☐ MONEY ORDER   ☐ VISA   ☐ MC

CARD NO _____ EXP. DATE _____

# A Victorian Romance

LINDSAY WELSH

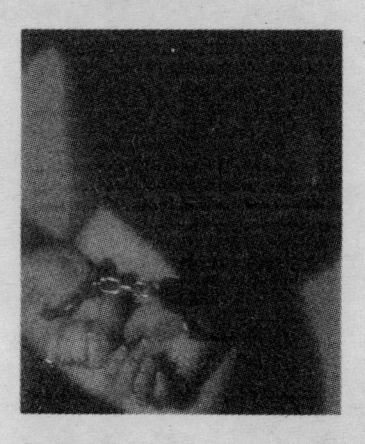

# THE TRAINER

"Ms. Adamson writes some hot, very heavy scenes...
She leads newcomers to SM gently through each scene,
but players of the hardest core of SM will also
find the read extremely satisfying."
—*Lambda Book Report*

LAURA ANTONIOU
writing as
SARA ADAMSON

# THRILL CITY

JEAN STINE

# WANDA

Her skin tingled with delight, and she was hungry for kisses and love

## ANONYMOUS